Praise for PL[...]

"Catherine McKenzie has reached new heights with *Please Join Us*, her propulsive thriller about secret organizations, hidden agendas, and the lengths one woman will go to reclaim her life. You won't want to put this book down!"

—Laura Dave, *New York Times* bestselling
author of *The Last Thing He Told Me*

"A superior crime novel. . . . Exceptionally crisp and clever."

—*Toronto Star*

"Catherine McKenzie's latest is a triumph. I was infatuated with this brilliant, tangled web of lies, coverups, and deception. Totally thrilling and empowering, *Please Join Us* shows how some people will stop at nothing to get what they want. McKenzie never fails to impress!"

—Mary Kubica, *New York Times* bestselling
author of *Local Woman Missing*

"I devoured this book in one sitting! *The First Wives Club* meets *The Firm* in a chilling, serpentine ride that will leave you breathless. *Please Join Us* belongs at the very top of your TBR stack."

—Liv Constantine, internationally bestselling
author of *The Last Mrs. Parrish*

"This searing take on professional networking from Catherine McKenzie is a fast-paced, intriguing, intense read that is as smart as it is suspenseful. Original and thought-provoking, it has plenty of twists and turns to satisfy even the most seasoned thriller reader, and the women of this tour de force will haunt you long after the final page is turned."

—Heather Gudenkauf, *New York Times* bestselling author
of *The Weight of Silence* and *This Is How I Lied*

"You can always rely on Catherine McKenzie for smart, complex, irresistible suspense. *Please Join Us* takes one sinister turn after the next—just when you think you have it all figured out, she turns the tables again."

—Jessica Strawser, bestselling author of *Not That I Could Tell*

"With a scintillating, timely premise, and McKenzie's signature page-turning style, *Please Join Us* is a winner."

—Robyn Harding, internationally bestselling author of *The Perfect Family*

"Another superbly plotted thriller from Catherine McKenzie, full of signature twists and turns, where readers are invited into the warm waters of a women's group, only to find it's not all sisterhood and solidarity. . . . Join if you dare!"

—Roz Nay, bestselling author of *Our Little Secret*

"Catherine McKenzie's *Please Join Us* is her best book yet. It's a page-turning blend of corporate intrigue, secret societies, family drama, and twists galore. You won't be able to put this one down or relax until the final series of reveals and double-crosses unfold . . . and even then, you'll walk away with your heart pounding. An intelligent, captivating thriller that really thrills!"

—David Bell, author of *Kill All Your Darlings*

"The claws come out! *Please Join Us* is a diabolical and fast-paced ride through a women's networking group. This twisty, captivating book will have you reading all night."

—Samantha Downing, internationally bestselling author of *My Lovely Wife* and *For Your Own Good*

"Stunning, propulsive, and sharp as a knife, *Please Join Us* is about a secret women's group and the members determined to get ahead at all costs—just like men do. With a creeping sense of paranoia and full of surprising twists, this smart, feminist thriller explores women's empowerment versus justice and the gray spaces we inhibit when success is on the line. This one's a knockout!"

—Christina McDonald, *USA Today* bestselling author

"Wholly original [and] utterly enthralling with gasp-worthy twist after twist, Catherine McKenzie's *Please Join Us* is an absolute masterpiece. This propulsive thrill ride about an exclusive, all-female club where nothing and no one is who they seem will have you glued to its pages, bingeing until you reach the explosive conclusion. *Please Join Us* belongs in at the very top of your summer reading list."

—May Cobb, author of *The Hunting Wives*

ALSO BY CATHERINE McKENZIE

Six Weeks to Live

You Can't Catch Me

First Street

I'll Never Tell

The Murder Game (writing as Julie Apple)

The Good Liar

Fractured

Smoke

Hidden

Spun

Forgotten

Arranged

Spin

PLEASE JOIN US

A Novel

CATHERINE McKENZIE

ATRIA PAPERBACK

NEW YORK   LONDON   TORONTO   SYDNEY   NEW DELHI

ATRIA
PAPERBACK

An Imprint of Simon & Schuster, Inc.
1230 Avenue of the Americas
New York, NY 10020

First Atria Paperback edition April 2023

ATRIA PAPERBACK and colophon are trademarks of Simon & Schuster, Inc.

For information about special discounts for bulk purchases, please contact Simon & Schuster Special Sales at 1-866-506-1949 or business@simonandschuster.com.

The Simon & Schuster Speakers Bureau can bring authors to your live event. For more information or to book an event, contact the Simon & Schuster Speakers Bureau at 1-866-248-3049 or visit our website at www.simonspeakers.com.

Interior design by Kyoko Watanabe

Manufactured in the United States of America

1 3 5 7 9 10 8 6 4 2

Library of Congress Cataloging-in-Publication Data is available.

ISBN 978-1-9821-5924-5
ISBN 978-1-9821-5925-2 (pbk)
ISBN 978-1-9821-5926-9 (ebook)

For the women in my Pride.
You know who you are.

The door to Athena's apartment is open.

I'm both relieved and petrified by this. Relieved because I'd been worrying on the frantic ride over about how I was going to get in without involving third parties—her doorman, the police. And petrified because it means that Athena's SOS message was real, that something actually is wrong, and she isn't simply being dramatic.

I stand in front of the open door with my heart beating like a bass drum. Athena's is one of two apartments on this floor; the other door is firmly shut. I can't yell—that might result in more third-party involvement, although I'm already on the security footage in the elevator and the lobby. I'd glanced up at the camera downstairs, and then away. The doorman knows me. I catalog all of this and conclude the obvious: there's no covering over the fact that I've been here, no matter what I find inside.

The seconds are ticking away in time to my heart, and Athena needs help. But still I linger. I don't want to know what's through this open door. I don't want my life to change in the way I know it will if I cross the threshold. If Athena requires an ambulance, she would've called 911. So it's bad, what I'm going to find, but final.

My phone buzzes. I'd put on dark yoga pants and a hoodie when I got Athena's message, dressing for a crime I didn't know I was about

1

to commit. My phone is in the pouch across my belly, its soft purr a tickle. I don't have to read it to guess who it is, nudging me through the door.

Karma.

I've been thinking about that word a lot lately.

My phone buzzes again and I enter, closing the door behind me gently. Even though there's no denying I've been here, I slip on the pair of surgical gloves I'd grabbed on the way out, moving quietly so I didn't wake my husband, Dan. I did anyway, and I murmured something about *work*, the lie slipping easily through my teeth. He turned over and went back to sleep, sadly used to the vagaries of my job.

My heart's been getting a workout tonight.

Athena's apartment is shrouded in soft light from a table lamp in the living room. I've always loved her home, the product of two classic sixes being knocked together to form something that feels both traditional New York and entirely original—a house inside a building, complete with a full rooftop garden. The downstairs is made up of a large living room, dining room, and a massive kitchen/great room that's bathed in sunlight during the day and stares at Central Park.

I walk quickly through the rooms, careful not to touch anything despite the gloves, hoping I'll find Athena downstairs, but with each empty room it grows more unlikely.

I search for anything out of place, my mind logging as I go.

—There's a man's coat laid over the end of the couch, folded neatly.
—There are two wineglasses on the counter in the kitchen, stained a deep red.
—The sliding glass doors to the balcony are locked tight.

I walk back to the staircase that leads upstairs, a modern combination of metal, glass, and wood, doing my best to keep quiet. I want to call out, to shout her name, to do one of those frantic, loud searches like you see on film, but I don't. I've been instructed to tell no one what I'm doing. Noise is the enemy. Silence and deliberation are required. It takes effort, though. I don't want to move toward whatever's waiting for me up these grand stairs. I want to bolt in the opposite direction, out into the night and the city, and then . . .

I steady myself against the wall, my hands sweating inside the gloves. There's a painting at the top of the stairs that I love: a body of water, maybe a pool, that perfect blue of the sea in Antigua. The lines are blurred, so it's hard to tell, but it's beautiful.

Blurred lines. That should be our anthem.

I reach the top of the stairs. Up until now, the whole house has been as still as a tomb, only the gentle hush of the central air letting me know that the apartment's alive, even if no one else is. But now my ears are picking something up—a plinking sound, water dripping, its landing muffled.

The bathroom. There are two of them, but instinct drives me to the guest bath to the left of me, the one right outside Athena's bedroom. I used it not that long ago, when we had a late night and I ended up sleeping over, calling Dan with my excuses, my lies, like I did tonight.

Work, work. I always blame work. It's the reason I've done all of this, the origin of this moment. Whatever this is. I only need to push open the bathroom door to find out.

My heart is thrumming again. I get another text. Again, I don't need to read it. **Open the door**, it will command, and for the first time I wonder—am I on camera?

I push that thought aside. The possibility of cameras leads to a cascade of thoughts that I don't have time for right now.

I open it. My eyes flit over the room, the collection of data my brain's focus.

—Athena, naked, hunched in the corner of the generous bathtub.
—The water slowly dripping from the rain head shower.
—The diluted streak of blood still circling the drain.

"Athena," I say, my voice steadier than it has a right to be. "Are you all right?"

Her dark-brown eyes are blank, her beautiful, famous face unmarred. She follows my gaze to the other end of the tub, watching the water drip into the basin, each drop thinning out the red to pink.

"It's not mine," she says in a hoarse whisper. "It's Jack's."

PART I

CHAPTER 1

It's Not Us, It's You

Then—June

I blame the points committee.

For those of you who don't live under the tyranny of yearly evaluations of your productivity and ability to bring in clients being plugged into a mysterious formula that spits out the number of "points" (i.e., money) that you'll receive each year, perhaps it seems silly to care. But when you've worked sixty-hour weeks since you were twenty-six—scratch that, your whole adult life—and you've made it, but you still haven't made it far enough, it's humiliating. Being a partner isn't good enough. Being in every "best of" lawyer publication doesn't cut it. Putting yourself out there in a million ways that make you uncomfortable doesn't mean shit. If you didn't bring in the clients and/or the billable hours, your points are cut. Doesn't matter that you helped build the place. Those years of two-thousand-plus billable hours and no time to yourself—well, thanks, I guess, but what does that have to do with today?

Nothing.

Your points are being cut, you're taking a step down, you're now in the loser tier, and if you don't course-correct, you're going to reverse lap the new partners in the most pathetic race ever.

Not that they said that exactly, but the sad turn of my mentor Thomas's mouth when he walked into my office and shut the door to deliver the news said it all.

Without some radical intervention, my days were numbered.

When Thomas left without giving me any advice on what to do other than to say that we'd "just have to wait and see" if my profile turned into files, I sat at my desk and stared at my computer screen as if it might deliver answers. What had gone wrong? Sure, the last year had been less busy, but that was because one of my main clients had gone bankrupt. It wasn't my fault—I wasn't their financial adviser. They were the kind of client you didn't replace in ten seconds, or in ten months. But that hadn't been taken into account.

I'd done everything I was asked to do and more, and it hadn't been enough.

What was I supposed to do now?

I needed to get out of my head, so I called Dan.

"Should I be putting pink champagne on ice?" he asked as a greeting, the answer assumed, his anticipation of our celebration palpable.

I felt the sudden need to cry. Dan had sung those words, like he often did, with the confidence of certainty. In thirty-nine years, Nicole Mueller had never failed, so I had to be calling with good news.

I turned my back to the glass door of my office so no one could see when the tears fell.

"Um, no, decidedly not."

"Wait, what?"

I could imagine Dan sitting in his own office in Jersey City. He was in-house counsel at a bank, changing paths five years ago when he didn't make partner. I'd supported his choice. We didn't both need to be working this hard, particularly if his firm wasn't going to recognize his worth. The bank paid well and let Dan have his weekends. It was an easy decision.

"They put me in the Samuel tier," I said, naming a partner who was one point away from being kicked out.

"The loser tier? No, you're shitting me."

"I wish I was."

I stared hard at my computer screen, blinking back tears. It was open to Facebook, a place I went when I needed to distract myself for a minute or ten with pictures of cute puppies and smart-alecky kids.

"Why?"

"My hours were down."

"But AlCorp. went bankrupt."

"I know."

"That wasn't your fault."

"I said that."

"They didn't give you any warning?"

I thought back to the meeting I'd had with the points committee in May. Everything was positive. In January, I'd been named as one of the top 40 lawyers under 40 and had been featured in a prominent lawyers' magazine. I'd made a bunch of other lists too; the clients loved me, my hours were down, but they were sure that was a blip. I was a model for others to follow, they'd implied—maybe even said— as Thomas nodded along like a proud parent. I'd left the meeting confident.

Getting their decision today felt like being in front of a judge who's made up her mind but doesn't tell you what she's going to do, so you have no way of convincing her otherwise. "No, there was no warning. Thomas seemed so . . . guilty."

Dan growled. "Fuck Thomas."

"Yeah."

"Seriously, Nic. You should leave."

I stared at my hands. My nails were chipped and ragged. Was I not polished enough? Was that why? I've never been big on personal grooming. That sounds bad. I'm a clean person, I dress well, and my shoulder-length chestnut hair is well-kept, but the extra primping that a lot of professional women seem to find the time to do? I've never had the patience for it.

"And go where?"

"Lots of firms would be happy to take you."

I turned away from Facebook, facing my windowsill. It was cluttered with the plaques they encouraged you to buy when you made all those lists. Best Lawyers, Chambers, Who's Who. I was in all of them. Future star. Litigation star. Consistently recommended. I was supposed to make full equity partner this year—that was the plan. Instead, I was moving away from that goal. "Not now. I should've taken Fosters up on their offer last year."

"What's changed?"

"Me. In the eyes of the legal world."

"You don't have to tell them about the points."

I smiled sadly at my own reflection. My dark-blue eyes were tired, and my hair was pulled back too tightly from my face, making me seem severe. I looked like a loser, despite Dan's optimism. It was one of the things I loved most about him—how naïve he still was, his Ohio earnestness firmly in place despite more than fifteen years in this city. It was why he didn't make partner. His firm didn't think he had a killer's instinct, and they were right.

"They probably already know."

"How?"

"Because people don't sit on this kind of information." My email pinged, dragging my eyes back to my screen. "Goddamn it."

"What?"

"I just got an email from Albert and Prince."

"The recruiters?"

"The recruiters for mid-level law firms, yes."

"It's a coincidence," Dan said, but he didn't sound like he meant it. Dan might be naïve, but he's not stupid.

"It's been five minutes since I got the news, and they already think I'm vulnerable enough to move my practice to a firm I didn't even interview at."

"Maybe they'd respect you more there? Big fish in a small pond and all that."

"Maybe."

"So?"

"I wouldn't be able to respect myself."

I hadn't meant to say that out loud, but it was true. I don't know when I turned into a law firm snob, but I was. It wasn't that those mid-level firms didn't do good work; they did. Lots of smart people I'd gone to law school with had ended up at that level. But it wasn't where you *chose* to be. It was where you washed ashore. Until now, I'd only had choices, not inevitabilities. But Dan had been at one of those firms, and he hadn't even made partner—

God I was awful, even in my own head.

"Sorry, I know how that sounds."

"It's okay," Dan said lightly.

I forgot sometimes, because his ego was so firmly in check, that he still had one. Bad enough that his wife was the star in the family. I didn't need to rub it in.

"No, it's not. How about this. Why don't you put that champagne on ice after all and I'll leave early, and we'll order from Kam Fung?"

"I thought you had to work."

"I did, but fuck it. Fuck them."

"That's my girl."

I smiled. "I'll see you at six, okay?"

"You betcha. Keep your chin up."

"I always do."

We hung up and I kept staring out the window. Midtown lay below—all that buzzing ambition, the striving, the aggressiveness. I'd loved it from the first time I'd visited for interviews in my second year of law school. I was top of my class at Yale, and even though I had zero contacts in the legal world, everyone wanted me. Taking me to dinners I couldn't afford and providing me with hard-to-get theater tickets. What was not to love?

My computer *ping*ed again. A Facebook notification. I'd tried a thousand times to turn the stupid things off, but I'd never managed it. I didn't ask the IT department to do it, because those guys were spies who were only too happy to report infractions to the managing partner.

Guess who's having a baby! my high school friend Tammy had written.

Oh God, another one? Ever since I turned thirty-nine, I noticed a peculiar phenomenon among my high school girlfriends who'd remained child-free until then—they were all getting pregnant for the first time. The Last-Minute Babies, I called them. Getting one in before they were forty. Dan and I had decided not to have kids, but it wasn't something you advertised, not unless you wanted to get interrogated about why, and told how babies were so wonderful and enriching and who was going to take care of us when we were old? And then everyone just assumed it was because you were too focused on your career.

As if that were a bad thing.

Dan never had to answer these questions.

If men ever wondered why women were angry all the time, they could start there.

Congratulations! I wrote, then turned back to my inbox. Fifty new emails had accumulated in the hour I'd lost to the points committee bomb dropping. I scanned through them quickly. Three recruiters had already reached out, and several of my partners had written short *Sorry!* or *That's crazy!* emails. No other content. No mention of points. Plausible deniability that they were criticizing management. Billings took a 75 percent drop on points day. Usually that pissed me off, which showed my lack of empathy. I probably had some apologies of my own to dole out. I certainly didn't care about billing today. Instead, I decided to clean up my emails then leave, even though it was the middle of the afternoon.

I spent an hour deleting and triaging emails so I could exit without a black cloud of guilt. When my inbox was finally under control, I stood and raised my hands above my head.

An email arrived. Please join us, read the subject line.

God, another drinks thing. I was already losing one to two nights a week going to networking events. But if I was going to turn this situation around, I couldn't turn invitations down.

I opened it and sat back down as I read.

Dear Nicole,

Have you ever wondered why your career hasn't progressed as far as it should?

Why others have continued to climb the corporate ladder while you've been stuck in place?

We've been there.

Despite years of hard work and all the talent in the world, our careers were stalled too.

Why?

Because the boys' club still exists. No one wants to talk about it, but it's true.

So we decided to do something about it, and that's how Panthera Leo was born. Women helping women succeed the way men have for centuries. Over the past twenty years we've become a network of CEOs, managing partners, executives, and money managers—every successful woman you know is probably one of us.

And that's why we're writing to you. You've been recommended to us, and we'd be delighted if you'd become a member. All it takes is a few minutes of your time to complete our application, which can be found at www.pantheraleo.com.

A few minutes, and everything you always wanted could be yours.

Our next experience is happening soon. Please join us.

Best,
Karma & Michelle

CHAPTER 2

I Have a Bad Feeling About This

Then—June

"You're not seriously thinking of going, are you?" Dan asked three hours later. We were sitting at our dining room table with the remnants of takeout and champagne. We were lucky to have a place that contained a dining room, although we almost never ate there. We lived in a pre-war building on the Upper West Side in a large three-bedroom apartment that had been in Dan's family for generations. Back when it was built, a maid occupied the small cell near the bathroom, and families sat down for dinner every night.

"Is it so crazy?"

"Um, yes."

"Why?"

Dan reached his chopsticks into the container of sesame noodles. We always got a double order, because it was the one dish we both couldn't stop ourselves from eating until it was done. We'd discovered that on our first date twelve years ago when a friend had set us up. It might've been the reason we went on a second one, not that either of us would admit it. What kind of origin story is that? We both love sesame noodles. Is that enough to build a life on?

"Because it's probably a cult," Dan said, the accusation serious; but he was laughing.

"It's not a cult."

"How do you know?" He sucked up a large mouthful of noodles, something I usually found adorable but that was getting on my nerves that night. Dan was often like a big puppy—with light-brown curly hair that was always too long, big brown eyes that didn't shield his emotions, and wide shoulders from his days on the swim team. He was loving and sometimes made a mess all over the place because he got too excited.

"I checked it out."

"How?"

I shoved a salt-and-pepper shrimp into my mouth. "I used my lawyer skills."

"Ha. I'm going to need details."

"I read their website."

It was slick and professional, with an application form and two "experiences" to choose from, one taking place at the beginning of July at a dude ranch in Colorado and another in November. It even had a page of endorsements from women like *Sally J., executive. My career took off once I harnessed the power of Panthera Leo!* Its Frequently Asked Questions page expanded on the information contained in the invitation: it was a referral network, and membership was by invitation only. There were no annual dues, but the experiences were pricey and yearly attendance was encouraged.

"And?"

"Standard networking stuff."

Dan pulled the noodle container closer. "Oh, well then, I guess it's fine."

"What's the worst that could happen?"

Dan took a moment to consider, then ticked off a list on his fingers, a smile dancing in his eyes. "Brainwashing, branding, sex trafficking."

I laughed. "Dan, come on. This is about business."

"Wasn't NXIVM called Executive Success Programs when it started?" Dan and I had been mesmerized by *The Vow*, and he'd done a deep dive on NXIVM after we'd watched it, reading several books by ex-members and listening to endless podcasts.

"I think you kind of want it to be a cult so you can put all that knowledge to good use."

"It's possible. But I do worry about you."

"You think I'm going to end up in a three-way with their leader?"

"Maybe."

"It's run by two women."

Dan cocked his head to the side. "Well, it could still happen. Just don't give them any money."

"Don't worry. Our down payment is safe."

We'd been saving toward a down payment to buy the apartment when Dan's aunt Penny died. But it had taken us both years to pay off our student loans—two Ivy League degrees each had produced a scary mountain of debt—so we weren't as close to that goal as we wanted.

A shadow crossed Dan's face. "Speaking of which . . . Aunt Penny isn't doing so well. She's in the hospital again."

My stomach dropped. Aunty Penny had been diagnosed with terminal cancer in March, but she was a fighter and had been responding well to treatment. "Why didn't you say anything?"

"I didn't want to ruin dinner."

"Dan . . . You know I love her as much as you do."

"I know."

"What happened?"

"Unclear. They found her unconscious in her room at the old folks' home."

"I'm so sorry."

Aunt Penny was my favorite member of Dan's family, and not only because of the incredible real estate she let us live in for a reasonable rent. Dan's mother was an uptight WASP, and while I'd grown up around the middle-class version of Louise, I never felt as if I was good enough for "her Daniel," even though the family business, Rawleigh Pharmaceuticals, had suffered a massive economic setback right as Dan was graduating from high school. Overnight, they'd gone from wealthy to the bank taking over. But that hadn't changed Louise's outlook on life. She was as exclusionary as many of my classmates at Yale, dismissing me because I came from a small town they'd never heard of and hadn't attended private school. Add in that I'd failed to produce any grandchildren and, well . . . you get the drift.

"We should go see Penny," I said.

"Don't worry; she said she spoke to her lawyer."

"Hey!" I reached across the table and punched him in the arm. "That is not what I meant at all. I'm worried about her. This is the third time she's been in the hospital this year."

"I know, but . . ."

"Yes?"

"You also love this apartment."

"So do you!"

"You're right, I do."

There was a lot to love. High ceilings, crown moldings, wide hallways. We had a large bedroom and our own personal offices. The property was wrapped up in a family trust that was set up so the ownership couldn't be transferred while she was alive, but Penny had always told us that she wanted us to purchase it when she died, and when she was diagnosed as terminal in March, she'd told us she'd given directions to her lawyer to do what was necessary.

The General Tso chicken had congealed into a sticky mess on my plate. "We should go see her."

"We will. Over the weekend."

"We don't have anything to worry about, do we?"

"No, I don't think so. So long as we can qualify for the mortgage."

"I think we can handle it." It was more of a hope than a certainty, because Dan's family was the type who'd exact a purchase price that hit the market value to a T. But I was generally a hopeful person. The points committee notwithstanding, nothing had gone seriously wrong in my life.

"Not if you give all our money away to the cult."

I looked up. His eyes were teasing me, but still. "It's not a cult."

"Betcha."

. . .

The next day at my desk, I sat staring at my bank balance, wondering if I had enough to retire. Or at the very least, chuck my job and find something else to do. This was precipitated by the slow drip of continuing emails expressing their condolences at my "situation," which were meant to be friendly but just rubbed it in. Added to which, Thomas came by to "check in on" me, something he'd only ever done once before when he found me crying in my office after my mother died.

This was not good. I wasn't the woman in the office who needed consoling. I was the one who told people not to take it personally, while quietly congratulating myself that it wasn't me.

God, was I that insufferable?

The answer from my bank balance was no—I did not have enough money to retire, definitely not. And no, I probably didn't even have enough money to cover us for long. Not in Manhattan. Dan's salary could support us in Jersey, in a house that would take me an hour to get to the city from, or in a Manhattan one-bedroom. That a perfectly good apartment wasn't enough made me ashamed, but I'd busted my ass since I'd graduated from law school, and it felt like I should have something more to show for it.

I started a line of regret for every expensive dinner we'd had, and the dresses I didn't need from Theory, some of which were hanging in my closet with the tags still on. I didn't have a thing for shoes, but I did for a certain kind of column dress—when I couldn't sleep at night, shopping was my therapy. I didn't want to know how much it had cost me. More than actual therapy, probably, and certainly too much for someone who wanted to be in a position to tell the partners to take this job and shove it.

Fuck.

Thomas had felt the need to spend ten minutes brainstorming with me about ways in which I could raise my profile. I could try teaching? I was teaching, I reminded him; the semester had ended in May. *Oh, right, right.* What about writing an article? *Ditto*, three articles published last year, and editing a book chapter that had taken up all of my free time. For a while there, Dan had started making typewriter noises whenever he saw me. *Oh, ha!* Thomas said. *That Dan, he's such a cutup! I like that guy.* Well, he was sure that if we continued to "put our heads together" we'd come up with something. *Don't give up, that's the important thing.*

I'd never said anything about giving up. It was just expected.

"Should I get my pom-poms?" I said.

"What's that?"

"Forget it. I'm on it."

"That's my girl."

I gritted my teeth. The #MeToo movement never hit the law profession. Instead, the old guys, the ones who grabbed asses and dated their secretaries, had been sent to the "departure lounge," a half-abandoned floor where they could wander around and tell their semi-racist and totally sexist jokes to one another. Which left guys like Thomas—men in their late forties and fifties who never crossed the line, but you knew they wanted to. A look, a possessive comment, a fatherly pride even though they were often the same age as you or near enough. Like you were their project. They wanted to help you overcome your main deficit—being a woman in a man's world—if you played along and didn't forget your place.

Only they never truly helped you. They never stepped aside and let you run things. When a client said they wanted someone with "gray hair" to oversee the file (thin code for a man, because what professional woman lets her hair go gray?), they never demurred and convinced them otherwise. For women to be at the table, some men needed to step aside, but they didn't do that, they never did that, and . . .

Ugh. Now I was ranting. I hated that rant, even though I believed every word of it.

Was it any wonder women were mad? Was it any wonder women were tired?

This woman was. Tired and mad.

And so, when Thomas finally left my office with an encouraging thumbs-up, I did some light googling about Panthera Leo. Besides their website, all I could find were websites about lions, because it was the taxonomic term for the species. In a way, I was happy to find nothing. If it was malevolent, there'd be something about them on-line. A blog, a negative review on Yelp.

Reassured, I opened up the email I'd received the day before and followed the link to the application form. I took my time filling it out, but when I got to the "experiences," I hesitated. The cost wasn't outrageous, about five thousand dollars, but Dan wouldn't be happy with me spending the money. My points going down meant that my income was going down too, and if Aunt Penny was truly dying, then our expenses were about to go up significantly.

I read through the brochure for the July experience again. Five days at a dude ranch in Colorado. Horses and vistas. A full gym and spa. I rubbed my semi-permanently stiff neck. I needed a massage. A thousand massages. And the firm should pay for them because it was their fault. A year away from forty and I felt like my body was breaking down piece by piece.

The firm. *They* should pay for it. They *could* pay for it. I pulled up a spreadsheet and checked. I had five thousand dollars left in my ex-pense account. It was meant for wining and dining potential clients, but that's what I was doing, right? I wasn't going there for my own amusement. I needed to up my game, and that's what this promised. Besides, no one ever checked expense reports. If they did, they'd have to acknowledge the strip clubs and three-thousand-dollar bottles of wine that some of the male partners put on there.

So, no need to worry.

I pulled out my corporate credit card and entered the information, then hit send.

Within a few minutes, I received a confirmation email. I'd made the right decision. I was *in*.

Your life is going to change, Karma and Michelle promised me.

I sure hoped so.

CHAPTER 3

Assume the Crash Position

Then—July

In all my preparations over the weeks before I left for the retreat, I forgot that I hate flying.

A stupid thing to forget. But with having to wrap up and pass off a couple of files quietly so that people didn't think I was on vacation for five whole days (God forbid), standing vigil at the hospital for Aunt Peggy, and deciding what I should pack for a dude ranch, I didn't have much time to think about it. My assistant booked the flights, and she knew my requirements, though not the reason for them—a window seat in the middle of the plane where I could stare at the wing the entire flight so that the plane didn't fall.

Don't judge. It's worked so far.

My departure took so much effort because there were no phones permitted and no internet provided at the ranch. Five days with no phone and no internet connection. Normally when I go away, I take my laptop, my iPad, *and* my phone. I'm connected the whole time and usually do three to four hours of work a day. Since that's less than half of my usual day, it still seems like a vacation. But not this time. This time I needed to *give in to the experience*. I needed to be *truly disconnected*. I needed to *let the outside world fall away*.

That's what the material I received in the weeks leading up to my departure said. And even though it had me rolling my eyes, it also had me excited. No one could reach me for five whole days? Like, not even a little?

Sounded like heaven.

But being in heaven required more planning than usual. I gave detailed instructions to the two junior associates I was working with, which included only asking my best work friend, Felicia, for help if they were stuck. On no account were they to tell anyone else that they couldn't reach me. They both had round eyes of apprehension as I spelled it out to them. Twenty-seven and already married to their jobs (or at least their phones), the associates couldn't fathom a moment of disconnection. I'd heard one of them say that she even slept with her phone under her pillow so she could answer Thomas's calls in the middle of the night if required. She'd given him a special ringtone and everything.

I'd heard that one in the bathroom, unseen in the stall. I wanted to tell her not to bother, that Thomas might make her think this type of loyalty was rewarded, but it was the semi-lazy male associate who tried to get you to sleep with him during orientation week who was going to make partner first. But what was the point? She'd learn that soon enough, and I didn't want to steal her hope. She wouldn't believe me anyway. Like a woman who married a cheating man, she thought he'd be different with her. She could change him. She could change the whole system.

I knew because that's what I'd thought myself.

The endless generational fight. One generation always thinks the younger one is lazy and naïve, and the younger one always thinks the people who came before are bitter and ruined everything.

Both of us are right.

But I had files to hand off and things to organize, and so I waited for them to leave the bathroom while I crested the wave of a particularly bad period cramp and kept my lecture to myself.

Maybe if I'd done that more often—held my tongue—I wouldn't

be sitting in a window seat anxiously watching the wing of the airplane that was about to take off. Who can say what changes in your life might make any other thing happen?

"I have Xanax."

"What?" I turned away from the window. The woman sitting next to me—mid-thirties, dark skinned, and beautiful in a way that made it hard not to stare—was familiar. Was she truly offering me drugs?

She smiled, her teeth perfect and white. "I used to be afraid to fly too. Then I spoke to my doctor about it and—"

"Xanax?"

"Yeah, it works. You want? It will change your life."

Now I knew who she was. Athena Williams, a thirty-five-year-old recently elected first-time congresswoman, one of only a handful of Black women in the House. She'd taken the establishment by surprise, a candidate who squeaked out a win on election night that no one could believe, even her. Because she'd been a famous model in her early twenties, her campaign had gotten national attention and a lot of derision. But since her election, she'd proven to be an effective questioner in committee and was deft at making her point on Twitter. There was already talk of her running for the Senate when a seat became vacant.

"Um, isn't that illegal or something?" I asked, trying to keep the judgment out of my voice.

"Definitely."

"Better not, then."

"Suit yourself." She reached into her bag and came out with a bottle of pills. She tapped one out and cut it in half with her fingernail, then popped it into her mouth, returning the other half to the bottle so quickly it was over in an instant. She turned to me, knowing I'd been watching.

"Half is enough for me. A full one and I feel like a zombie."

She leaned back, closing her eyes. Did Xanax take effect that quickly? Maybe I should have taken the pill. I felt queasy. I'd had my eyes off the wing for the last few minutes, and who knew what had happened in the interim? I stole a glance out the window. The wing was still there, the ground crew shoving the last of the luggage into the hold.

"The wing won't fall off," Athena said.

"I know." It wouldn't because I'd be making sure the whole flight.

"You can't keep it from falling off with the power of your mind."

"How did you—"

"Fellow sufferer, I told you."

I watched her for a moment as the cabin crew announced that the doors were closing and we'd be taking off in five minutes. Anxiety crept up my neck. I checked my phone one last time and texted Dan an airplane emoji. He sent back a heart and wrote **you'll live.** I sent a heart back, then put my phone in airplane mode.

"Have you been to Colorado before?" Athena asked, her eyes still closed, her hands resting on her flat belly. She was wearing a pair of hiking pants and a Lululemon long-sleeved tech shirt. Aside from the very expensive purse, she was dressed as if she was ready to go on a backpacking trip. I was wearing my Manhattan summer weekend wardrobe: black capris, a T-shirt, and a black sweater for the cold airplane. I'd already felt as if I stuck out while waiting for the flight, surrounded as I was by tall, fit people in hiking shoes and wicking fabric.

"No, you?"

She turned her head toward me and opened her eyes. They were a rich brown with small flecks of gold. Eyes that had stared out from dozens of magazine covers, looking like they knew you personally. "A bunch of times. You'll love Aspen. What are you going for?"

"Oh, I . . ." I panicked, and not just because we'd pushed back from the gate and were taxiing along the runway. Once my application had been accepted, I'd gotten a glossy PDF that had stressed the values of community, and also discretion. Panthera's existence wasn't a secret—they had a website. But it still felt as if I shouldn't tell anyone where I was going.

"It's okay," Athena said, smiling. "I know."

"You do?"

"Panthera Leo, right?"

"How did you figure that out?"

"Karma and Michelle have a type." Her eyes were unfocused, the Xanax kicking in. "They know who'll fit into the group. And that's important because at its core, PL is a friendship."

"But for business?"

"Yes. A group of friends working together to achieve a common goal."

"World domination?"

She smiled at the joke and closed her eyes again. "I'm going to get some sleep if you don't mind."

"Oh, sure."

"You should try to sleep too. The next couple of days will be intense." She said the word *intense* casually, as if she were speaking about a workout.

"Not going to happen," I said.

"Okay."

She laced her hands in her lap, and I went back to my vigil as we accelerated and lifted off the ground. I tried to focus on the world we were leaving behind getting smaller, to distract myself from the fact that we were defying gravity.

—The ball field that looked like it was built for toys.

—The pools in the backyards of the suburban houses.

—The puffy clouds we were reaching for.

It was going to be okay. Whatever I was heading to, it was benign. Athena Williams was a member, for Christ's sake. Someone so public couldn't be involved in anything bad.

Right?

. . .

"Hello, folks. This is your captain speaking. We're going to be heading in for our landing in a few minutes. If you've never flown into
Aspen before, you're in for a treat. That being said, there's also going
to be some turbulence. So buckle up and enjoy the view."

My head snapped up. Against the odds, I'd fallen asleep, but I was
awake now.

"Maybe I should've taken that Xanax," I murmured.

"Told you," Athena said.

"I didn't mean to wake you."

"You didn't. And the captain's right. The view is amazing."

I eyed the window. The wing partially blocked the view, but I
could still see the mountains, tall triangles capped in snow. I'd seen
pictures before, but they didn't do it justice.

"The first year I came here, we climbed that," Athena said, pointing to a high peak. "Maroon Bells. Two days."

"That's terrifying."

"It kind of was."

The plane shuddered and made a loud *bump*. I cinched my seat
belt tighter, feeling sick. I'd never thrown up on an airplane, but
there was always a first time.

"You okay?"

"Tell me about the climb."

Athena shifted in her seat. "You know that book, *Into Thin
Air*?"

"About Everest? Where all those people died?"

"That's the one."

"I read that. It was great."

"Yeah, well—"

The plane *bump*ed again. I gripped the ends of my seat. How long
could it take to land? Five minutes at most? We were very close to the
mountains now. Surely, we weren't going to hit them.

"Anyway," Athena said. "I loved that book too. But it wasn't great
feeling like I was inside it, which was what the climb was like. I was
worried I wasn't going to make it down. I thought I was going to die

on the mountain and be some stupid headline. It was one of the hardest things I've ever done."

I forced my gaze away from the window. "Why do it, then?"

"Because it was there?"

"That's what they say about Everest."

"I know. I'm joking." She checked her perfectly manicured nails, a red high gloss that I could never pull off.

"Oh, sorry."

"It's fine." She smiled. "Close your eyes."

"Why?"

"It'll be easier, trust me."

I closed them, not quite sure why I was following along. Athena had that effect on people, I'd learn. It was one of the reasons she was an effective politician. She had a way of speaking that made you want to do what she was asking, no matter how far outside your comfort zone.

She made an encouraging sound, and I squeezed my eyes shut even tighter. It wasn't instant darkness. Instead, I saw floating points of red light that slowly faded away, as if I'd been staring at the sun.

"So," Athena said. "One thing I learned on that hike was that I needed to take in the moment. I'd done this thing that was super hard and scary. I'd used up all my energy and then some to get to the top, and the view was incredible, but I couldn't appreciate it. All I could think about was that there was weather coming in and how were we going to climb down all those steep pitches we'd come up and what the hell was I thinking doing the hike in the first place? There's even this picture of me at the top, and I'm miserable."

"You were scared."

"Sure, but I let my fear defeat the experience. I let the fear win."

I pressed my fingers against my eyelids. "Why are my eyes closed?"

"Because I want your full attention. It's this thing we do sometimes, in PL. To make sure we're listening to each other."

"Okay, I'm listening."

"Good. Because it's important, Nicole. You can't let your fears govern you."

"I don't."

"Sure you do. We all do. That's why you spend flights staring at airplane wings."

"It's not a big deal."

"It is, though. Because if you do this for something as innocuous as flying, think about how much it must be affecting the rest of your life. All the small and big ways that you're letting your fear rule you."

I wanted to fight back, but I held my tongue. I didn't know this woman and she didn't know me, and this whole thing was getting kind of weird.

The plane jolted.

"What was that?" I asked.

"Open your eyes."

I did, slowly. That same transition from darkness to light, a few red flashes, and *oh*. "We're on the ground."

"Yes."

"I didn't notice."

Athena smiled again. It wasn't a smile I recognized, not the one from her campaign posters. It was more genuine than that. Closer.

"Was that the point? To distract me until we landed?"

"It was one of them."

We arrived at the gate and the seat belt sign was turned off. She stood and started to gather her things. She had one of those tech backpacks that was always being advertised to me on Facebook, one that had enough storage capacity to keep your whole life in. It was appealing and organized. I resolved to get one as I turned to check the view. It was incredible. Beautiful mountains and an endless blue sky.

I turned back to Athena. "Is that what I'm going to learn during the next five days?"

"It'll be one of the things."

"And the rest?"

Athena's smile stayed in place, but her eyes shifted back to their public version. She reached up and fiddled with a small pin on her lapel. "Nicole, I couldn't even explain it to you if I tried."

The line of passengers waiting to get off started to move, and I watched Athena walk away, then stood to gather my things. As I shuffled off the plane, I replayed our conversation, how she'd lulled me into calm. She was right. My fears did tend to rule my actions. It wasn't just the flying; it went deeper than that. The whole reason I was on the plane was rooted in the fear that I'd lose my place in my career. Operating from a place of fear wasn't productive, and I resolved to work on that, pleased with myself about the choice I'd made to join Panthera though it felt like going out on a limb.

And maybe that's why I didn't think to ask how Athena knew my name.

Now—October

"Jack's blood?" I say to Athena in her bathroom.

Athena's head lolls to the side. Has she passed out? No, she's just out of it. Drugs? I've never known Athena to do serious drugs—just an occasional Xanax—and drugs weren't something I usually dabbled in. But I could use something tonight, something to blur this reality and make me forget what I'm seeing.

"Athena!" I say sharply, close to her face, my hand ready to slap her into reality if necessary.

It isn't. Her eyes focus and she turns her head toward me. "Can I have a towel?"

"What?"

"A towel. I need a towel."

I lean back and grab one off the rack, tossing it to her. She stands unsteadily and tucks it around her body, then glances disdainfully at the remnants of the stain at the other end of the tub. She has bruises forming on her thin upper arms, as if someone's grabbed her forcefully, maybe to shake her, maybe to hold her still.

She steps out of the tub without saying anything.

"Athena! What the fuck?"

She checks herself in the mirror, fluffing her hair back into place. There are dark rings under her eyes, as if she hasn't slept properly. "Thank you for coming."

"Where is Jack? Why is his blood in your tub? What's going on?"

Athena sits on the thin edge of the tub. Her shoulders sag, and she gets that unfocused look again. If I don't get some answers in a minute, I'm going to lose my fucking mind.

"I texted you?" Athena asks.

"Yes."

"I forgot."

"Athena. Please focus. I need some answers. Quickly."

Athena holds her hands out in front of her. Her nails are the same signature red as when we'd first met. But one of them is missing, ripped off, and another is cracked. She tucks her fingers inward and curls her hands in her lap.

"I met Jack on Radius," she says.

She's not answering my questions, but at least she's talking. I need to be patient.

"I remember." I think back to the night she'd connected with Jack. The app was supposed to be exclusive, and I'd marveled at the people I recognized who were members, some of whom were married. Wasn't it supposed to be a dating app? Was everyone screwing around? Plus, staid, very married Thomas had been there. How picky could they be?

"Did Jack do something to you?" The bruises on her arms. The coat downstairs. The wineglasses in the kitchen. The blood. Jack's blood, she'd said. "Where is he?"

Athena's eyes travel to the wall. Behind it is her bedroom. I know with 100 percent certainty that I do not want to go in there. But it doesn't feel like I have any choice. I'm here to help Athena. I've learned that asking too many questions isn't a good idea. And Athena's returned to her almost catatonic state, so I leave her and walk slowly toward the door. It's ajar, a crack of light on the wall.

I stand on the threshold wondering, not for the first time, how I got here. What series of decisions led me to this, about to walk into a room to discover—what? Everything else in my life before this feels like a straight line. I checked this box, and I got this result. Binary. That's what my life was *then*. Expected. Even.

Now . . .

I push open the door. It drags across the thick carpet. The air is still, but there's a tangy smell. Something metallic.

Blood.

My hand flies reflexively to my mouth as I walk slowly through the room. Again, my brain takes an inventory.

— The bed is rumpled, but not with sleep.
— There's a pile of clothes in the corner, as if they've been thrown there.
— There's a man's shoe lying at a weird angle on the floor at the edge of the bed.

I want to close my eyes. I want Athena's soothing voice talking me through this, distracting me so that when I open them again, I'll be somewhere safe, the danger behind me. But I'm alone. This is my task to complete.

No, not entirely alone.

I turn the corner of the bed. There's a foot attached to the shoe.

And the foot belongs to a man who's quite dead.

CHAPTER 4

Outside Now

Then—July

I sat in the van that took us—Athena, me, and three other women—to the ranch outside of Aspen like a small child with my face pressed up against the window. The mountains, the sky, the green rolling grass waving in the breeze. It was as if we'd stepped into a postcard, like everything around us had been filtered and retouched.

But as we bumped along the highway, I couldn't help but wonder: Who were these women sitting with me? Athena I knew, and yet didn't. I'd seen her campaign videos, those highly produced and moving "introductions" that go viral on Twitter. She was a prominent Black model who broke several color barriers in terms of mainstream coverage, then left that life behind to go to Harvard. Some lost years after she graduated when she rambled around, trying to find a purpose. Then her shift to politics, to give back and change the world. She'd unseated a thirty-year incumbent to gain her seat. It was an impressive accomplishment for someone her age.

Were all the other women of this caliber?

The woman sitting next to me introduced herself as Connie Chu. That name had a familiar ring to it, too. In her early fifties, her hair was pitch-black with fine streaks of white and blunt cut to her chin. She was also dressed in athleisure, and I wondered if I'd missed the memo. Thank God I'd packed some yoga clothes, the tags still on, that I'd ordered in a panic a few days before I left, when I realized that none of the workout clothes I'd bought during my healthier pandemic days fit me. It felt as if, overnight, I'd gained in weight what I'd lost in the points committee's decision. Had I really put on fifteen pounds without noticing? Was that why I felt slightly out of breath all the time? Because my clothes were cutting off my circulation?

We passed another stunning view of the mountains and I whipped out my phone and took a shot, then sent it to Dan. **What you're missing**, I wrote. He sent back a rude emoji and made a joke about having to castrate himself to get there. I smiled and put my phone away.

"It's beautiful, isn't it?" Connie said. She had a smattering of freckles across her nose, like a small trail of footprints in the sand. The reason her name was familiar came back to me. She was the founder of a huge security company that used hackers to protect systems rather than attack them. I'd seen her name across hundreds of documents I'd had to review early in my career when her company went public. Some idiot had misidentified her as Connie Chow, and I'd had to go through each document and put in a corrected page because everything had already been printed and collated, and fixing it was someone's idea of a good, humbling task for me.

"It's amazing. I can't believe I've never been out here before."

She smiled. "That's what I thought the first time too. I was so lucky to shelter in place here during the first wave of the pandemic."

Dan and I had spent the spring 2020 lockdown working at the dining room table and arguing over whose turn it was to go to the bodega to forage for whatever food was available. I cleaned every inch of the apartment with old cleaning supplies and logged hundreds of hours on the Peloton app even though I didn't have a Peloton, just an old exercise bike I couldn't stand up on. All the senior partners had decamped to the Hamptons and complained in unguarded moments about how they missed their housekeepers and nannies.

"Wish I'd been here. Am I the only newbie?"

"Why do you ask?"

"I don't want to be the only new person."

Connie focused in on me. "Are you afraid of being in unfamiliar situations?"

My shoulders crept up. Was every conversation going to turn into therapy? "I think it's normal to be apprehensive about spending five days with a group of strangers."

She patted my hand. "Don't worry; everyone I've ever met in PL has been amazing. Like Athena."

I glanced over my shoulder. Athena was sitting in the third row with another woman in her mid-thirties who was also vaguely familiar, but that might have been because she resembled half the professional women in New York. Long dark hair in beachy waves. Manicured hands. Pilates-class thin. The requisite yoga pants and a tank top that showed off her toned arms and shoulders.

"I worked on one of your IPOs," I said to Connie.

"Are you in venture cap?"

"No, I'm a lawyer. It was for . . ." I searched my memory banks. "Felidae, I think?"

She smiled. "My first corporate baby. Now on its way to being a Fortune 500 company."

"Oh wow, amazing." I wanted to kick myself. I sounded like a moron and felt out of place. What did this group want with me?

"You're wondering why you're here?" Connie said.

"Well, yeah."

"Because you're worth it."

"How do you know? We just met."

"Because you got picked."

"They never make a mistake?"

"Michelle and Karma? Not that I've known. Not about people. They're . . ." Connie played with the ring on her index finger, a simple platinum band. Like Athena, she was wearing a pin on her lapel—a watchful lioness on its haunches. "They're very good judges of character."

"Ranch up ahead," the driver said as he slowed down. He was in his mid-fifties, rugged and Western, his cowboy hat pushed back on his head, his denim shirt tucked into his jeans under a wide belt buckle. He'd held a sign that said PANTHERA RANCH at the airport and introduced himself as Gary.

He turned off the highway, and we drove along a long dirt road through a field of tall green grass filled with yellow wildflowers with black centers. The mountains loomed in front of us, so close it felt as if I could touch them if I reached through the glass. After a minute, we approached a set of high iron gates. There was a large lioness laid out across the middle of them.

The gates parted and the van kept moving. The road was dusty, and we were soon enveloped in a haze of it. Later, I'd wonder if the dust was allowed to accumulate on purpose, if even that part of our entrance to the ranch was manipulated, planned, timed.

Then, I thought only that someone should wet the driveway to keep the dust down.

The van stopped, and Gray said, "Everyone out!" in a weird militaristic way, and we climbed out into the swirling cloud.

It fell to the ground slowly, a misty light receding.

When it was gone, two women were standing there holding their arms out in greeting.

CHAPTER 5

The Arrival

Then—July

After a brief introduction to Karma and Michelle, we were shown around the ranch, and then to our individual cabins. They were spread out in a horseshoe across the property like small brown beads. Inside mine was a bed made of birch logs, a small matching dresser, and a sink. No bathroom. No shower. Those were in another building, and communal. Showering together wasn't how I wanted to build a community, but it was only for a few days.

I'd been up since four to get my flight, and I was tired. The first scheduled activity was the "Greeting," whatever that meant, which was still a couple of hours away, so I spent a few minutes putting my stuff away in the dresser, then lay down on the block-patterned comforter on the narrow single bed and fell promptly to sleep. I wasn't a napper, but that afternoon I slept hard for two hours despite the bright sunlight streaming in through the windows.

I don't remember dreaming, only the insistent buzzing of my phone that snapped me awake.

"Dan?"

"Aha! I knew it."

"What?" I sat up slowly, feeling dizzy and disoriented.

"You have your phone."

"I do."

"You said you wouldn't."

"Are you cross-examining me right now?"

Dan chuckled. "I wouldn't dare."

"We have some free time before the Greeting. I guess we'll lose our phones then?"

"What's the Greeting?"

"No idea. Everything has been pretty vague up to now."

"You should've brought a burner phone with you."

"Like a drug dealer?"

"So you can stay in touch," he said lightly.

I ran my hand through my hair. It was a mess and I smelled like the plane. "Dan, you'll never guess who's here."

"Oprah?"

"No, dummy. Athena Williams."

He took a beat to process. "The Athena Williams?"

"Yes. And another woman—Connie Chu—that I did a deal for years ago. You know, the one who started Felidae, that security company?"

"Wow."

I worked out the kink in my neck and stretched my arms over my head. "Admit it, you were kind of hoping for a juicy story."

"It's early days."

"True." I got up and walked to the window. The view was striking: more rolling grass, a large pasture, horses, and purple and yellow wildflowers. I set the phone down on the dresser and put it on speaker. "How's Aunt Penny?"

"Sleeping."

She'd never left the hospital. She had good days and bad days, but she spent a lot of time sleeping, and we knew it wouldn't be long until she was gone. I'd almost canceled the trip because of it, but Dan encouraged me to say my goodbyes while she still knew who I was. It had been an emotional hour in her private room a few days earlier, and the effects still lingered like a bad hangover.

"Are you at the hospital?"

"Yeah. My mom's here too, and my sister."

I breathed in and out slowly. Dan's sister, Katherine, was a pain in the ass who was still mad we were living in Aunt Penny's place even though she lived in Cincinnati. Dan's mother, Louise, favored her, though she'd always said she didn't want to take sides between her children. But when one child is a jerk and the other is the nicest person you've ever met, well, you *are* taking sides if you let the jerk get away with whatever they want under the guise of family unity.

"Sorry I'm missing it," I said.

"Sure."

"Well, I'm sorry I'm not there for you."

"It's fine. She's had a good life." I could hear the catch in his throat.

"She has. And Dan—"

"If we don't get to keep the apartment, it'll be fine."

Tears sprang to my eyes. It was the first time either of us had said it out loud. It was a stupid thing to get emotional about—real estate—but we'd been there for almost ten years, the whole time we'd lived together. We'd gotten married there. We'd made every large decision that we'd made together there: careers, whether to have kids, whether to stay together when we'd had a rough patch five years ago. I knew our marriage could continue outside its four walls, but I wasn't ready to face that possibility.

"You promise?" I asked.

"Yes. Now open your suitcase and check the inside pocket."

"Why?"

"I left you a surprise."

"Hold on." My suitcase was on a small stand in the corner. I opened it and felt around until I found the inside pocket where I usually kept my travel toothbrush. Instead, there was something small and rectangular. I unzipped the pocket and pulled it out.

"You got me a burner phone?"

"I did."

"What am I supposed to do with this?"

"Hide it."

"In case of?"

"In case of emergency."

"You're nuts."

An announcement sounded behind him. Someone was needed urgently in room 627. Not Aunt Penny's room.

"Maybe," he said. "But I love you and I don't like the thought of not being able to reach you for five days. Not in a creepy way—I promise."

"I know." I clutched the phone in my hand, feeling sad and loved. "Thank you."

. . .

I didn't get a good look at Karma and Michelle when I'd arrived; they'd said hello, then spun off into the dust that was still swirling every time a gust of wind blew. Gary had been the one to give us our tour. At the end of it, he pointed to a large log structure at the center of the compound and told us to show up there at sunset after we'd had dinner.

When I got off the phone with Dan, I read the printed schedule on the dresser and was relieved to see it was time to eat. I changed quickly into my new yoga wear, taking a fleece with me since I suspected it would cool off as soon as the sun went down.

The communal dining room was in a large log building in the middle of the string of cabins. On one side were the showers, fitness room, and spa; the other was the dining room and a library/lounge area. Inside, it had a similar vibe to the cabin I was staying in—minimalist rustic, with walls and furniture made of bleached logs and not much in the way of decoration other than an occasional Navajo printed rug and one striking needlepoint of a lioness in full roar.

This is what my law firm is paying five thousand dollars for?

Though no one had promised luxury accommodations. "Luxury thinking" was the point, whatever that meant.

The dining hall had two long tables set parallel to each other. A large wall of windows framed the mountains—the astounding view almost justified the price. There was a generous buffet set up on a table underneath the windows: two large salads, cold poached salmon, grilled vegetables, fluffy dinner rolls. It reminded me of the spreads we had at law firm events, expensive but bland. I thought briefly of the work I'd left behind. I shoved it aside and filled my plate, then turned to find a seat.

Connie and Athena were at one of the tables, deep in conversation. The two women I didn't know were at the other. I wanted to sit with Connie and Athena—I'm an extrovert, though I have a cap on how many new people I can meet in a day—but the brunette from the van motioned for me to join them, and this was about building community, so I did.

"Hi, I'm Samantha Cole," she said when I took a seat across from her. She had half the amount of food on her plate that I had, and I felt embarrassed by my gluttony.

Samantha held out her hand and gave me a firm shake. Eye contact, an open expression.

"Nicole Mueller," I said.

"What do you do?" the other woman asked. She had pale skin and a halo of orange hair around her head that reminded me of Orphan Annie. She also wore a sullen expression, but maybe she was just tired from the travel. There were dark circles under her baby-blue eyes, and I guessed her to be in her late thirties or early forties.

"I'm a lawyer."

The redhead sat back in her seat in a challenge. "A lawyer, huh?"

"Yep. Hit me with your best lawyer joke. I can take it."

Samantha laughed. It was a pleasant sound, almost a giggle, which was at odds with her forthright manner. "I like lawyers."

"Not many do."

"I play one on TV."

For the umpteenth time that day, I felt like a dummy. That's why she was familiar. Not because I'd seen her around Manhattan, but because she was on that show, District Attorney, half my firm was obsessed with. I'd never watched it because I didn't need to watch what I did all day on TV. When I had the time, I wanted an escape into things like zombies and postapocalyptic futures where people disappeared and then reappeared with special powers. I knew those things didn't happen. But trials did. Watching fake trial prep made me anxious.

"Your show is very popular," I said. "Congratulations."

"You don't watch it though, right?" Orphan Annie said.

"I didn't catch your name."

"And you didn't answer the question."

My shoulders crept up. "You're right, I don't watch. Sorry."

"It's fine. You can't take things like that personally."

I smiled at her. "I agree."

"Her name is Heather Davis," Samantha said.

"Nice to meet you, Heather."

Heather picked at the food on her plate. She'd taken a generous portion like me but had barely eaten any of it. "Sure."

"She's not very friendly," Samantha offered.

"Do you two know one another?"

"We were sitting next to each other on the plane."

I watched Heather hunt a stray piece of lettuce around her plate. She didn't seem to mind us talking about her like she wasn't there, but something about her whole vibe was off. Everyone else was excited to be there. Heather seemed pissed. Like she was there against her will.

"What do you do, Heather?"

She raised her head with a sigh. "I'm in corporate finance. I specialize in hostile takeovers."

"Ah."

"I know who you are."

"Have we met?"

"New York is a small town."

If someone had told me that fifteen years ago, I would've said they were nuts. How could a city with eight million people be a small town? But I knew now what she meant. When it got down to it, there were circles within circles that made it seem as if everyone knew one another. I'm always running into people I know at restaurants or browsing in a store on a Saturday.

"What firm are you at?" I asked.

"Young and Fine."

That explained it. They were clients. Young & Fine purchased companies through aggressive tactics that often ended up in litigation. That's where we came in. It wasn't my specialty, but everyone in the firm had to work on some of those cases.

"How did you end up here?" I asked.

Heather smiled for the first time. "That's a long story."

"Feels like we have time."

Someone clapped their hands together sharply. "Okay, ladies! The moment you've all been waiting for!"

Gary was standing at the head of the room holding what looked like a pillowcase. He'd added a black puffy vest to his cowboy uniform and his boots were dusty.

"Oh God," Heather said.

"What?"

"You'll see."

Had Heather been at the ranch before? I'd assumed she was a newbie like me, but clearly that was wrong. Come to think of it, Connie had never answered my question about that either. Maybe I was the only new recruit.

"Cell phones, please," Gary said.

"Oh," Samantha said. "I guess they were serious about that?"

"As a heart attack," Heather said.

I took my phone out and checked it. There was a rush of email messages which I scrolled through quickly. Nothing urgent.

"Ladies, let's go!"

Everyone at my table was doing the same thing as me—sending last-minute messages. Connie and Athena had their phones in their hands but weren't looking at them. I felt ashamed. Cell phones were like yawns—contagious—but still. I'd handled everything at work, and Dan had thought ahead and given me an escape route if I needed it. I could give up my phone.

I stood and walked toward Gary, taking inventory as I went.

— The calm certainty of Athena and Connie.
— The way Heather clutched her phone to her breast.
— Gary's air of authority.

I didn't know what it added up to, but collecting information I might need later reassured me.

Up close, Gary had a dark shadow across his chin where his beard was coming back, and eyes that were almost black. He was strong, fit, and powerful. Not a man to be trifled with. He nodded at me and held open the bag. I placed my phone inside, trying not to feel like I was giving up a limb.

It's only four days, I thought.

Not enough time for anything significant to happen.

CHAPTER 6

The Greeting

Then—July

Night stole into the compound like a thief. One minute I was watching the most amazing sunset I've ever seen, and the next it was so dark it was hard to see my hand in front of my face. It was a moonless night, and the stars were thick in the sky, the Milky Way a shimmering wave.

"Is that Venus?" I asked, pointing to the brightest star.

"Fuck if I know," Heather said.

"This way," Athena said briskly. She pointed toward an even darker part of the compound. We followed along single file, Connie, Samantha, Heather, me, and Athena bringing up the rear. The path was a narrow rut in the dirt. When we turned a corner, there was a large open structure looming against the inky sky and a roaring fire beneath it, the sparks reaching up into the night, the wood crackling. The fire was made from a sweet-smelling wood—an apple tree, maybe, with a hint of something else. It was calming, and I let out a slow breath, like I'd learned in the yoga classes I no longer went to, deep and from the solar plexus.

"Take a seat," a woman's voice said. It was low and soothing, like chimes tinkling. It was hard to see who was speaking in the dark. There were two figures standing side by side across the fire from us, their faces in shadow. They were both wearing long, flowing garments that made them appear shapeless.

We followed her instructions and sat a few feet apart from one another on the two low logs that were set up around the fire. I slipped my fleece on, glad I'd thought to bring it.

"Welcome," the woman said once we were all seated. "I'm Michelle Song." She stepped forward. The fire lit up her gray-blond hair, which she wore in a long side braid over her shoulder. While I hadn't recognized her when I met her briefly that afternoon, once I heard her last name, I knew who she was. "Welcome to Panthera Ranch. And welcome to Panthera Leo. We could not be happier that you've accepted our invitation to join our little community."

Michelle shared a bemused look with the woman standing next to her—Karma. Connie and Athena joined her in a laugh. "We may be little in numbers, but we're outsized in influence. That's the goal, anyway."

Her words flowed like music, which made perfect sense. Michelle Song was the lead singer of the Songbirds, one of those eighties groups that played ubiquitously throughout my childhood. She was over sixty now, but she still had the Kelly-green eyes that gazed out from her three multiplatinum albums. She'd dropped out of the music business in the early 2000s after a brief comeback album.

And I ro-oh-am through the grass . . .
And I ro-oh-am through your heart . . .
And I ro-oh-am through my life . . .
Wishing, wishing, wishing that I had another song to sing.

That was the chorus of her last earworm, which my mother had played on repeat while she danced around the house. She would be so excited if she knew that I was this close to Michelle Song, but she'd died ten years ago, so all I could feel was her loss.

"Influence," Michelle said. "Do you know how important that is in the world? You might think you do, but it's more than you know. That client you didn't get, Nicole? That part that went to someone else, Samantha? That deal that fell apart, Heather? That's not because of a lack of talent or motivation or hard work. Maybe for others, but not for you. We've vetted you. We know."

Michelle looked at each of us directly. When I met her eyes across the fire, it felt as if she were looking directly into my heart, my ambition. As if she knew all the plans I had for myself were slipping away.

"You lost those things because of influence, or its lack. Influence is everything. It's the boys' club, the inner circles you don't even know are there. If you're lucky, you might break in. More often than not, you don't, and sometimes it's without even knowing it. We've felt that in our own lives. You think I got credit for writing all our songs? The record company insisted I give equal credit to my ex-husband because he was the tortured-artist type. He was *believable* as the auteur of our hits. Me? I was the candy floss that made it palatable. I was a mother. Mothers don't write hit songs, *that's not cool, man.* I butted up against that for ten years, and then I'd had enough. I was tired of it all. I'll bet you're tired of it too."

I was. My God I was *so tired*. Beneath all the frustration and anger at what the points committee had done to me was exhaustion. I'd worked myself to the bone for years and it didn't seem to be enough. Why was that? It wasn't just the boys' club. But it wasn't *not* the boys' club, either.

"I was tired and frustrated, and all I could think to do was drop out and leave it all behind. Being a wife and mother and a superstar was weighing me down so much I felt strangled. And then I met Karma," Michelle said, smiling at the woman who stood slightly behind her. She was in her mid-fifties and tall. Her shoulder-length hair was dark, thick, and wavy, held back from her face with a band made of the same pattern as the rugs in the lodge. Her skin was burnished, and her eyes looked black in the night. She was wearing something similar to Michelle—a long flowing tunic made out of natural fibers in a deep russet color.

"As fate would have it," Karma said with a smile.

"As fate would have it," everyone but Samantha and me said as one, while I shivered in my fleece.

"Maybe you read the stories," Michelle said. "How I dropped out of my record deal and went to Tanzania to find myself? Those articles always had a certain tone about them. Like I couldn't take it. Like I was drying out from too many parties and too many men. Nothing could be further from the truth." Her melodic voice turned steely. "The media has such a failure of the imagination where women are concerned."

She spread her arms out wide. "I wasn't there to find myself. I was there to return to myself. To get back what the media and the fans and my ex had taken from me." She thumped her chest. "My courage, my creativity, my ambition. And when I'd peeled away the layers that I'd cloaked myself in, I knew a few truths: You don't have to be in the spotlight to get what you want. You don't have to be loud to wield power. You can achieve everything you want if you know one simple thing. We are stronger together."

"Together we are one," Connie and Athena said in response, sending a chill through me.

Silence fell. I watched the crack and pop of the fire and followed a shower of sparks up to where they met the horizon. I shivered again, goose bumps climbing up my arms. Michelle's words resonated. I'd felt alone in my career for reasons I couldn't quite explain, and even before then, in college, in law school. The idea that there might be others who'd have my back no matter what filled me with a sense of hope.

"What this means in practice is simple," Karma said after a moment, her voice deep, almost masculine. "We work together to advance our interests. We champion one another. We're like Emily's List. With teeth."

Laughter rippled around the circle like dominoes falling.

"Speaking of teeth . . ." Karma said. "Most of you know this, but for the uninitiated, you may have noticed our symbol around." She stepped closer to the fire and pointed to the pin on her left shoulder that was holding her wrap in place. It had the same lioness on it that I'd seen Athena and Connie wearing. "Panthera Leo. That's our name and our emblem. The female lion. Because she's the one that gets things done in the Pride. Without women, the men wouldn't eat, they wouldn't have the 'lion's share' to take. That's true for humankind too, but often unacknowledged, even today. 'The woman behind the man,' sure. But she's supposed to be nice and polite. She's not supposed to be primal. Gentle, not vicious. Only men are allowed those attributes."

Karma held out her hands to the fire. "But don't worry, you don't have to be outwardly fierce. It's a metaphor for what we stand for. Being in charge and getting what we want. We don't need to take the credit. Let the men take that if they want to, when they need to. When it counts, your contribution will be recognized."

"So, what does this mean in practice?" Michelle said, stepping up to Karma. The two of them formed a pendulum, swinging back and forth in harmony. "It means that if you need anything, you come to this group. To your Pride. You are a family, one without a formal leader. Women don't need to fight for their dominance; they join together willingly to achieve the best result for all. When one of us asks for help, we say yes without hesitation or excuses. We don't put up barriers or question choices. We let our fellow Leo know that we are there for her and we will do whatever it takes to resolve her issue."

A log tumbled from the pile and released another cascade of sparks. Karma raised her arms up in a welcoming motion. "Enough talk for now. We'll discuss more of this tomorrow after you've had a chance to sleep and process. We know you're all tired from your journey. A few last words to explain the Greeting."

Michelle dived quickly down to the ground to pick something up. A round wooden bowl that she held in her hands like an offering. "Leos are our symbol and our guide. Their method of greeting is personal and comforting. A simple rubbing of their heads. Like this." She turned with the bowl in her hands to Karma, who leaned her forehead in until it was touching Michelle's. They moved their heads back and forth slowly, reminding me of an Inuit kiss, or *kunik*.

"Please rise." Karma stepped back from Michelle and motioned for us to stand.

We did, one by one.

"Turn toward each other."

I faced Heather. She rolled her eyes at me quickly and I gave her a small smile.

"Lean in."

We did as instructed. Heather smelled like sandalwood and possibly weed. Our foreheads touched and I swept mine back and forth. It was a strangely intimate gesture, much more so than the standard cheek kiss that I'd never liked.

"Please give the Greeting to everyone, then come and take a sip from the bowl," Michelle instructed.

We did as she asked, leaning into one another, learning each other's scents, the feel of their hair as it brushed against our cheeks. In the back of my mind, Dan was laughing at me, but I banished him. So the ritual was a bit hokey and not my thing. Who cared? I'd spent my whole life trying to conform to the male ideal of how a woman in business should be, and where had it gotten me? Less points, that's where. Maybe a bit of hokey was what I was missing.

When we were done, we lined up in front of Michelle, who was cradling the wooden bowl in her hands. "Don't be worried; this is a simple, natural sleeping draft that we learned to make in Tanzania many years ago when Karma was researching products. It will help ease your mind into sleep quickly so you can get the most out of your time here."

I shifted nervously from foot to foot. I'd turned down Athena's Xanax because drugs weren't my thing. *But what could it hurt?* It was going to be hard for me to sleep after that nap, and I was exhausted. I needed a break from my brain.

When it was my turn with the bowl, I took a large, bitter gulp.

That's what Michelle and Karma had said Panthera was about, right? Accepting help without question? Or was it the other way around?

I was suddenly too tired to tell.

CHAPTER 7

The Workout

Then—July

I slept the sleep of the innocent but was woken by the sun at the ungodly hour of six a.m.

The first thing on the schedule wasn't until that afternoon—a hike ominously called the Hunt. I hoped this was a metaphor. Although I ate meat, I didn't want to kill it.

Regardless, I needed to find something to do with myself until then. I was like a child who didn't know how to entertain herself without screens.

I grabbed some freshly squeezed orange juice in the dining room and headed to the gym. If I was going to get two extra hours in the day, I should work on my fitness. And by work, I meant start doing something about it again. Forty was just around the corner, and my recent wardrobe discovery meant I wasn't going to be able to rely on my metabolism to keep from having to buy an entire new set of clothes if I didn't change some things soon.

I expected to be alone in the gym, but Heather was already there, running red-faced on a treadmill at a speed I knew I'd never attain. I waved to her in the mirror and got on the other treadmill. A fast walk seemed like the right way to start.

After five minutes I was panting and cursing myself. How had I let things get this bad? I resolved to exercise for thirty minutes every day, even if it meant having to forgo a bit of sleep. And to cut out that second glass of wine that had snuck into my daily dinner routine. Surely that should be enough?

"What do you think of the place?" Heather said, thumping her arms onto the side of my treadmill.

I reduced my speed because I knew I couldn't walk that fast and talk at the same time. "It's beautiful."

Heather wiped her face with a towel. Up close you could see that her complexion was freckles with milky-white skin underneath. She had her hair in two braids and looked more like Anne of Green Gables than Orphan Annie.

"I meant, what did you think of Michelle and Karma? Last night's spiel, etcetera?"

I glanced over my shoulder, though I wasn't sure what I was worried about. "I like the underlying message."

"You're cautious. I get it. You're a lawyer."

I slowed my treadmill down even further. "So far, it's not what I expected."

"What did you think it was going to be?"

"Not sure. Meetings. PowerPoint presentations on how to build up our referral networks."

"It's more like an intense corporate team-building retreat."

I checked the treadmill's screen. I hadn't even walked a mile and my legs felt like they were dying. I wanted to reach for the speed button again, but I didn't want to show weakness in front of Heather. Those corporate raiders were all the same—ultra-aggressive without much thought for the consequences. Litigators lived in other people's consequences. It was our job to fix their mistakes.

"Have you been here before?" I asked.

"I have, but I didn't end up joining Panthera the first time."

"Why not?"

"I had to leave for a work emergency. No big deal."

"You thought it was worth it? To give it another try?"

She passed her towel over her face. "I guess I did."

"Do you know Karma's story? Michelle's, I know. My mother was obsessed with her when I was growing up. But there wasn't that much information about Karma on the website."

"She's Good Karma."

"The wellness brand?"

"Yep. But that's just where she started. She's got an umbrella of companies now in the personal care and holistic pharmaceutical industry; some she started herself and some she's acquired. Last year she made the list of female billionaires."

I scrolled through the mental images I had of the CEO of Good Karma, a frequent Instagram presence who came off as a slicker, more corporate version of Gwyneth Paltrow. Yet here, she was distinctly granola. Was either of them real?

"How did she and Michelle meet?"

"In Tanzania. Karma sources a lot of her ingredients there. You know, all those tree-bark-sap facials and whatever?"

My treadmill beeped. I'd finally walked a mile. I was either going to have to start running or do forty-five minutes every day in order to get any decent mileage.

"Why did they start Panthera?"

"To fight the patriarchy." Heather smirked. "But that didn't stop Vic Sullivan from trying to take over Good Karma five years ago."

I'd heard of Sullivan—he was an inventive genius who'd started numerous companies that all seemed to turn immediately to gold. But he'd had some legal trouble in the last couple of years and had been ousted from his first company, SulliVent, a massive biotech firm that was on the cutting edge of using tech to deliver medication.

"Your firm worked on the deal?"

"Yep. Putting men in charge of women's companies is one of our specialties. Diversity this and diversity that and sensitivity training and you know what's changed? Exactly nothing, that's what. If you have a vagina, then you're handicapped. God forbid if you have a kid or show an emotion at work."

I felt my blood starting to boil. "Emotional women, right? That is such bullshit."

"So much bullshit. It's men that do most of the violence. It's their emotions we need protecting from."

"Sing it, sister."

Heather looped her towel around her neck. Her face was as red as it had been at the beginning of our conversation. I wondered how long it stayed like that. "Anyway, Karma fought off the takeover, and I think that prompted them to get more aggressive with recruiting people into Panthera. She wanted to consolidate a wall of female power to stave off any other men who thought they knew better. And it's worked as far as I can tell. Those assholes all respect her now."

"That's cool."

"Yep."

"Does your office know you're here?"

"Hell to the no. They'd have kittens."

"Where do they think you are?"

Heather raised the corner of her mouth. "Rehab. Can you believe that shit? It's the only way to take a real vacation these days. And since the men do it too, they can't say anything about it."

"That's fucked up."

"It's life. Do what you need to do to get by. Your firm know that you're here?"

"Not exactly."

"Where do they think *you* are?"

I checked the screen again. I seemed to be entering a hill section and the treadmill was creeping slowly upwards as my calves protested. "Um, well . . ."

"That's what I thought. Anyway, I should take a shower. See you later."

She left, and I thought over what she'd said. I hadn't lied about where I was going, but I hadn't told the full truth, either. A networking conference, I'd said, and that *was* the reason I was here. But I also knew that if I'd told Thomas what I was doing in detail and asked for permission, he wouldn't have given it.

So I didn't ask. It's always easier to apologize after.

So long as your apology is accepted.

CHAPTER 8

The Hunt & The Dunk

Then—July

At lunch we gathered around one of the communal tables and got to know one another—establishing career paths and people we knew in common. Things we did not talk about:

- —Fashion, shoes, or beauty treatments.
- —Whether we looked good or fat.
- —Where to find a man.

When we were done, we changed into hiking clothes and assembled by the ashes of last night's fire. I'd developed a small, lingering headache, and I had my doubts about the innocence of the concoction I'd imbibed. Then again, it was equally likely to be device-withdrawal. Either way, I'd had a good if short sleep and was about to exercise for the second time that day. This group was already giving me benefits.

We waited for Karma and Michelle in the hot sun. It got cool at night, but it was full summer, the temperature during the day in the mid-eighties, though the air was dry, so different from the mugginess of home. The sky felt a million miles high, clear and blue and endless.

Gary arrived and handed each of us a small pack that contained a rain jacket, water bottle, compass, granola, first aid kit, and a map, then left us. The ranch appeared to operate on minimal or very discreet staff, as I hadn't seen anyone other than Gary and a few people working in the kitchen. I wondered what the place was used for generally, or if it was exclusively for the group.

Once we'd settled our packs on our shoulders, Karma and Michelle appeared. Both of them had traded their flowing robes for more practical hiking shirts and three-quarter leggings with sturdy hiking shoes. They passed quickly through us, giving us the Greeting from the night before.

"We'll be hiking out there," Karma said, pointing to the tall green grasses that were lilting in the breeze beyond the dusty courtyard. She was wearing a pack that had a rifle attached to its side. "But first, a bit of information. Who can tell me how a lion hunts?"

"It stalks its prey," Samantha said. She was wearing black hiking shorts that ended at her knees and a matching ball cap with her long hair pony-tailing out the back. Her legs and arms were toned in a way I'd never achieve even if I worked out daily for hours. I was glad I was in a profession where that kind of dedication to my body wasn't necessary.

"That's right," Michelle said. "Quietly, in tall grasses, it waits for the right moment before it pounces. It's a stalker. Not for its own pleasure, but to survive. It requires enormous patience and cooperation, two traits that are important to develop in yourselves. If you have them, you'll be rewarded."

"So that's what we're going to do today," Karma added. "Work on our ability to move through things together to obtain a reward."

"Is that what the rifle is for?" I asked.

"It's for protection. This isn't New York City."

Athena smiled. "Lots of people have guns in New York City."

"What are we stalking, then?" Heather asked.

"Life."

Karma turned on her heel and started walking through the courtyard. We followed her one by one, kicking up dust until we entered the tall grass, which was sharp and caught exposed flesh if you didn't approach it the right way. As we hiked, Karma and Michelle pointed out elements of our environment that we would've ignored. A patch of bent grass that meant an animal had rested there. The way the wind carried scents. How to stand in a formation that would allow the group to have a three-sixty view of the landscape and signal to one another about what surrounded us. It reminded me of Girl Scout training, the badges I'd earned a distant memory. We didn't see much wildlife beyond some birds and an errant jackrabbit, its white tail flashing through the grass, but I felt much more aware of my environment and my place in it. I appreciated the lesson in complete stillness, how to freeze in place and listen. Total concentration was a skill I already used in my job, and it felt good to flex that muscle.

"When you stop to listen," Michelle said, standing with her arms out wide, her fingertips fluttering over the tops of the long grass, "life is all around you. The more you know about it, the more you can shape it to your will. Pick your target, learn everything you can about it, and then go in for the kill." She turned in a circle, looking each one of us in the eye. "Understood?"

We nodded, and she smiled in response. Karma flicked her wrist, pointing across a rolling expanse, motioning us to follow her. Sweat ran down my back as the sun covered us, the ground deceptively challenging. We hiked silently for thirty minutes until we arrived at the cool shade of a stand of aspens. There was a river nearby, its bubbling an invitation. I put down my pack and I reached gratefully for my water bottle.

I was going to walk/run for forty-five minutes every morning from now on if it killed me.

We formed a natural circle around Karma and Michelle, who didn't look winded or hot. They probably ate perfect organic diets and never fought over the last helping of sesame noodles.

"How can you apply the lessons we learned over the last few hours to your life?" Michelle said.

"Know your enemy?" Samantha said.

"That's right. It is good to know as much as possible about anyone who's standing in your way. Information is a tool. Anything else?"

"Be aware of your surroundings," I said.

Michelle turned to me, her focus sharp. "Another good suggestion, but unpack that a little."

"If you know your environment well, you can use it to your advantage. Or at least not let it get in your way."

"Excellent. Anyone else? What about instincts?"

"We should trust them," Heather said.

"You should trust your Pride," Karma said. "Instincts can lead us astray."

"How?"

"Take today," Karma said, pointing to the field. "If that had been a real hunt, if we were truly stalking a dangerous animal, your instincts might have been telling you to give up, to flee from the danger. But trusting in your Pride would keep you in place and on task."

Trust others, she was saying; let them help you. It made sense to me. It was probably why I'd acted uncharacteristically and accepted the invitation in the first place.

"There is much to learn from Leo," Karma said. "And from each other. In order to do that, we need to build trust. To strip away the barriers that divide us, both emotional and physical." Karma pointed toward the creek. "That water is never more than sixty degrees, even in the hottest summer. Right now, it's even colder. That's why we'll be going in. We'll strip away our clothes and the fears we cover ourselves in. Only when we're naked before each other can we build absolute trust."

I stared at the creek. The water was rushing through the rocks, and if there are two things I hate, it's cold water and being naked in front of others. I'm one of those women who went into the curtained-off changing room in the gym. I never understood the women who had no compunction in removing their clothes in a room full of strangers, and who lounged around with their towels around their waists as if they were men.

"Won't we get hypothermia?" Samantha asked. "I had to go into a river on a shoot once and that totally happened."

"We'll only be in for thirty seconds. Enough time to fully immerse yourself and feel the experience. Then you'll walk here to the sunlight and let nature warm you."

That satisfied Samantha, but not the riot of complaints in my mind. I didn't even take cold showers during the worst days of summer. The last time I'd willingly gotten into freezing water was during a polar bear swim when I was fourteen. It did not go well.

"What if we have a medical condition that prevents us from doing it?" I asked.

Michelle gave me a bland expression. "Do you?"

"Well, not diagnosed, but I think I have a low threshold for hypothermia."

"It's your choice. Just as it's your choice to join us or continue on your merry way. But I would ask, why did you come here?"

"To get what you mentioned in your email: the advantages that men have in the workplace."

"That's honest. And did you think you wouldn't have to work to get those things?"

"No. But—"

"What does jumping into freezing water have to do with getting ahead in the workplace?"

"Yes."

"It's not linear, Nicole. I cannot promise you that if you do this, then you'll achieve the results that others have. But I can promise you that if you don't, you won't. It's up to you." She held her hand out. My hand raised almost automatically to meet it. When our fingers touched, hers were cold, like she'd already been in the water. "We can do it together. All right?"

I gazed into her eyes and felt the power of persuasion that she possessed. That certain light of accomplishment. She could see past this moment, and I wanted to.

"Yes."

She smiled and released my hand. She started to undress. I wanted to turn around to do the same, but I had a feeling that wasn't the point. So I picked a spot just past her ear and slowly removed my own clothes, letting them fall at my feet.

"Let's go, everyone. You too," Michelle said.

I willed myself not to look around. Not to think about the fact that I hadn't shaved my legs in a week or gotten that bikini wax I was supposed to. This wasn't a date, and no one cared about my personal grooming. I shouldn't care either, though most of these women had better bodies than mine. Was it easier to be nude when you had better personal self-esteem? Then again, most women probably hate something about their bodies. I'd never heard a man talk about that. How did that happen?

"Ready?" Michelle asked. Her shoulders were pale, with only a half moon of darker skin where her neck was normally exposed.

"Ready," I said with confidence I did not feel.

She reached out again, and I took her cold hand. We walked down the bank in our bare feet, the rocks scraping at our tender flesh. The closer we got to the river, the more powerful it seemed. The water hurried loudly through large rocks and was about three feet deep. The air smelled cold.

"There's a deeper pool over there," Michelle said in my ear. "If we can get to those rocks, we can drop right in, then climb out."

I tried to see where she was pointing. On the far side of the river, about fifty feet away, there was a circle of rocks where the current seemed less violent. I'd have to take her word for it that it was deep enough to jump into without breaking a leg.

She let go of my hand and stepped onto a large rock, then another. I followed her from rock to rock. I held my arms out from my body to keep from falling. I couldn't hear my heart beating over the roar, but I could feel it. When I checked my watch, my heart rate was at 140 beats a minute—higher than I'd gotten that morning on the treadmill.

We reached a large flat rock near the circle that Michelle had pointed to. There was enough room for both of us to stand on it, but our sides were touching, my hot body lining up with her cool one. I couldn't believe I was about to do this. But I'd come this far, the water wouldn't kill me, even if it felt like it might, and the one thing I couldn't abide was failure. That's what had been driving me toward this. The sense that I was about to fail for the first time in my life.

No, fuck that. I wasn't failing. I was jumping.

"Ready?" Michelle said in my ear again.

"Let's do it."

"Three . . . two . . ." She tugged my arm and pulled me in after her, not bothering to wait for one.

The water felt like a slap. It stole my breath and clung to my bones. The pool was deep enough to sink all the way over my head, and it was black beneath the surface. Sound cut out and I tried not to panic as the breath rushed from my body. My feet hit the bottom, and I instinctively kicked up until my head broke the surface.

Michelle was treading water next to me. She grabbed my arm. "Twenty more seconds."

I nodded as my teeth started to chatter and I began to count in my head. Each second was agony, a test of my will not to panic and let the water pull me under. I'd never felt so cold; the polar bear swim was nothing compared to this. It didn't matter. All that mattered was the cold, the cold, the motherfucking cold.

"And out!"

Michelle released me and I slipped beneath the surface. I kicked up and two sturdy hands reached down and lifted me out, enveloping me in a metallic space blanket that felt like tissue paper.

"Wrap that around you tight," Karma said, "and walk back to the sun."

I did as she instructed and stepped past Samantha who was next in line and was not looking happy about it. Heather was behind her, staring into the woods, doing her best not to see what was coming. Athena and Connie weren't there, but I guessed they'd already done this part.

I walked with my teeth chattering back to the field, slipping on the rocks, the space blanket barely covering me. I had no heat to hold in and it felt as if I'd never get warm again.

I climbed up the bank to where I'd left my clothes. Athena and Connie were sitting there, sunning themselves like life was a picnic.

"You made it," Athena said.

"I . . . g-g-gue . . . sss . . . s-s-sooo . . ."

"You need help warming up?"

"W-Whhhh . . . d-d-did . . . y-y-y . . ."

Athena stood and walked to me. She took the blanket and tucked it around me quickly, so I didn't have time to be embarrassed, then took my left arm between her hands and started rubbing vigorously. It hurt, but I could also feel a bit of warmth spreading through my hands.

"Connie, help me out. Her lips are blue."

Connie took my other arm, following Athena's example as they moved me into the sun. After a few minutes, my teeth stopped chattering. Just in time for Samantha to emerge from the woods looking like I must have: blue lips, white skin, space blanket like a cape.

"Help her," I said, clenching my jaw to keep my teeth from clacking.

They listened to me, and I lay down on my back in the grass, using my clothes as a pillow. I watched the cloudless sky, willing the sun to leach into my bones and warm them. In a few minutes, Samantha joined me, then Heather, her teeth still chattering rapidly.

Then Michelle sat on the ground, dressed back in her clothes. She seemed calm and much warmer than I did. "How do you feel?"

"Cold," Heather said.

"Anything else?"

"Like I survived something," I said.

"You did. You survived something together. And even though you were afraid, even though you didn't want to do it, you did it without question. Well, without too many questions."

We laughed.

"Look behind you."

We turned. Standing in the field about a hundred yards away was a large mule deer. It had a thick rack of antlers that sprouted up about a foot above its head, not a full adult. It was staring at us, placidly chewing on some grass, not a care in the world, and certainly no fear of us.

"Wow, that's cool," Heather said.

"Is it dangerous?" Samantha asked.

"Not unless you charge it or threaten its young," Karma said, emerging from the woods. She'd changed back into her clothes as well, though her hair was wet. Had she jumped into that water just for fun? "Let's get dressed, everyone. We still have a ways to hike."

We obeyed her without protest. I climbed back into my clothes and twisted my hair up in an elastic. I wished I'd thought to bring a ball cap. The sun was still beating down and it was making my headache worse. I put my sunglasses on and took a sip of water, then put my pack back on.

"Gather round," Karma said, and we formed a by-now familiar circle around her. "We were talking earlier about how Leo hunts. How it stalks its prey. It likes the element of surprise. It waits for the weak animal to wander off from the herd, and that's when it pounces. Sticking together is important to ward against that sort of attack. Sticking together is what protects you. Don't get separated from the Pride. Because otherwise, you might end up with your neck snapped."

I shivered even though I was warm.

"Too gruesome for you?" Michelle asked, sensing my unease.

"It's fine."

"No use in hiding from reality," Karma said, stepping out of the circle, her gaze on something in the distance. "That's how lionesses kill. When they find their prey, they snap its neck and sink their teeth into its throat." Then she pivoted and pulled the rifle out of the side of her pack in a fluid motion. She put her eye to the sight and pulled the trigger.

Boom!

I turned in time to see the bullet connect with the deer we'd seen earlier. It stared at us in stunned silence for a moment, then toppled to its knees and disappeared in the grass.

And for the first time, I felt afraid.

Now—October

Like the deer that Karma shot without warning, Jack was also taken down by a bullet.

His head is tilted to the left, arms splayed out. There's a red stain on his chest. I look away from the violence, concentrating on other details to quell the horror.

—He's wearing jeans and a black cashmere sweater.
—His watch is pulling away from where it usually rests on his wrist, revealing a white tan line.
—His hands are bruised, like he's been in a fight.

Fuck.

I pull out my phone and open the encrypted app I've been receiving text messages through.

There's a dead man here.
Are you sure?
Yes.
Stand by.

Stand by? Stand by? I'm standing over the body of a dead man my friend almost definitely killed in the middle of the night, and I'm supposed to wait on hold as if I'm trying to activate my cell phone?

I've been taking too many orders tonight. Too many orders in general. It's time I got some answers on my own.

I move gingerly around the bed, making sure to give a wide berth to the body. It takes an act of will not to call 911, and it's only because I'm certain that he's dead that I don't. No ambulance can save him now.

But I need to do something.

Think, think, think!

He was shot. That means there must be a gun. My eyes sweep the thick rug. No gun. I bend down and lift the skirting that's concealing the underside of the bed, using the flashlight on my phone to search the darkness. Dust bunnies, an errant elastic, but no gun. I stand and walk quickly but carefully over every inch of the room, but there's no gun in here. Could it have been in the bathroom and I missed it?

"Athena?" I whisper loudly, though I'm not sure why I'm whispering at all. The walls between these apartments are thick. Thick enough, obviously, to muffle the shot that took out Jack and the fight that preceded it.

I walk out of the room. "Athena," I say more loudly this time.

She pokes her head out of the bathroom. She looks almost normal now, her hair pulled back, some color returned to her face. "What?"

"Where is the gun?"

"The gun?"

"You know what I'm talking about." Athena only looks at me blankly, and I wonder if it's the shock or if she truly doesn't know what I'm asking. "Jack. The man you shot in your bedroom."

Athena's head snaps back sharply. "Is he dead?"

"Yes."

"Are you sure?"

"I don't have time for this. Where's the gun you used to shoot him?" Athena's eyes lose focus again, and I'm worried I'm going to have to slap her to knock her back into reality. Not that I'm above doing that, but there's been enough violence tonight. "Where is it, Athena? I'm not kidding."

"I didn't mean—"

"I know," I say, even though I don't know. "You can tell me what happened later. Right now, I need to find it."

She gets that blurred look again, then turns away from me and walks down the hall and then down the stairs. I follow in her wake, wondering if it's in the living room, if I should've searched it properly when I arrived, even though I didn't know what had happened then, or what to look for. But Athena doesn't stop in the living room. She's walking toward the kitchen. When she gets there, she doesn't turn on the lights or hesitate. She walks to the wall of white cabinets and touches one of them. It slides open on a soundless mechanism. I come up next to her.

It's the garbage chute.

"Down there," she says, pointing a delicate finger. "It was trash."

Then she throws back her head and laughs.

CHAPTER 9

The Cleanup

Then—July

"**W**ell, that was gruesome," Samantha said that night at dinner. "I mean, I've been covered in blood before, but it was fake."

"Ugh, I can barely eat," Heather added, pushing her plate of food away.

I agreed with them that butchering the deer had been an ordeal, but I'd oddly had no problem eating. When we'd returned to the property, I was ravenous.

After Karma had checked that she'd gotten a clean shot off and the deer was dead, she'd pulled a set of boning knives and saws out of her backpack, arranging them on the grass in an orderly fashion. Then she'd strung the deer up in a tree with Connie and Michelle's help, and started giving instructions on how to disembowel it. Heather had tried to protest that she was a vegetarian, but a look from Karma silenced her.

It had been a grueling three hours of work, hard and physical. When we were done, the smell of blood filled our nostrils in a way we wouldn't soon forget. I'd wondered how we were going to get the hundreds of pounds of flesh back to camp, dreading the thought of having to lug it ourselves, when Gary appeared on a 4x4 with a large cooler on the back. He said he'd take it from there, and we hiked silently away from him, exhausted.

When we got back to the ranch, we headed without discussion for the communal showers. I had no issue stripping down in front of the other women this time. I put my clothes directly in the trash. There was blood spatter around my shirt cuffs that was unlikely to come out without major elbow grease, and I had no desire to try. I stepped into the warm spray and scrubbed every inch of my body until the water ran cold. Then I wrapped myself in a towel and walked back to my cabin.

That night's menu was simple: Caesar salad and garlic bread and spaghetti. It was exactly what I needed, and I piled my plate high, carbs be damned. I had a moment's hesitation when I realized there was a meat sauce, but it looked and tasted like beef, so I was okay with it. Whatever it was, it tasted delicious, and I went back for seconds, willing myself not to care what the others thought, if they noticed at all.

"You should try the garlic bread," I said to Heather. "It's great."

She wrinkled her nose. She looked like one of those women who never ate enough, her head too big for her body, even her spandex shirt loose on her arms. They all did, really—the others. I was the only one who had any extra meat on my bones.

Oh no. Wrong thing to think about!

"What was that all about?" Samantha asked Athena. "Bonding through butchering?"

Athena chuckled. Even though she'd spent the day doing exactly what I had, she was polished and put together. Some people were like that; they looked good right after they worked out or woke up. I was never going to be that person, and it was long past when I should've stopped caring about it. "Something like that."

"I thought there'd be seminars," Samantha said.

"Karma and Michelle aren't big on that sort of thing. They believe that you already have all the knowledge you need within you. You just have to find a way to harness it."

"I thought I was going to be getting massages and spa treatments," I said. "Silly me."

"I could use a spa treatment," Samantha said. "Butchering was murder on my nails."

Connie gave a deep belly laugh, and Samantha looked happy that she'd pleased her. I wondered, briefly, if they knew one another outside the group, then dismissed it.

"Have you done that before?" I asked Athena.

"That exact thing? No. But things that have taken me out of my comfort zone? One hundred percent."

I thought about what she'd told me on the plane. "Like when you climbed the mountain?"

"Maroon Bells," Athena said, her smile dropping. "That was nuts."

Heather looked at the window, where the mountains were framed in the fading sunlight. "You climbed that?" Heather said, pointing to the highest peak. An airplane was flying overhead, and from that angle, it seemed like it was flying at the same height. Maybe it was.

"We did."

Heather shook her head. "No way I'm doing that."

"It's best not to say what you will and won't do," Connie said gently. "That's not what we're about."

"Slavish obedience, then?"

"No, of course not. But a 'no' is usually a roadblock. A hard stop. It's not the way the group works. If we're confronted with a challenge, then we'll discuss it and come to common ground. We'll make a decision together about whether we're going to do it or not."

It occurred to me that we hadn't been consulted about either of the things we'd been asked to do that day. But maybe that came later? I was too worn out to decide. Tired from the day, but also in general. Tired of making decisions and solving problems. Let someone else take the wheel. That was the whole point of a Pride, wasn't it? That no one person was responsible for everything? That sounded good to me. That sounded great.

"That didn't happen today," Heather said petulantly. "I really am a vegetarian." She pointed at the plate that she'd pushed away, which had plain pasta and some salad on it. "Butchering an animal is against my principles. And really fucking gross."

"Nature is death—that's a fact," Athena said. "You don't have to eat the deer if you don't want to. At least it was free until it died."

"But it didn't have to die."

"You're right; it didn't."

"So why kill it, then?" Heather was on the point of tears.

"To teach us a lesson," Athena said matter-of-factly. "To test us."

"Did we pass?" I asked, trying to ease the tension.

"That wasn't the Test," Connie said.

"What's the Test?"

Connie twirled her spaghetti elegantly around her fork. "Every member of PL is put to the Test at some point."

"How?" I pushed, because you cannot change a lifetime of habits in a day.

"It's different each time."

"But it wasn't what we did today?"

"No," Athena said. "During the retreat, the Pride is put through a series of smaller challenges to solidify us as a group. But that's not the Test. That's a bigger challenge. Something that's life changing."

"Like going to the North Pole?" Heather said, half-joking, half-sarcastic.

"You'll know what it is when it happens," Connie said. "It will be impossible to miss."

"In a good way?" I asked nervously.

"All challenges achieved are good for us, whether they were hard when we did them or not."

"Right," Athena chimed in. "Take today. Last night, we were sitting at separate tables, but now, we've been through something together. Something we can use as a foundation to build our Pride, so we know that we can trust each other. Things between us are already different. I can feel it, can you?"

Athena was right. These women were strangers yesterday. Now they were in my life in a way I couldn't quite explain. "Yes, I feel it."

"That's good." Connie put her fork down. "I'm going to head to bed, and I suggest you all do the same. Big day tomorrow."

I wanted to ask her what was coming, but she rose so quickly I didn't have the chance. And ultimately, what did it matter if I knew what it was in advance? A night of worrying about it wasn't going to change anything. Better to sleep and start fresh tomorrow.

I watched Connie leave the dining room as the rest of the group resumed eating and talking of lighter things. I retreated into myself, which I tend to do sometimes. In a group but not, participating but removed. We were connected, I could feel that, yet I also felt some distance. I listened to their chatter without contributing, and I filed away the fact that Connie hadn't wanted to discuss the Test, what it involved, or what its purpose was. Not to mention the fact that this was the first time I'd heard anything about it.

But it wouldn't be the last.

CHAPTER 10

Invisible Cracks

Then—July

The next morning, I woke up early again, having had no trouble going to sleep without whatever it was that Karma and Michelle gave us the first night. I'd been worried I was going to be haunted by the ghost of the deer we'd dismembered, but I was asleep soon after my head hit the pillow in a way that usually only happened when I was ill.

I stretched out my body in the narrow, hard bed, feeling creaks and cracks in unfamiliar places, and remembered my resolution from the day before. Morning exercise every day. Better get to it. I sat up and pulled out a clean set of clothes. I felt the phone Dan had left me in the hidden pocket of my suitcase as I rooted around. I took it out and sent him a quick text: **Alive. Having fun! See you in a couple of days.**

I waited a second for him to respond, then hid the phone away. On my walk to the gym in the crisp morning air, I admired the view and meditated briefly on the nature of truth. Was I having fun? Yesterday I would've said no. But today, with yesterday's tasks behind me, I felt a sense of accomplishment. I'd done it. Two things I'd thought

I'd never do and was glad I'd stuck to. Maybe this place wasn't going to fix my career, but there were lessons I'd retain regardless.

I was the only one in the gym that morning, putting in my time and miles on the treadmill. I decided to try running for five minutes and then walking for five, with the goal of reaching three miles by the time the forty-five minutes I was now committed to were over. I barely made it, but it felt like progress. Somewhere around the thirty-minute mark I started to feel less like garbage, my body finally warming up. It reminded me of how I felt when I was Peloton fit.

Back in my little cabin, I gave myself a good once-over in the mirror. I was chubbier than the last time I had examined myself closely. My shins were covered in bruises from the jump into the water and the scramble out. I ran my hand along my jaw. It was slacker than the last time I checked, like I was slowly transforming into my mother, or the memory I had of her from childhood. I'd be turning forty soon. That both freaked me out and didn't. I'd never cared that much about age, but I was starting to feel a generational split between myself and the associates. Priorities, cultural references—it was the little things at first, but they added up. That transformation from feeling entirely at ease with where you were to feeling destabilized. Insecure. Passed by.

I turned away from myself and searched my luggage, looking for something to wear. Again, my hand hit the phone Dan had secreted away. I pulled it out, feeling like an alcoholic about to take a drink. I was so addicted to my phone. I could admit that. If I misplaced it, I felt anxious until I'd located it.

I checked if Dan had written me back.

Relief, he wrote. **I miss you.**

I was surprised he'd written that. Dan was affectionate in actions but not so much in words. I was always teasing him when I'd been away on a business trip. "Did you miss me?"

"Potentially," he'd say, grinning.

"Admit it—you did!"

He'd shrug and put his feet on the coffee table. "More sesame noodles for me."

"Fucker."

Eventually I'd beat it out of him, but it's never as nice as a spontaneous message.

I wrote him back. **Miss you too. Just worked out!**

This time, he wrote back immediately.

Wow. A miracle. How's it been?

Good. Tiring.

All the goat sacrificing too much?

I shuddered. That was too close to the bone.

They're not Satanists.

Why tired then?

Long hike yesterday.

Ooh, you hate hiking!

I did hate hiking. I'd hidden that from Dan at the beginning of our relationship, the way you do when someone you're into loves something you don't. As I result, I'd ended up on a brutal hike with him in the Adirondacks. He quickly realized I'd been less than honest, and he was okay with it. I had other qualities apparently.

I do!, I wrote.

And yet . . .

One for all and all for one!

You're a musketeer?

Nope. It's more like we're a pride of lions. Lionesses.

So, you're wild now?

Wilding, maybe.

Someone knocked at my door. "Breakfast in ten."

It was Gary. I hid the phone behind my back reflexively. I knew Gary wouldn't be pleased if he found me with it.

"Okay, thanks!" I called back.

"You're meeting with Karma and Michelle at ten."

"Alone?"

"Yes. Is that a problem?"

"Nope! Where do I meet them?"

I moved closer to the door, feeling ridiculous shouting through it. The phone vibrated in my hand—another text from Dan. I held it tighter.

"At the fire pit."

"Okay, great. Thank you!" I said it as dismissively as I could, hoping he'd walk away. The sound was off, so he couldn't hear me texting, but I didn't like the thought of him lingering outside my door. I listened, frozen, until I heard him leave and knock on the door one cabin over.

I checked the phone.

Where'd you go?, Dan had written.

Here! Sorry. Don't worry.

I do worry.

I know. How is Aunt Penny?

He sent me a sad face emoji.

I'm sorry, I wrote.

It's okay. We always knew we couldn't have her forever.

That almost made me cry too. I'd started letting my walls down, and look what was happening.

I have you forever tho, right?

Yes, Dan wrote. **Forever. Whether you want me or not.**

Good. I've got to go to breakfast.

Text me later?

I'll try, but if I don't, don't worry. I'll see you soon.

K.

I put the phone away. I was glad we connected. Whether he missed me or not—and he did; why else hide the phone despite all his mock concern—I missed him, and that was a good thing. We hadn't always been so solid.

Five years ago we'd almost split. Small changes could have consequences between two people. Dan not making partner, moving in-house, other stuff I'd tried to file away. We fell out of step for a while. Took each other for granted, and that didn't feel good. Other couples might have left each other, but we decided to try and fix it. We had.

But what I forgot to pay attention to was that when your foundation's been shaken, small fissures remain, no matter how many times you paper over the cracks.

CHAPTER 11

Walk the Line

Then—July

In the daylight, the fire circle lost some of its magic. There was a pile of white ash in the pit, and I could see that some of the beams that created the structure above it were worn and cracked, like the wood it was made of was older than the rest of the ranch.

Karma and Michelle lost some of their mystery too. Not that I hadn't seen them in the daylight; I was naked with Michelle the day before. But back in this space that I knew by instinct they found sacred, I missed the theatricality of the robes and the night and the fire. Spandex and hiking shirts didn't have the same dramatic flair.

"How are you doing this morning, Nicole?" Michelle said with a smile as she gestured for me to sit on the bench across from them. "What did you think about yesterday?"

"It was good. Hard, but good." My body creaked as I sat down, a preview of my forties.

"You've been using the gym?" Karma said. She had a blunt way of talking, almost without affect.

"Both mornings."

"That's a change for you?" Michelle asked. She was thinner than she'd been when she was at the height of her fame. Her legs and arms were sinewy and strong.

"Yes. But a welcome one."

"That's good. We love change."

"You do?"

"It makes you confront what isn't working in your life and hold on to what is."

I nodded, but inside, I wasn't so sure. I'd been in the same job since I graduated from law school. I'd been with the same man for more than a decade. My personal style had crystallized at twenty-three. I wasn't someone who changed much, and I'd always assumed it was because I was comfortable with what I had. But maybe I was afraid? Maybe it was easier to stay in one place rather than risk something new?

"You don't agree?" Karma asked. She was the stronger of the two, her shoulders broad, her face lined from sun and hard work.

"Well . . ."

"You can say whatever you're thinking," Michelle said with a slow smile.

I looked away from Michelle's penetrating gaze. I could smell the lingering scent of the fire, like the morning after a party, and feel the hard wood bench I was sitting on. This place wasn't set up for comfort. "I think that sometimes people change just for change's sake. And that's not necessarily a good thing. It's easy to think that the grass is greener on the other side, but it isn't always better, just different."

"Are you talking about your marriage?"

I brought my eyes back to Michelle's. "Not specifically, no. But sure, we've had our moments."

"And you chose to stay?"

"I did."

"Why?"

"Because I love Dan."

"Or you were afraid to be on your own?" Karma said.

I stared down at my hands. They were swollen from the altitude, and my wedding band felt tight on my finger, the flesh rising up around it. "Sure, isn't everyone?"

I felt the betrayal to Dan in those words. I didn't think they truly applied to me, but how did I know for sure? How did anyone know whether they stayed with the person they were with because they wanted to or because it was easy?

"I think many people are fine alone, and many people are not," Michelle said. Her blond-gray hair was still thick and wound together in an intricate braid. "When I left my husband, it felt like the hardest thing in the world. In fact, the whole world was against me."

Karma murmured her agreement, and though it seemed like hyperbole, I knew what she was talking about. My mother had cried when Michelle and her husband split up after twenty years together, breaking up the band in the process. It was one of those breakups that was all over the news, full of speculation, with coverage that went on for weeks. It gripped my mother like few other things did then. I remember telling her to get a life—who cared about some celebrity breakup? But a lot of people felt like my mother. Many others were invested in the relationship, one that had lasted when most of their peers' couplings had crumbled. They were a sign of stability, pop-rock royalty, something to admire. All an illusion, I was sure, but we love to put people on pedestals then tear them down.

"That must've been hard," I said.

"So hard," she said, almost singing the words. "But it led me to better things. The moment my plane landed in Tanzania I felt a huge weight lift off my shoulders. No one knew me there. I could be Michelle without all the expectations and judgment. I could be myself without having to be in a couple. A few days after I arrived, I felt something I hadn't felt in a long time. Happiness."

"Happiness is in short supply, don't you think?" Karma said.

"It most definitely is," Michelle said. "But it doesn't have to be."

I crossed my arms over my chest. Happiness. What did that feel like? I was happy when I won a case, but the feeling was preceded by the intense anxiety of flipping through the electronic pages of the judgment that appeared in my mailbox without warning, setting my heart racing in a way that couldn't be healthy. Lazy Sunday mornings with Dan; those made me happy. A good container of sesame noodles. But these were transient things. I didn't need therapy to know I wasn't happy on a regular basis.

"More happiness in the world would be good," I said. There was a pause while I waited for them to ask me if I was happy. Was I going to lie? Somehow it felt as if they already knew the answer. "Is that something that happens in the group?" I said to fill up the silence. "Does it promote happiness?"

Karma nodded slowly. "Group structures do promote joy, particularly for women. Did you know that men are happier married, and women are not?"

I'd read that. It seemed like a broad generalization. "Men like to be taken care of."

"And women get used up taking care of them," Michelle said. "That's where we come in."

"You're going to take care of my husband?" I joked.

"No, but we are going to help you with some of the other things in your life. Worrying about your career. Trying to figure out how to stay relevant, to keep climbing the ladder—all of that will be much easier for you now."

"And that will give you space," Karma added, "to focus more on yourself, to find the things that can make you happy."

"That sounds great. What's the catch?"

"We don't think about it like that."

"Sorry."

"It's fine. We get it. This is unusual." Michelle waved her hands around. Whether she was indicating the ranch, or Panthera, wasn't entirely clear. "As we said before, we expect our members to help one another when required. That's not a catch; that's a promise."

"I got it."

"You sound hesitant."

"I'm just trying to figure out why you picked me. All of these other women are so accomplished."

Karma frowned. "You don't think you're accomplished?"

"Well, yes, I've done some things. But I'm not in the same league as Athena or Connie."

"We know."

Ouch. "So what am I doing here?"

Karma leaned forward with purpose. "They weren't who they are now before they joined their Prides either. They're the evidence that this works. Us working together, being there for one another, being a women's club in a boys' club world. Doing overtly what men have been doing forever. You can reach the same heights as they have."

"I'm flattered."

"You don't need to be. You've worked hard."

I had, goddamn it. I'd worked so hard. Too hard. "I have."

"What do you think is holding you back?"

The points committee, I wanted to say, but they were the symptom, not the cure. "Honestly, I don't know. Sometimes I feel like it's me. Like I'm too aggressive or rub people the wrong way. Like I don't fit in. I'm too picky, I know. I care too much."

"These are good qualities," Karma said. "They should be valued in your organization, not a handicap."

"You're right."

"But it happens to women all the time. The same things that we value in men are seen as a deficit."

"It's true."

"You sound skeptical."

"I'm not, I just . . . This is hard to explain, but I grew up with the idea that we could be genderless, you know? Like if we were competent and didn't focus on that stuff, then everyone would treat you like that too."

Michelle smiled gently. "Has that been your experience?"

"Sometimes. I mean, I see differences. I know that there are guys who can get away with things that women can't. But it's better than it was. At least the men are mostly trying now."

"And yet, you feel like you've hit a wall. That you're going backward in your career."

"Yes, but that's happened to men in my office, too." It had happened to Dan.

"I'm sure it has, but it doesn't have to happen to you."

I felt an overwhelming sense of relief. If what they were saying was true, it was exactly what I needed. I wanted my career to keep going forward, not back. To feel valued, as if everything I'd worked for hadn't been in vain. I wasn't someone who liked asking for help, but I needed it.

"I'd really like that."

"Good. It's yours for the taking if you like."

"I would."

They smiled. "We're so happy," Michelle said.

"Is that it? I'm in?"

"If you complete today's challenge, yes," Karma said.

I thought back to my conversation with Connie and Athena at dinner. "Is that the Test?"

"No . . . the Test is something . . . larger. More significant." Michelle moved her hands in a reassuring way. "But that will come later. We think it's important to put our members through a series of trials. To assess your resolve and your commitment. We want to be sure that you'll be able to weather what you need to in the future. So today's challenge will be a test of sorts, but you'll continue to be tested in other ways throughout your time in Panthera."

"Will it be hard?"

"It will be a challenge. But we have faith in you."

"And your Pride will be there to help you," Karma added. "You'll do it together."

They were trying to encourage me, but I couldn't help eyeing the mountains behind them, so impossibly tall and far away. I was in terrible shape, my whole body aching from two days of exercise. There was no way I was going to climb a mountain like the one Athena had, regardless of what kind of support I got from the others.

"We're confident that today's challenge is something you can accomplish," Karma said, reading my mind.

"I hope so."

"We know so. And it will begin this afternoon. Meet back here at four. You'll find a backpack in your room. Pack for overnight."

"Any other clues?" I asked as I stood to leave.

Karma laughed for the first time, a deep sonorous tone that resonated in my chest. "Now what would be the fun in that?"

CHAPTER 12

Into the Woods

Then—July

What did packing for overnight mean? I tried to think back to that camping trip I'd taken with Dan, so many years ago. We were supposed to hike into the backcountry and camp overnight at a place he'd gone as a child, and then complete the rest of the climb to the top of Mount Marcy the next day, the highest peak in the Adirondacks.

But when we'd gone into the lodge to register, a ranger had spoken to us about the bear situation and how we had to have all our food packed away by four p.m., and even Dan had been unenthusiastic. So we'd pitched our tent at a campground nearby and then hiked the entire ten miles from base to peak in one day. It wasn't a technical climb, and I was in better shape back then, but ten is a lot of miles, and when we got to the top, the wind was ripping across the blasted rock, and there was still snow in shady spots. I was cold and miserable, and I burst out crying when my hat blew away. Dan wrapped me in his rain jacket and promised to never take me hiking again, and we made it down and past my deception, which he still liked to kid me about now and again.

None of this provided any insight into what I should pack. I understood the idea of challenges—at least, I thought I did—but I still didn't have a handle on what the Test was. Something big, obviously. Something I'd know was happening when it happened, Connie said. I wished I knew more so I could study and plan. So I could control the outcome.

But no, that's what I always did. Looked ahead and thought of all the things that could go wrong. Disasterizing, I called it. Seeing the tornado before it formed, the hail before it fell. It was supposed to help me deal with what was to come, to make me less anxious when it inevitably did. But it didn't work. Instead, I suffered twice. It was something I knew I had to work on, so I vowed to concentrate on the task at hand and I took out my warmest sweater, the rain jacket Dan had suggested I pack, a pair of long underwear (ditto Dan), and a puffy vest I'd forgotten about but found at the back of my closet. Extra underwear, hiking shorts, and some T-shirts went in too. And as a last-minute addition, the phone Dan had given me, buried deep inside the pack, in case the disaster came.

• • •

"So, this is the plan," Karma explained when we'd assembled at the fire pit with our gear. At four o'clock, the sun was still beating down hard, the thinner atmosphere making it feel stronger than it did in New York, but without the humidity. "Gary will take each of you to a separate corner of the property. You'll be blindfolded on the way there so that your location will be unknown to you. You'll have a map and a compass. You need to find one another before dark, set up the tent, and spend the night."

"Is that all?" Heather asked in a tone halfway between sarcasm and nonchalance. Her hair was in a thick French braid, and she had a strip of sunburn across the bridge of her nose.

"I'm glad you feel you're up to the challenge, Heather," Michelle said.

I smiled at Michelle, and she gave me an answering smile back. That afternoon, I saw the advantage of her long flowing robe, which seemed to create its own breeze and was a good screen from the elements. She'd put on a broad straw hat as well; all she needed was an English garden to lounge in.

Heather shrank into herself, chastised.

"Are blindfolds really necessary?" I asked nervously. I might've decided to let go of my control issues, but there was a limit. I'd never been into any kind of blindfold, metaphorical or otherwise.

"We want to make this as challenging as possible," Karma answered. "To assess your ability to adapt and follow instructions. If you do, then you should have no issues."

Gary was standing behind Michelle and Karma, smirking slightly.

What was the appeal of Gary? Did it matter? I was feeling hostile toward him because he was the one who was going to blindfold me. He hadn't done anything to invoke my ire except follow instructions.

"Does everyone know how to use a compass?" Karma asked.

"Why don't you assume we don't," Samantha said with a nervous smile, "and explain it to us like we're children."

Athena laughed. "Compass for dummies?"

"Precisely."

I was glad Samantha had spoken up. My time the in the Girl Scouts was a long time ago, and I didn't want to find out that I'd forgotten how to read a compass when it was too late.

Karma took hers out and went through the basics, showing us how to find north, how to get to a point on a map. I concentrated as best I could, but I continued to feel anxious. At least we weren't climbing some massive mountain. Mount Marcy had nearly sunk me, and it was something that people ran up on a regular basis.

When Karma was done, Gary handed us our supplies for the night.

—A package of food that could sustain us for twenty-four
   hours if necessary.
—A two-liter water bottle.
—A sleeping bag.
—Part of a tent.

"You'll all need to come together to have true shelter tonight," Michelle said. "Otherwise, you'll be sleeping under the stars."

We nodded grimly. It was already four thirty. It got dark at nine. Depending on how far apart we were dropped, it was going to be a struggle to get to where we should be on time.

"Can I have a flashlight?" Heather asked.

"Or matches?" Samantha added.

"You'll have both," Michelle said, holding out a box. "There's a headlamp for each of you, and matches in the food packet, as well as a collapsible cup and iodine pills. Follow the directions if you need more water than what's in your water bottles."

"You'll need more water than that," Karma said. "Most hikers who get lost die of dehydration. Don't be one of them. There's plenty of water out there. Water should be your first priority."

"Even over finding each other?" I asked.

"Both should be a priority. Remember, you're stronger together."

"Wasn't that your campaign slogan, Athena?" Heather quipped.

"Something like that."

"Well, if it worked for Athena, it must be the right way to go," I said, and Athena grinned at my positivity. "Anyway, should we get this show on the road? Sun's a-wasting."

"I appreciate your enthusiasm, Nicole," Michelle said. "All right, then, load up."

We each took a headlamp, put the supplies Gary had given us in our packs, and lifted them, heavy with food and water, onto our backs. Then we climbed into the large four track Gary had pulled up. Gary moved among us with a set of bandanas, tightening each one across our eyes with a sure knot at the back of our heads. It let the light in, but it was muted and smelled vaguely of sweat.

When each of us was blindfolded, Gary started the engine and put it into gear. As we kicked up a cloud of dust that I could taste rather than see, and left Michelle and Karma behind, Michelle's assumption that I was embracing this task with zeal lingered. Because as much as she seemed able to intuit about me, she'd gotten that one wrong.

I wasn't enthusiastic.

I was afraid of the dark.

. . .

Thirty minutes later, after Gary removed my blindfold and made sure I had all my equipment, he drove off with the others and I was alone. I took in my surroundings, enjoying the fresh air, the scent of the grass, and the mild perfume of wildflowers with something feral underneath. I was standing next to a log fence. On the other side of it was a large herd of cattle. There were barbed wires between the logs, but I couldn't tell if the fence was electrified, or if the cattle were happy to stay inside their enclosure. I'd never seen cattle up close before, other than in a movie, and I wasn't prepared for their size and smell. They were fascinating to watch, but the sun was racing across the sky, and I had two and a half hours to find the others before I'd start getting panicky, so it was time to get a move on.

Karma said that the priority was water. I had a lot of it, though, so I was okay for the time being. I checked the map I'd been given. By my admittedly easily wrong calculations, the point I was headed for was three miles away. At a normal walking pace, that should take me an hour or so, but I'd never walked with this much weight on my back over uneven terrain, and I could already feel it slowing down my steps. There also wasn't a path to follow, just a field full of tall grass. To the right was a wooded area, and somewhere in there, again, if I was reading the map right, a stream. Maybe the same one we'd gone for a dunk in the day before. I had a terrible sense of direction, and the blindfold hadn't helped.

It occurred to me that it might be easier to walk through the woods than the field. Or at least along the edge of the woods? I didn't know, but I knew someone who did.

I dug into my pack and pulled out Dan's phone. No bars. That idea was out the window. I put the phone away and willed myself to concentrate. I had to walk northwest for an hour and then I should be there. I could do this. I put the compass in my hand, found my direction, and started walking.

It didn't take long for me to come to the first barrier: another fence with more cattle on the other side. I didn't know much about hiking, but I knew that getting into a pen with thousand-pound animals was a bad idea. I walked along the fence line, and ended up at the woods after all. I stopped for breath, wiping my face with my shirt, and then took a long drink of water. It was still cool in the canteen, and it felt so good in my throat that I had to will myself not to drink too deeply.

I checked the compass. I was now off course, but not too badly. Once I got past this obstacle, I'd be able to track back to where I needed to be. The worst thing about following the map, though, was that I had no idea how far I'd come and no way of judging it. There weren't any road signs out in the woods, no distance markers. I realized too late that I should've started a walk on my Apple watch—it didn't have cell service on it, but at least it could track how far I'd gone. I opened the exercise app and started an "outdoor walk." I'd already been hiking for twenty minutes, so hopefully the measurements wouldn't be too far off. A mile, maybe. I took another drink of water and walked into the shade of the trees. The air smelled like rotting wood and cold water, and it felt odd to be alone in the woods. My footsteps sounded loud. And there were other sounds—shuffles and creaks, cries and grunts that got my imagination working overtime.

Lions and tigers and bears, oh my.

Lions were impossible—though maybe I was wrong about that. Were there mountain lions in Colorado? Maybe? Bears, on the other hand. Oh God. How had I not thought about bears? There were definitely bears around. Why hadn't they given us bear spray? Or a whistle? Did that even work?

"Breathe slowly," a voice said behind me, making me jump. I turned around, but I already knew who it was.

"Athena! Where did you come from?"

She gave me a friendly smile. Her hair was in a braid and held back from her face with a thick cotton headband. She looked comfortable in her hiking boots, like they were part of her usual attire. Her water bottle was hanging from one side of her pack and there was a machete hanging off the other. *She should shoot a campaign video out in the wild,* I thought. She looked so outdoorsy and approachable.

"I got dropped off near here. Then saw you heading into the woods and thought I'd make sure you were okay."

I put my hand against a tree to steady myself. "I feel like I'm having a heart attack."

"More likely a mild panic attack. But don't worry. I have bear spray."

"How did you know I was thinking about that?"

"You were muttering out loud. 'Lions and tigers and bears . . .'"

"Oh, ha. Yikes, I didn't realize." How embarrassing. I kept putting my foot in it around Athena. Something about her made me insecure in a way I hadn't felt since I was starting out as a lawyer. And yet, she'd been nothing but friendly and welcoming to me.

"It's okay. There are bears around. Here, take this." She handed me a lanyard with a whistle hanging off it. "The whistle scares the bears. The bears don't want to eat us. They just want us to stay away from them."

"Let's do that, then."

Athena checked her watch. "We should get going. Still a couple of miles to go."

"Am I at least heading in the right direction?"

"You are."

She started walking, and I followed her. In a few minutes, we'd skirted the cattle pen and were back in the field. "We need to go there," Athena said, pointing to another stand of trees that looked small in the distance. The path between us and that point seemed clear, if far.

I checked the time. It was already close to six. "Will we make it before sunset?"

"We should. But we have to cross the river."

"Another river?"

Athena smiled grimly. "You didn't expect it to be easy, did you?"

"No."

"So one foot in front of the other, and we'll get there."

"I'm glad you're here."

"We're a team."

She walked ahead of me. She had fantastic posture, her shoulders unbowed by the weight of her pack. She strode with assurance, like she knew where she was going, which maybe she did.

"Have you been here before?" I asked, coming up next to her.

"In this exact place? No."

"But you know the area, right? You've spent a lot of time here?"

"Some. Why do you ask?"

"Just making conversation."

She glanced at me. "Hoping to keep the bears at bay?"

"That's right."

"You do seem to have a lot of fears, Nicole."

I looked down at the ground. My boots were caked with mud, the laces twisted with the long grass we were walking through. Before this trip, I wouldn't have classified myself as someone who was fearful, but all Athena had seen were my fears. Life was like that sometimes. It conspired against you in a way that made someone feel as if you were one way when you really weren't.

"I have some, just like everyone does. You do too, right? Hence the Xanax?"

"True."

"I *was* worried we were going to have to climb that mountain."

Athena shook her head. "They never repeat themselves."

"That's good." We walked in silence for a few more minutes. "Has the group helped you? I mean, I'm sure it has, but how specifically?"

"Well, for one thing, I can say with one hundred percent certainty that I wouldn't be a congresswoman if it weren't for them."

"They're that powerful?"

"Michelle and Karma encouraged me to run and put me in touch with the right people in the party to get behind my candidacy."

"That's impressive."

"They're proof that if you put your mind to it, you can get what you want."

"And everyone gets these kinds of results?"

Athena adjusted the straps on her pack. "If they put in the work and trust the process, yes."

"How many people are in the group?"

"Only Michelle and Karma know. Everyone is divided into Prides of five, and we interact with them individually."

"How long ago did you join?"

"Four years ago."

"You were in another Pride before this one?"

Athena stopped and pulled out her water bottle. I followed suit, mindful of keeping hydrated. My bottle was now half-full.

"I was."

"What happened to it?"

She smiled. "Nothing. We've all been put in different Prides. It's a way to share knowledge with new members. Prides are made up of experienced members and newer ones."

Ahead of us, the tall grass was waving in the sunlight. "And we don't all get together at some point? No jamboree?"

"I've met some other members, and I know the old members of my Pride. You can recognize them by the pin"—she motioned toward the lion pin that was attached to the strap of her pack—"but there's never been anything organized, no."

"Why not get us all together?"

Athena put her water bottle away and started hiking again. I kept expecting her to get frustrated with my questions, but she seemed happy enough to answer them.

"I'm not sure, honestly. The organization's not secret, exactly, but Michelle and Karma prefer discretion. That being said, Karma is fond of saying that sometimes it's better to operate quietly, because if they see you coming, then they can try to stop you. But if you're just there, steadily working away, then you can get things done before they even know what's happening."

I tucked my thumbs under the straps of my pack, pulling them away from my body. My shoulders were starting to kill. "I get it."

"It's a tactic I use in Congress. A lot of new members show up with big proclamations about what they're going to get done, and then they run into the same old slow-down-you-move-too-fast crowd."

I laughed. "Now that would be a good campaign slogan."

"Ha. Sure. No one wants to know how the sausage gets made, though."

"True."

"Anyway, I got some advice from another member early on. Don't tell people what you're going to do, just do it. And so that's what I've been doing, and it's working."

"That's great."

"It is. And it will be great for you too."

A deer loped out of the forest, startling us both. We stopped to watch it, its white tail pointed upwards. I flashed back to yesterday, the explosion of the gun still loud in my mind.

"So everyone keeps saying," I said when the deer had galloped away.

"You don't believe it?"

We dipped into a hollow in the grass. That same feral smell I'd encountered at the cattle pen filled my nostrils, like an animal had been there recently. Fear crept back into my bones. "It's not that," I said, looking left and right, my ears alert. "I'm just cautious. I got some bad news at work a couple of weeks ago and I'm still feeling tender. I want to believe it can all be turned around, but I'm skeptical."

"The points committee are a bunch of idiots."

"True, but wait, how did you—"

"Stay still!" Athena ordered, and I froze. I heard hissing, saw a flash in the grass, felt something whizzing by my ear, and then there was a great *thwack*!

Athena was in front of me on her knees, the machete in her hand and a dead rattlesnake cut in two laid out before her.

She'd reacted so quickly.

But I'd never even seen it coming.

CHAPTER 13

Survival of the Fittest

Then—July

Athena and I rolled into camp around seven, sodden from having to ford a fast-moving river that stood in our way. Connie was there already, and Samantha soon joined us. Only Heather was missing.

"Should we look for her?" I asked.

Connie shook her head. "We don't know where she was dropped off. We're better off setting up the tent and building a fire so she can see us."

"But then anyone will be able to see us," Samantha said.

"We're not hiding," Athena said.

Samantha laughed at herself. "Oh, right. Too many movies."

"Why don't you and Nicole set up the tent, and we'll make the fire?"

"Sure," I said. "But do we have all the pieces? We were each given a different part, right?"

"Good point," Athena said. "Let's see what we've got." We pulled out our sections of the tent and laid them on the ground. "Looks like we're missing the tent fly. That's good news."

"So long as it doesn't rain," Connie said, looking up. The sky was starting to darken, the setting sun highlighting the gathering clouds.

"Let's get the fire made and hopefully Heather will be here before that happens."

"What if she doesn't make it?" I asked. "We just let her stay outdoors all night?"

"She has a sleeping bag, food, water, matches. She'll be all right."

I shuddered, thinking of the snake we'd encountered earlier and the bears we didn't. Even if she didn't run into a predator, it still sounded dangerous.

Samantha tugged on my arm. "Let's get the tent set up, okay?"

"Sure."

We walked away from where Connie and Athena were gathering wood for a fire and found a relatively flat spot.

"Have you ever put one of these together before?" I asked Samantha. "I have not."

"My family used to go camping all the time when I was a kid."

"Thank God."

"Here, give me the ground sheet." She pointed to what looked to me like a tarp. I handed it to her, then helped her unfold it. It was large and heavy, and I was glad it hadn't been in my pack, which I'd gratefully abandoned the minute we got into camp. Taking it off had briefly made me feel as if I were floating, but I was back on earth soon after.

"Now let's spread out the tent base."

When we were done, it barely looked big enough to hold five people.

"That's going to be a tight fit." I shivered. I'd taken off my wet boots and socks and changed into running shoes and dry clothes. Though the water hadn't been as cold as for the full dunk, I was still feeling its effects. Added to which I was tired and hungry. I knew I hated camping for a reason. "What do we do next?"

Samantha explained how to thread the poles through the tent, and we soon had a raised structure that was made mostly of mesh.

"That doesn't look like much protection," I said.

"That's why we need the fly."

I checked the time. It was past seven thirty. "Where is she?"

Samantha hugged herself. "I'm worried about her. She doesn't always handle pressure well."

"They should've given us radios." I gripped the lanyard around my neck. "We could blow our whistles."

"No," Connie said, coming up to us with a piece of wood in her hand. "The point is to make it here on our own."

"I though the point was working with each other," I said petulantly. "And I had help. Athena got me here."

"That was happenstance," Athena said, joining us. "And frankly, I probably should've stayed behind you and observed you from afar."

"I'm glad you didn't."

She nodded. "Look, we've got enough wood for the fire now. We'll light it and if it's close to getting fully dark, we can blow our whistles."

"Do you think that's a good idea?" Connie said. "I mean—"

"We have to do something," Athena interrupted her. "Come on, let's light this."

We walked to where they'd built the fire ring out of rocks. Connie bent down and struck a match, holding it to the aspen bark that was spliced through the miniature log cabin she'd made of sticks. Before long, the flames were dancing merrily, and Connie added wood carefully. "We can't make it too big. There's always forest fire danger around here."

I hauled my pack over to the fire and sat down on it, reaching my hands and feet out to the warmth. I could feel the shape of Dan's phone beneath me. Maybe I'd have a signal? If Heather didn't show up by dark, I resolved to check, regardless of the consequences.

"Does someone have their map?" I asked. "Mine got damaged in the river."

"I do," Athena said. "What do you want it for?"

"I think we can figure out what direction she's coming from by seeing where each of us was dropped off."

"Good idea," Samantha said.

Athena took the map out of her pack and unfolded it. "I was dropped off here," she said, pointing to a spot about a mile away from where I'd been left.

"I was here." I pointed as best I could to where I thought Gary had dropped me, based on where the river was and where we were now.

"Here, I think," Connie said, pointing to the other side of the map.

"And here," Samantha said, pointing to the middle.

I puzzled it out. "So, if we were all put about a mile from each other and equidistant from the meetup, then she should be . . ." I scanned the map and did some calculations in my head. "Here," I said, pointing to a place that was south of where Connie had indicated.

"Are you sure?" Samantha asked.

"It's like one of those LSAT problems. The ones with patterns. I'm good at those."

"Okay," Athena said, "so she also had to cross the river down here." Athena tracked the blue line down the map. "That was tricky, even for two of us. Maybe she got stuck there?"

Connie pursed her lips, then checked her watch. "If we search for her now, we might all get caught out there in the dark."

"Just two of us could go," I said. "And two could stay here. But we should decide fast, because every minute we talk we're wasting time."

"She's supposed to get here on her own," Connie said stubbornly, making her same point from earlier.

"But we're also supposed to be learning to work together. To make group decisions because we're stronger together. So I think we should make a group decision."

"We vote?" Samantha said.

"Karma and Michelle like us to discuss until we reach a consensus," Athena said.

"There's no time for that. Unless everyone agrees right now, we need to vote." I looked at Connie. Her expression hadn't changed.

She didn't want to search for Heather. But would she give in if the vote was against her? Could she stop us?

"Let's vote," she said.

"All in favor of two of us going?" I raised my hand, as did Samantha, and after a moment, Athena. Connie didn't raise hers.

"Okay, so we go. Athena, why don't you and I go, and Samantha and Connie can stay here?"

"No, I'll go," Connie said. "Come with me, Samantha."

They put together a pack quickly and put their headlamps on, and without any further discussion they marched out of camp. Their departure didn't make me feel better, but at least we were doing something.

. . .

It was an anxious hour waiting by the campsite, searching the horizon as the sun set with a suddenness that didn't happen in New York. While I fretted, Athena calmly made dinner and served it to me—a casserole made up of half the food from each of our food packets. It looked disgusting but tasted okay, and I ate it perched on a log, watching the horizon.

I tried not to think about what would happen if they didn't come back soon. To cast the idea that this was a horror movie I was living in—and the field was the basement one character after another found themselves going into with none coming back—from my mind.

Thoughts like that weren't helpful.

I ate as slowly as I could, postponing the moment when I'd feel as if I had to go out into the darkness and search for them myself. Athena fed the fire, and it was a sharp tower of light. They should be able to see it, even from far away. They should make it back before it got too late. So long as Heather wasn't hurt. So long as none of them got hurt and the bears or the lions or whatever else was out there didn't reach up and grab them.

And then, right as I was giving up hope, as the minutes that I'd allowed until I had to do something other than wait wound down, I heard a noise and saw a headlamp, and the three of them stumbled into camp.

"Hallefuckinglujah," Heather said as she sank down onto the log beside me and reached her hands out to the fire. Her pant legs were thick with mud, and she was shivering.

I put my arms around her and hugged her quickly, then let go. "I'm glad you made it. I was worried."

Heather looked surprised at the affection, then smiled. "Me too."

"What happened?"

"Got lost. Eventually found the river, but have you seen that thing? I tried crossing it but turned around halfway in because it was getting dark, and the current was crazy."

"Yeah, the river was intense."

"Thank God Samantha and Connie showed up. I never would've gotten across it by myself."

"You want some food, Heather?" Athena asked.

"Definitely." Athena handed her a plate. Heather lifted it to her nose and smelled it. "Is there meat in here?"

"Oh yeah, sorry. I put in the tinned tuna."

Heather expelled a breath, then picked up the fork. "Fuck it. I am so hungry I don't even care."

I laughed. "We won't tell anyone."

Heather shoveled some food into her mouth. "This looks disgusting but is surprisingly good."

"Right?"

Connie and Samantha took seats around the fire, each with their own plate.

"What were you going to do for the night if they hadn't showed up?" I asked Heather.

"I had the tent fly. I was going to put on every piece of clothing I had and then wrap myself in that."

"Why not make a fire?"

"It was too wet where I was. No wood, either. I figured it was a bad idea to start wandering around looking for it."

"It's good you didn't," Connie said. "You did the right thing staying by the river."

"I was pretty happy to see your headlamps coming, I have to say." Heather scraped the last of the food off her plate into her mouth, then reached down and undid her boots. "These things are killing me." She pulled them off, letting her socked feet rest by the fire. Steam rose up from them. "What about you guys? Did you have any trouble?"

"A snake almost killed us," I said. "Thank God for Athena."

Heather shivered next to me. "I hate snakes."

"Who doesn't?" Samantha said, finishing her noodles as she stared at the fire. I was impressed with her quiet efficiency. She was the opposite of the actress-diva type I expected, which I appreciated. "So what now?"

"What do you mean?" Connie asked.

"Do we get a medal?"

Athena gave a small laugh. "Not quite a medal, but yes, we all made it."

"As fate would have it," Connie said.

As fate would have it, I repeated in my mind. But it wasn't fate that got us to the rendezvous; it was working together. It was disobeying the command to do it on our own.

"Oh," I said.

"What?" Heather asked.

"We were supposed to help one another."

Connie turned to me. "How's that?"

"We were given contradictory instructions. Get to this location on our own, but a Pride works as one. And that's how we all got here safely. Athena helped me. You guys helped Heather. We worked together and we made it. That's what they were testing, right?"

Athena smiled. "You're pretty smart, you know that?"

"Sometimes. Connie?"

"That was the purpose of the exercise," Connie said. "To put you under stress and see how you'd react. If you'd rely on each other or try to go it alone."

"So why put it to a vote, then? When we wanted to search for Heather, you didn't vote for it."

"You didn't?" Heather said. "Thanks a lot."

"That was part of the exercise too," Connie said. "Bucking against authority. We tend to obey a dominant person and that happens in Prides too. But often, in order to succeed, it's important to stand up to the person who's trying to lead. To assert yourself, even when you're being told you might get in trouble. That you might not get what you're fighting for."

I found it interesting that Connie was casting herself as the dominant person. I mean, she was, but I wasn't used to people being so upfront about it. "Doing the right thing in the face of adversity. That's what you mean?"

"Yes. You all have goals, and we want to help you achieve them. But it might not always be easy. It might not always be linear or obvious how to get there. You need to keep that in mind and learn to figure out where resistance is necessary."

"Well, I for one am glad that you stood up for me, Nicole," Heather said. "Thank you."

"Is this the Test, then?" I asked.

"No," Connie said. "The Test is something . . . larger. At some point, your loyalty to the Pride will be at issue. How you come through that, what choices you make, that will be the Test."

"Why is that necessary?"

"Because that's how life works. Michelle and Karma prefer to be realistic about it and to control for it. The Test doesn't have to be physically challenging. It's about doing the right thing when presented with a choice. It's about choosing your Pride above all."

We watched the fire for a moment, letting her words sink in.

"We should clean up and get some rest," Athena said. "Enough lessons for one day."

We agreed and made quick work of cleaning up after dinner and putting the fly on the tent. Then, one by one, we climbed in, our bodies crowded against one another. It warmed the tent quickly, and though the ground was uncomfortable beneath us, I was content. We were safe. We'd passed this challenge, and soon we'd be home and reaping the benefits.

I turned onto my side and dropped into a dead sleep like I'd fallen out a window, too tired to think anymore.

Too tired to question why a Test was necessary at all.

CHAPTER 14

The Covenant

Then—July

In the morning, we packed up the tent, ate a quick breakfast, and, with a map that Connie had on her, made the six-mile hike back to the ranch. Without the disorientation of the blindfolds and the ticking clock, it was a relatively easy hike on a flat road. We arrived at lunch, ate, and separated to get clean and recover from a night on the hard ground.

After a long shower and a nap, I checked in briefly with Dan, then spent the afternoon exploring the property, something I hadn't had time to do before then. I walked around the stables and watched the horses exercising in their paddock, their scent strong in my nostrils, bringing back childhood memories of riding lessons with my mom. She would've loved the ranch—she was always the one pushing us to do outdoorsy things, while my sedentary father would have preferred to watch football. He'd been felled by a heart attack at sixty, and at his funeral my mother had looked broken, but also free.

"I'm going to travel," she told me later at the house. "Go to all the places your father never wanted to go."

It was my first year at the firm, and I was exhausted from the work and from the loss of my dad. He'd worked a lot too, all my life, leaving me mostly alone with my mom. I'd always meant to find the time to get to know him as an adult, but my time had run out.

"That's great, Mom. Where will you start?"

"Italy, no question."

I hadn't thought she was serious, but she was. She took six months to sort through all their things, sell the house, and plan her trip, and then she was off. I followed her travels for the next year, always expecting her to tell me she was done and heading home. Instead, I'd received a call from the hotel she was staying at in London. She'd died in her sleep of the same thing that had taken my dad, no warning.

I lost two parents in eighteen months, and the total time I'd taken off to mourn them was five days. I knew at the time that this wasn't right, but I'd shoved those feelings away and gone back to my practice. Ten years later, standing in a tall grass field, staring at mountains that had been there before man had arrived and would be here long after we'd passed into history, I knew I'd made the wrong choice. I should've taken the time to heal, to travel, to stop and smell the wildflowers. Maybe that's what this time was. An opportunity to refocus on what I wanted from life and how to get it. After only four days, I already felt close to this group of women, particularly Athena. Dan was my family, but I had room in my life for other people, other connections. I felt different in this place, a good different.

It remained to be seen if that was a feeling that followed me home or got lost in transit.

· · ·

"Welcome, welcome, welcome," Michelle sang to us that evening as we gathered once again around the fire circle as the sun set behind the mountains. We started with the Greeting, and we quickly moved through the group, rubbing foreheads. It felt intimate, even more so for having spent the night together in a cramped tent. It also felt less alien, though I couldn't imagine doing it outside of this setting.

"How did you all fare?" Karma asked when we were done. She was wearing a different robe that night, made of a dark hemp material and cinched at the waist with a thick belt. Michelle's was made of a light, creamy, flowing material. Together they looked like yin and yang, the darkness and the light, though I didn't think either of them particularly dark.

"We made it," Samantha said cheerily.

"That's great," Michelle said.

"Any difficulties?" Karma asked.

"I almost got bit by a snake!" I said. "But Athena saved me."

"And I got lost," Heather said. "But they found me."

"How fortunate," Michelle said. "Teamwork is a blessing." She smiled at each of us and we visibly relaxed. I felt like we were schoolchildren who'd been caught doing something naughty and our teacher had just let us off the hook. Not because she didn't know what we were doing, but because she'd decided on benevolence.

"Perhaps this challenge was too easy," Karma mused.

"Not on my back," I said with a smile, and the tension broke so quickly I thought it might be all in my mind.

Karma nodded. "As you know or have guessed by now, we believe in challenging our Prides. It's easy to work together when there's no true challenge. But under stress, the cracks show, and real leaders emerge. That is what we've been showing you over these last few days. But while you will formally come together as a Pride tonight, the challenges are not over. Each of you will be put to the Test at some point. You'll be faced with what appears to be an insurmountable obstacle. You might be afraid. You might think about giving up, but the solution exists. And it lies within your Pride."

Karma swept her arms out. "Rely on each other, call on each other, trust in each other. If you do these things, you can overcome any test that we, or life, might throw your way." She brought her hands together, palms touching. "I'm sure you have questions." She looked at me and I tried to hold my gaze steady. "But learning to put those aside is part of the Test. If your mind is clouded with questions, you won't be searching for solutions. When the Test occurs, do not spend your time wondering why it is happening. React, respond, reach out, solve. The reason for everything will become clear once the Test is accomplished."

Karma dropped her hands and smiled at Michelle. "Let us begin."

"This is our last night together," Michelle said. "A beautiful evening for the pin ceremony."

"As fate would have it," Athena said.

"As fate would have it," we all said together.

Michelle held her hands out wide while Karma put a large log on the fire. Michelle motioned for us to form a circle, holding out her hands on either side and encouraging us to lock hands with each other. Heather was on one side of me and Samantha on the other. Heather's hands were cold, Samantha's the same temperature as mine. I gave them each a smile and squeezed an assurance.

"Our Pride is complete," Michelle said. "It has come together through adversity, and each has her role to fill. You were chosen for your compatibility, but we cannot ensure that you'll survive and thrive. Only you can do that. Only you can decide to work together and create success. Are you ready?"

"Yes!" Athena and Connie said enthusiastically, raising their hands and pulling us along with them.

Michelle cupped her hand to her ear. "I can't hear you!"

"Yes!" we said together.

"Whatever life throws at you from here on out, you have each other to face it. You have each other to fight it. Are you ready?"

"Yes!"

"Good," Michelle said with a smile, and we laughed. We lowered our hands at her motion to do so, and a hush fell on us. "Now, close your eyes and listen."

I did as she asked, experiencing that strange change from light to dark that I had on the plane with Athena. The fire crackling, the wind in the trees, the creaks in my back—I felt and heard and smelled them all.

"Repeat after me. We promise," Michelle said in a deep, sonorous voice.

"We promise," we repeated.

"To put the Pride before all."

"To put the Pride before all."

"To fight for what we deserve."

"To fight for what we deserve."

"To receive our rewards."

"To receive our rewards."

"With humbleness and grace and discretion."

"With humbleness and grace and discretion."

"We promise," Michelle said, "to say yes to our Pride, no matter how challenging."

"And protect them from those who would seek to do them harm."

"We will celebrate our victories and learn from our defeats."

"And move through the world with love."

Silence again, weightier this time.

"Let's embrace our sisters," Karma said.

I opened my eyes as I was enveloped in an enthusiastic hug from Samantha, then a less enthusiastic one from Heather, and then all of us in a tight circle. We released one another and re-formed our larger circle.

Karma was holding a small box that she opened slowly. Inside, three pins were nestled in velvet. "Each of you will receive one of these. Wear it at all times. It's your way of showing your pride, and of letting others who you might meet along the way know that you're a member of the group. It's also a reminder of the promise you took today. Nicole, come forward."

I walked toward Karma as she reached into the box and took out a pin. She placed it in my hand. It was gold, a lioness at rest, and warm to the touch. Karma cupped her hands over mine and squeezed. The needle at the back pierced my hand.

"Ouch."

Karma smiled. "A little pain to remind you of today. You should wear it visibly every day so that you can be recognized by others in Panthera. If you see someone with one, you know you can trust them."

She pulled her hands away and plucked the pin from my palm. A small bubble of blood rose up, but the pain was already receding. She wiped the pin on a small cloth that was inside the case, a small streak of red against the white, then pinned it onto the breast of my fleece.

"I promise," she said as she pinned it in place.

"I promise," I replied, then walked back to my place in the circle as she called up Samantha. I raised my palm to my mouth and tasted the blood that was there, sucking it away without too much thought.

By the next day, I wouldn't even be able to see where she'd pricked me. Proof that something doesn't have to be visible to leave a scar.

Now—October

"This isn't funny, Athena," I say.

"No?" She slaps her hands against her sides. "No. It's not funny. I feel weird." She's pale, and there's a blue tinge to her lips.

"It's the shock."

"What?"

"You're in shock. Are you cold?"

"So cold."

"Go sit in the living room and turn on the fire. Wrap yourself in a blanket."

Athena nods but makes no move to follow my instructions. She's only a few years younger than me, but right now it feels like she's my child.

"Go, Athena. Do you need help?"

"No. I got it. Fire. Blanket. Yes, good idea."

She walks out of the kitchen, and now I'm alone with the ticking clock on the wall that tells me I have only seconds to act or I'm going to be in trouble. Forget that. I'm already in trouble.

My phone buzzes. I check it reflexively. **Go get the gun.**

She knows what I should do. She always has. She's monitoring me somehow. Through cameras? Through my phone? Who knows. It's not important. What's important is that I obey.

Obey. It's a word I didn't even use at my wedding, and now here I am, feeling as if I have to do so or face the consequences.

But that's wrong too. Because I'll face the consequences whether I obey or not. At least someone is guiding the process. Someone knows how this is all going to go and has seen around the corners I didn't know were there.

That's the thing about obedience. It feels safe.

But it's only safe if the person has your best interest at heart.

And here, my interest doesn't matter at all.

PART II

PART II

CHAPTER 15

Home

Then—July

Life sped up after I stepped off the airplane from Denver. Dan was at the airport to meet me, which was a surprise, something he'd never done before, and I knew in an instant what it meant.

Aunt Penny was dead.

He folded me into his arms, and we cried there in the airport baggage claim while people watched us, wondering what our tragedy was. We didn't look like a joyful reunion, and we weren't.

"Why didn't you tell me?" I asked when we were in the car he'd borrowed from a friend, snarled in traffic.

"You were doing your thing. I didn't want to ruin it. How was it, by the way?"

"It was good."

That felt like an understatement, but it was hard to sum it up in a few words. Not life changing, but life something. When we'd gotten our phones back at the airport from Gary, we'd exchanged contact information, and Connie had created a group text thread in one of the encrypted apps that she'd developed. *Women Killing It*, she'd called it, and I'd laughed at her enthusiasm. Our first meetup was scheduled for a week later, and I had a check-in with Michelle on the books too.

"So much excitement," Dan said, his hands confident on the wheel. He looked paler than when I'd left him, his tan faded after spending four days at the hospital. Penny had died the day before, slipping away peacefully with only Dan in the room. There had been no deathbed wishes or regrets. She'd simply gone to sleep and never woken up.

"I'll tell you about it later," I said. "Right now, I just want to be sad."

He reached over and squeezed my hand. "Me too."

I leaned my head against the window and looked out, watching the world crawl by. It was hot and muggy, a haze settling over the city. It was a blanket that I could feel being pulled over me, a weight I wanted to kick off.

"When's the funeral?"

"On Friday."

"Family coming in for it? Or are they still here?"

"Mom and Katherine went home on Friday. They'll be back Thursday."

"Fantastic."

Dan squeezed my hand again. "It'll be okay. You know they never stay long."

"Sure," I said. But I didn't believe it.

. . .

Somehow, I knew I'd regret going to Penny's funeral before I stepped into the black dress that I pulled from the back of my closet. The weather seemed to agree with me—an unrelenting rain was forecast for the entire day, and the sky was so dark I'd slept until my alarm shattered me awake, something that almost never happened.

I hated New York when it rained. In small-town Connecticut, where I'd grown up, the summer rain seemed like a cleanser, nature's street cleaner. When it was over, the air was fresh, and the trees felt greener. In Manhattan, rain heightened the smells and grime you learned to ignore most of the time, creating a thick sludge in the gutters and clouds of humidity that clung to you.

But it wasn't the weather's fault that I felt down and tired. Other than Dan, Penny felt like the only family I had. My parents were only children, and I'd grown up without cousins or grandparents, just our tight family unit. I'd never warmed to Dan's family, and the crush of work meant I hadn't kept in touch with most of the friends I'd made in law school other than through Facebook. Even my best work friend, Felicia, often felt like a friendship of convenience. It was probably my fault, but the reality was that I was lonely, something I hadn't thought much about until I started receiving daily texts from my Panthera Pride.

Good luck today! Athena had texted earlier. The others had quickly added their heart emojis and thumbs-up signs. It felt good to have them in my corner. I texted back my own series of hearts and tried not to dwell on what I had to face today.

— His family.
— Saying goodbye to Penny.
— The reading of the will.

Dan's family on his mother's side, old-money WASPs who'd lost most of their wealth during various economic downturns and most spectacularly when Dan was in college, knew how to follow the protocol and heighten the drama in all circumstances. His mother, for example, was probably happy about the weather. It meant Louise could limit her time by the graveside and stay in her fortress of solitude under a large umbrella held by the driver hired for the occasion. I knew better than to suggest this to Dan, but he also knew better than to challenge my moods when his family was in town.

Dan's dad, a jovial, nice guy with a ready smile and corny jokes, had died five years ago after a brief illness. I'd always wondered why Louise hadn't moved back to New York then. She'd been born here and had lived in the city until she'd gone to Ohio after she'd married. It was something she talked about constantly, making her twice yearly pilgrimages to reconnect with her "roots." But Louise and

Dan's sister, Katherine, had *the business to run*, apparently, and so she *simply couldn't*.

I'd breathed a sigh of relief, but the excuse was ridiculous—the part of the family pharmaceutical business that was left was run by competent people who answered to the bank, although they gave Katherine a position because clients liked thinking they were dealing with a family company rather than a cold group of bean counters. In my opinion, the most likely reason that they were staying put was that Louise ran the country club and Katherine had no connection to New York. She went to Berkeley for college and Wharton for her MBA. Neither of them liked being a small fish in a big pond, let alone a fish out of water.

Whatever the reason, I was happy to see as little of them as possible.

Despite the alarm, we were almost late. Our coffee maker chose that day to give up the ghost, and Dan insisted on buying coffee from a coffee shop because he couldn't face the day uncaffeinated. The only good thing that had happened so far was that my dress fit less snugly than I thought it would. I'd kept my promise and had hit the gym in the building every morning since I'd been home, getting in forty-five minutes on the treadmill. It sucked, and I walked a lot, but the times when I was running were starting to last longer. I'd coupled that with trying to be a bit more disciplined about my eating, and I could already feel a difference.

But even that nice bit of news felt petty. It was Penny's funeral. Who cared how I fit into my dress?

I helped Dan straighten his tie and we left the building, bolting into a cab to avoid getting soaked, then running into the Brick, the Presbyterian church Dan's family had been going to for centuries—a soaring structure of white pillars and red brick. Inside, we shook the water from our umbrellas and found seats in a pew near the front. Louise and Katherine were already there, twenty-seven years and one face-lift apart in appearance. Both icy blondes, and too thin to be healthy, their limbs were permanently tanned from too much tennis.

Dan hugged them both dutifully, while they gave me a half-bow, as if they were German. I'd (mostly) stopped being offended by their standoffishness. I was grateful that they'd decided to stay at the Thompson instead of with us, as I feared they might.

The organ played and the service followed its usual progression — the call to worship, the Prayer of Invocation. We weren't regular churchgoers, but I appreciated the comfort of the ritual. I recited the Lord's Prayer, and it gave me peace. Dan read a hymn and an old family friend spoke well of Penny, a great lady. I cried twice and tried not to notice Louise's dry eyes, Katherine's head unbowed. I didn't need to be underlining all the reasons I didn't like them. Instead, I leaned my head against Dan's shoulder and reached for the tissues he'd been thoughtful enough to bring.

I looked down at the program in my hands. It had a portrait of Penny taken at her eightieth birthday on its cover. We had a copy sitting on our mantel at home. She gave it to us in a silver frame when we moved in.

"I can watch over you," Penny had said with a husky laugh laced with the cigarettes she still snuck sometimes.

"You don't have to leave," I'd said, hugging her from the side.

"No, my dear, it is time." Penny had waved her small hands around, her heirloom diamond flashing on her left hand. "Out with the old and all that, you know."

"We could share the apartment. We can stay in the spare room."

"I wouldn't hear of it."

I pulled her closer. She smelled of Shalimar and the lavender she kept in her room to help her sleep. She'd been so nice to me from the first lunch Dan brought me to at her club. Insisting I have a glass of wine with the meal and "hang the bosses!"

"Thank you so much for letting us live here."

She smiled at me, her wrinkles real and earned. "Dan's the best of the lot."

"I know."

"Don't forget it."

I promised her I wouldn't, and she left, her driver coming to collect her bags. We had her over once a month for dinners on Sundays and shared holiday meals. She was our family. I was going to miss her like crazy.

The minister started the Benediction, and I mouthed along.

May the Lord bless you and keep you, Penny.

Thank you, Penny, I added, always needing an amendment to everything.

. . .

The reception was at the Colony Club. There was a full bar, and the air was thick with gin and tonics and smoked salmon sandwiches. There was an informal reception line that we stood in for a while, Dan knowing everyone, and me repeatedly having to explain who I was. An all-too-familiar feeling, being the outsider, the person who never fits in no matter how hard they try, the one whose name no one remembers. The first few times I'd brought it up to him, Dan told me I was exaggerating, so I'd stopped trying to explain. He didn't *not* want to get it, but he was one of those guys who fit in wherever he went, so he couldn't really understand.

Two hours on the dot after the reception began, everyone started to say their goodbyes, as if a bell had sounded before they'd been called into the theater. But they were the ones leaving before the play started. The entertainment was still to come.

As the waiters cleaned up, the family was ushered into a side room with six elegant wing-backed chairs set up in a circle.

"Will Poirot be joining us?" Dan quipped as he settled himself in one of the chairs.

"Daniel," Louise said without humor.

"Sorry, Mom."

I took his hand as Ms. Coates, the family lawyer, sat down in the chair at the top of the circle. She had shoulder-length silver hair held back with a black headband and was wearing a well-cut suit. She looked remarkably like the wills and estates partner from my firm, one of that tough, older generation that had to be more masculine than the men to survive the profession.

My phone buzzed in my purse at my feet. It had been doing that all morning, a workday, another inconvenient day to be away from the office. Instinct made me check it, since I'd been ignoring it for the last several hours. It was a text from Thomas: **We need to talk.**

Fantastic. Was Thomas breaking up with me?

At funeral.

Still?

It's a family funeral and I will be gone all day. Can we discuss on Monday?

There was a pause while he likely recovered from the shock of me not leaving a funeral to talk to him.

9. My office.

See you then.

I put my phone away and caught a disapproving look from Louise. I shrugged and mouthed *work*, then turned away.

"Are we all set?" Ms. Coates said, another reproach.

"Ready for you, Pauline," Louise said.

"Excellent. Sorry for the dramatic setting." She waggled her hand at the room. There was a roaring fire behind her despite it being the middle of July. The club kept the air at a frigid sixty-five degrees. Black rain plinked against the windows. "Penny had a sense of the dramatic sometimes. Not that she's in charge of the weather."

We all smiled as we were supposed to.

"Yes, well, ahem. She wanted me to summarize the will for you, and so here we are."

"And?" Louise prompted with her fake-sweet voice.

"Well, as you know, Penny's assets were in a trust set up by her late husband, Archibald, and the beneficiary of the trust, her having no children, is you, Louise, and then on your passing it's split equally between Katherine and Daniel."

Dan gripped my hand more tightly. We knew about this part, it wasn't controversial, and it was out of Penny's hands, Dan's uncle controlling assets from the grave. The important part was the direction to the trust to sell to us.

"Does it say anything about the apartment?" Katherine asked, leaning forward in her seat.

"It's in the trust as well. She left the contents to Daniel and Nicole."

"Are there no further instructions?" I said in small voice.

"No."

"What does that mean?" Katherine asked, but I knew.

"Louise owns it," I said. "And she can do with it what she wants."

Ms. Coates gave me an appraising look. "Well, the trust does, but yes, Louise is the beneficiary of that trust, so it's Louise's to determine what to do with it."

"And there's nothing else?" Dan asked. "No direction to sell it to us? You're sure?"

"No."

"Mom?" Dan said, turning toward her. "Did you know about this?"

She looked down, her cheeks pink, and picked a piece of invisible lint from her pristine black suit. "Well, Daniel, I don't know about all of these legalities."

"But you know that Penny wanted us to have it. You can sell it to us. For the right price. We'll have it appraised, get a mortgage. That's what you're going to do, right, Mom? Or we can just keep renting."

Louise played with the hem of her skirt. "Well, I don't know. It does seem as if you've had the apartment for a while now, and Katherine's been offered a job in New York with this marvelous company, so we thought . . ."

I didn't need her to complete the thought. She wasn't going to do it. Whatever Penny had told us, she hadn't done it. I never knew Penny to lie to us before, but I couldn't blame her for letting it slip her mind. She was dying. Real estate wasn't her priority.

"But Penny told us," Dan said, "that she'd set everything up so we could stay."

Ms. Coates rubbed her hands together. "Perhaps you were confused? She did have me arrange with the co-op board for you to be there legally when you moved in, since their rules are quite strict and only the owner is supposed to be living there."

"You're moving to New York?" I asked Katherine.

She gazed down her straight nose at me. "I've been offered a VP position at Linnaeus, and they're doing some very interesting work on a new protein that might be able to boost the immune system, so I thought I would."

"When?"

"Well . . ."

My head started moving again, unbidden this time. She was already in Manhattan, biding her time at the Thompson until she could displace us.

"How long do we have?" I asked.

"I thought thirty days would be reasonable."

Dan began to protest, but it all faded away to so much noise.

There's an expression I heard once when I was working with a lawyer from France on a file: *les cordonniers sont toujours les plus mal chaussés*, which, roughly translated, means "the shoemakers are always the worst shod."

Dan and I are lawyers. If we'd followed up properly with Penny and helped her to follow through, all of this could've been taken care of. But we were too shy to insist, too polite, despite our worries.

And now we were going to be without more than shoes.

CHAPTER 16

That's What We're Here For

Then—July

"**W**hat's up, Thomas?" I asked him on Monday morning at nine a.m. on the dot in his cavernous corner office. I'd brought him his favorite coffee from the shop downstairs as a peace offering, and though he'd smelled it appreciatively, he greeted me with a stern look.

I'd spent the weekend mourning our apartment and stressing about this meeting. I'd unburdened myself in the group thread, tentatively at first, then the whole story had come pouring out. How we'd been planning to buy the place for years, how Dan's family knew that, but they were refusing to sell it to us or even let us stay. Everyone was sympathetic, and Heather started sending me real estate listings and offering to go with me if I wanted, because she "loved being a real estate looky-loo." I'd told them about the meeting with Thomas, too, and this morning Heather had sent me a **you got this** text that had been followed by little bursts of support from the others that felt good to receive. Our daily text exchanges had already become something enmeshed in my day.

"Where were you on Friday?" Thomas said.

I pushed myself upright in his visitor's chair, making myself as tall as possible.

"I told you. I had a funeral to go to. Dan's aunt died."

I left out the great-aunt part, because his facial reaction at the word "aunt" was enough to indicate that he wasn't impressed with even that level of familial relationship.

"His whole family is in town for the funeral, and we were close. We live in her apartment," I added, my voice shaking, not ready yet to change that to the past tense. Thomas doesn't like emotions, but if used strategically against him, they can be effective.

And the emotions weren't faked. Dan had pleaded with his sister and his mom to let us stay, but they were immoveable. We'd *had our turn*, Katherine said, crossing her arms in a way that meant she wasn't going to budge. Dan and I talked it over, late into the night, parsing every conversation we'd had with Penny. It felt desperate and upsetting and it wasn't going to change anything. We had thirty days to find somewhere new to live. The prospect was exhausting.

"It couldn't be avoided," I said to Thomas when he didn't say anything. "I'm sorry."

I hated myself and Thomas, too, for making me apologize.

Thomas tipped his chair back. His corner office had a 180-degree view of Midtown at his disposal.

"All right, but coming on the heels of your other absence, it was very badly timed."

"I couldn't control when she died," I said, instantly regretting it.

"I'm aware of that, Nicole."

I clamped my jaw shut and met Thomas's eyes. He looked slightly chastened as he took a sip of his ridiculously expensive coffee. I shouldn't have brought it. My peace offering only ended up making me feel subservient.

"What did you want to speak to me about?" I asked. "When you called me?"

"Ah, yes. Some of your business expenses have been flagged."

"I'm sorry?"

"The managing partner asked me to speak to you. Charging vacations to your expense account is frowned upon."

"I didn't do that," I said, feeling nauseous. "What vacation?"

"Your little trip to Wyoming."

"I was in Colorado." I had only put in the report on Thursday. How had it already been reviewed and flagged? Was our managing partner that bored?

"Regardless. An alert occurred because you were at your limit. And I have to say, Nicole, I'm surprised at you."

"But it wasn't a vacation. I went to a women's networking event. I got invited to join the organization shortly after the points committee made its decision, and you said I needed to think outside the box and find a way to jump-start my career. That I needed to do something different to bring in business, and so I thought it was a good idea."

"What women's networking thing?"

"It's called Panthera Leo. It's the technical name for lion."

"That's odd."

"Any more so than Kiwanis?"

"Well, I've never heard of it. This lion thing."

"Athena Williams is a member. And Connie Chu. You know, the founder of Felidae? She's a client."

"Ah, yes. She is impressive."

"Yes. And one of the leaders is Karma Rosen, the owner of Good Karma."

"And your membership in this organization, will it bring in business?"

"That's the idea."

"Any leads yet?"

"I only just joined. The trip to Colorado was an intensive they have for new members. Can you please give me a bit of latitude to translate this into business?"

Thomas played with one of his cuff links. I remembered when I first met him almost fifteen years ago when I was still a law student. He'd taken me with him to court for the day, trying to woo me to sign with the firm. I was top of my class at Yale, and they weren't the only firm who was throwing things my way to recruit me. But Thomas was the only one who'd taken the time to convince me personally, outside of the usual interview and cocktail circuit. I'd appreciated it and accepted their offer. Since then, he'd been my mentor, but he'd also been a barrier.

"How long do you need?"

"You know bringing in clients is not like pushing a button, but I swear to you I am doing my best."

"And what about this?" Thomas said, holding up the printout of my expense report.

"Can you please tell him the expense is legitimate? I swear to God, Thomas, you can look back as far as you like. I've never put anything that shouldn't be on a report. Never."

"This points thing has you rattled."

"You'd be rattled too. But committing fraud on my expense report? For five thousand dollars? I'm not a moron."

Thomas put the paper down, thinking about his next words. "Can I be honest with you?"

I nodded.

"I'd hoped—we'd hoped—you'd be further along by now."

I tried not to sink into my chair. This was exactly what I had feared was going on. Even though it had all been rosy until this last year, I'd seen it happen time and again. Once the bloom came off the rose, you were a dried-out husk before you knew it.

"I'd hoped so, too. But I'm doing something about it, I promise."

"That's a promise I suggest you keep."

I nodded again and stood, knowing I was dismissed, feeling both tired and angry. I'd kept every one of my promises to the firm. They were the ones who'd broken theirs to me.

But I'd made a new covenant now, one that would hopefully, finally, put me in a space where Thomas and the points committee couldn't touch me.

. . .

Athena had offered her place for our first meeting. She lived in one of those soaring buildings made from weathered limestone on Central Park West. The doorman was expecting me, and I was the first to arrive. Athena answered the door barefoot but wearing one of her congresswoman suits—expensive gray fabric that fit her perfectly, a crisp shirt, a chunky necklace at her collarbone. She was on the phone and motioned for me to wait a moment while she finished up.

"You think we can break through in that market? I don't want to waste money chasing after ghosts." She nodded while the person responded. Then put her hand next to her head in the shape of a gun and shot herself. "All right. We'll discuss more tomorrow. I'm out for the night."

She hung up the phone and put it face down on a credenza made of glass that lay along the hallway wall.

"Sorry about that. You want the ten-cent tour?"

"Sure."

She showed me around. As we circled through the kitchen, she gave me a glass of white wine and then took me up the back steps to the roof. It was the best view of Central Park I'd seen since I'd been in New York.

"This is amazing."

"Isn't it? Sometimes I can't believe I live here."

"Not your usual public servant digs."

She laughed. "You should see my apartment in DC." She got an alert on her phone and tapped at it. "The others are here. And through the wonders of technology, I can let them in from up here."

"Great," I said.

"Is this where the party's at?" Heather said a minute later, coming onto the roof with Samantha and Connie in tow. Everyone was dressed in their "work" clothes—a collection of suits and column dresses for everyone but Samantha, who was wearing a light poplin summer dress that made me want to push for casual summers.

"One hundred percent," Athena said.

At Connie's prompting, we gave each other the Greeting, then spent a few minutes admiring the view, pointing to landmarks like tourists.

"Shall we sit?" Athena said, nodding to a set of lounge furniture. There was an outdoor kitchen near it, with a small buffet of food and a wine fridge.

We followed her lead and helped ourselves to food and alcohol. When we had our drinks, Athena raised her glass. "To Karma and Michelle."

We lifted our glasses and repeated the words. We all took a drink, then picked up where our text thread had left off earlier that day.

"I got that job," Samantha said, glowing with happiness. Her hair was pulled back in a tight bun at the base of her neck. She'd told us earlier that her show had wrapped in the spring and hadn't been renewed, but she was up for a large part in a new series that could lift her career to the next level, if she got it.

"What's the part?" I asked.

"It's the lead in the new *Law & Order* spinoff."

"Oh wow, that's fantastic," Heather said. She bit into one of the hors d'oeuvres that Athena had served us. "Athena, if you made these, I'm going to have to kill you."

"They come out of a box."

"That makes me feel better."

"I never would've gotten the part without Connie," Samantha said, raising her hands into a praying pose and bowing toward her. "Thank you."

Connie tipped her glass toward Samantha. "I made a few phone calls, that's all. What's the point of having connections if you don't use them? And you wouldn't have got the part if you weren't talented."

Samantha sipped at her wine. "Talent is fifty percent of the equation. Probably less."

"How about you, Heather?" Athena asked. "Anything to report?"

Heather popped another hors d'oeuvre into her mouth and washed it down with some wine. "A new file came into the office, a company ripe for a takeover. Do I have Connie to thank for that as well?"

Connie shrugged. "As fate would have it."

"Fate, my ass. It's plain old influence peddling, and I love it."

Athena smiled nervously. "Not a term you should throw around a congresswoman."

Heather pushed her hair back. It was frizzing in the heat. "Oh you know what I mean. We're doing what the men have always done. So thank you, Connie. I'll make a killing off this deal if it goes through."

"*Women Killing It*," I said.

"Precisely. When I get my bonus, we're going to Masa and eating the most expensive sushi in the world."

Masa was a six-hundred-fifty-dollar minimum. I'd never eaten there, only listened to the stories from the higher-ups who played credit card roulette. "I'm going to hold you to that," I said.

"And you, Nicole?" Athena asked.

"We're so sorry about your aunt," Samantha added, patting my arm.

I put my glass down. "It's not only that; it's the move. Dan's tried to convince his sister to let us stay there, but she's been a total bitch about it. So we have less than thirty days to find a new place, and work is crazy, though not as crazy as it should be, and I . . ." My throat closed up and I felt near to tears. "I'm sorry, guys. I'm a mess."

"What's going on at work?" Athena asked.

I hadn't had the time to fill them in on that morning's meeting with Thomas.

"Management thinks I've been cheating on my expense reports. And Thomas finally filled me in that the points-cutting was just the tip of the iceberg. They're re-evaluating me." I reached for my glass and took a large gulp of wine.

"What does that mean?" Samantha asked.

"They're watching me and waiting for me to fuck up. Anything I do that isn't perfect in their eyes is going to feed into this narrative that they made a mistake with me. That I'm not living up to my potential and never will. I'm worried I'm going to get kicked out of the partnership."

It was the first time I'd even voiced the thought, but it was true. I'd seen them do it to other former rising stars. Other firsts in their class who didn't quite make it as fast as the partners wanted.

"No, come on," Athena said. "Haven't you been there your whole career?"

"Yes, but that doesn't matter."

"I thought being a lawyer was a steady job?" Samantha said.

"Sure, any old lawyer. Some corporate drone. But when you're a partner, it's different. It's hard to explain. You have to constantly prove yourself. Your last file doesn't matter. If you don't measure up right this minute, it can all be over in an instant."

"Now that," Samantha said, "I can relate to." She put her hand on my back. "Just breathe, okay? It'll be all right."

"Why didn't you come to us?" Athena said. "That's what we're here for."

"I just found out this morning. I've been trying to process."

"Well, these are solvable problems, aren't they?" Connie said. She pulled out her phone. "Where do you want to live? I own several rental properties on the Upper West Side. You had a three-bedroom, right?"

"I can't afford something that big."

"Do not worry about that. We'll work something out that makes sense. How about I send you some listings and my agent will take you around to them on the weekend?"

"That soon?"

"It sounds like you don't have a moment to lose."

"Thank you."

"No need to thank me. It's what we do. And we can help you on the work front, too. A company whose board I sit on is looking to move a large, high-profile litigation file. They aren't happy with their current counsel. It's a two-month trial that's scheduled for late October. That sound like something you can do?"

"Yes, definitely. I don't have any trials scheduled till spring." It was one of the reasons I was in trouble with the partnership. That's where the real money was made—in actual litigation.

"Consider it done."

"Just like that?"

"Just like that."

I felt a flood of relief. "Thank you."

"We don't thank, we do."

Regardless, I got up and hugged her. She was surprised but appreciative, I thought.

"What about you, Connie?" Heather asked when I sat back down. "Everything okay with you?"

Connie stole a glance at Athena. "Life continues apace."

"Is that another saying?" I asked.

Athena reached for the wine bottle.

"It just means that life is life. Anyone need another drink?" Heather put her hand up and Athena filled her glass, and then her own. "I do have a mission for all of you, though. Can you tell me where I can find a man who won't tank my re-election campaign?"

We laughed then, as she meant us to, and the suggestions came fast and thick from Samantha and Heather, both single and deeply steeped in the New York dating scene.

My phone buzzed. It was Dan.

How's the branding ceremony going? Dan enjoyed teasing me, but he'd admitted the other day he was glad I joined the group.

It hurt, but we might get an apartment out of it.

For reals?

Half of it is true.

Tell me.

When I get home.

Which will be?

I glanced up, feeling the stares of the others on me, their words cutting out. "Sorry, it's just Dan." I texted **Soon**, then put my phone down.

"Tell us about Dan," Samantha said. "You haven't said that much about him, but I'm jealous."

I smiled. "I'm sure you have your pick of guys."

"Actors? Ugh. They're the worst."

"We'll have to meet him sometime," Athena said lightly.

"Yes, he'd like that."

The moment shifted back to dating advice. Heather seemed intent on finding Athena a man. There was always NotADateNight .com when she was feeling horny. Her words.

I sipped my wine, listening to their chatter, their excited suggestions, laughing at their terrible dating stories, secretly happy that I didn't have to participate. I'd never liked dating, which always felt fraught and stressful.

Laughing there with the other women, I didn't know what an understatement that would turn out to be.

CHAPTER 17

Imagine Your Life Here

Then—July

"**W**e can't afford this," Dan whispered to me as we toured our second apartment near the High Line that Saturday. This one was in Hudson Yards, newly renovated, with amazing floor-to-ceiling windows with views of the city I'd only dreamed of ever having access to. I never thought I'd like a modern apartment, especially after living at Penny's with all its pre-war charm, but I felt lighter the moment I walked in. The ceilings soared, and the furnishings were minimalist, with an extremely comfortable-looking gray chenille couch dominating the living room in front of an enormous gas fire. Sunlight flooded through the massive windows, and a three-fold door opened onto a patio filled with resort-like furniture.

"But if we could?"

"We can't."

"The building has all the amenities," the real estate agent said. Her name was Sylvia, and she was around forty-five, rail thin, with dyed purple hair. She was wearing an immaculate white suit that I would've been too nervous to even try on. A familiar pin sat on her lapel. "Gym, spa, pool, parking. Anything you could wish for."

"If I had a billion dollars," Dan sang.

"Hush."

He shook his head at me but stayed quiet throughout the rest of the tour of the three-bedroom luxury digs. With each minute I spent in it, I wanted it more. We'd each have an office. The kitchen was to die for, with a six-burner stove and an extra oven. We could have parties in this place. Not that we'd ever done that, but now that I had friends, we could.

I took out my phone and quickly took a picture of the thousand-square-foot living room/kitchen/dining space. I sent it to the Panthera thread, my sharing immediately rewarded with a flurry of *omg, fantastic!* and a roaring lion emoji from Heather.

I wanted the apartment badly, but Dan was right—we couldn't afford it. Even if things were going well at work, the monthly rent and fees were out of our league. I resolved to see some of the places Dan had circled in the Sunday paper, reasonable apartments with half the square footage we had now. Or we could move to the suburbs, he'd suggested. He had friends from law school who lived in cute towns in New Jersey where the public schools were great.

"Did you have any questions?" Sylvia asked. She tapped her red lacquered nails on the pristine counter.

"We need to think about it," I said.

She clucked her tongue. "Think quickly. These units don't last long."

"Got it."

She handed me the one-sheet and her eyes tracked to the pin on the strap of my cross-body purse. I'd put it there because it would've looked silly on the T-shirt I was wearing.

I scanned the one-sheet to the monthly rent and other costs for the gym, spa, and pool, and I felt sick to my stomach. It was more than double the highest number I'd let myself imagine. The dream was dead, like too many others I'd had. Taking the world by storm, for one. That's what I was supposed to be doing. Or changing it. Hadn't

I wanted to change it when I'd applied to law school? And now I just wished I made enough money to be able to live in this palace. What was wrong with me?

Sylvia took us downstairs and left with another admonishment to act fast, leaving us alone in the cavernous atrium. The roar of the water fountain made it hard to hear, so we stood close to one another.

"It would be nice, huh?" Dan said.

"Imagine your life here . . ."

"Is our life so bad?"

"No."

Dan pulled me in for a hug. "There's always New Jersey," he said into my hair.

"All those couples with kids."

He leaned back, searching my face. "Meaning?"

"Is that what this is about? You want kids now?"

"Not sure how you got from property to kids."

"Come on, Dan. I know you."

Dan looked at the floor. "Well, okay, yeah, it has occurred to me. I mean, if you aren't on the partner track anymore, then you'd have time for that, right? We'd have time."

"Dan."

"What?"

I touched his face. "Us not wanting kids wasn't about not having enough time. You know that."

"I know."

"So what's this about?"

"Penny's dying got me thinking."

"About carrying on the family legacy?"

Normally Dan would've laughed at that. He hated his family's reliance on the past for currency in the present more than I did. But not that day. "Is that so crazy?"

Yes! I wanted to scream. It is crazy to suddenly decide you want kids at thirty-nine, especially when you're not the one who'd have to carry them.

"It feels kind of crazy, Dan. I know things are a bit unsettled now, but remember during lockdown, how many times we said that we were lucky not to have kids? All that Zoom schooling and laundry and everyone on top of each other? Is that what you want?"

"It wasn't like that for everyone. Some people were happy to spend that time together as a family."

Show me, I wanted to say. *Show me the ones who were.*

"But we were happy just us. Aren't you still?"

"I am."

"Then why change things? Why risk it?"

Dan tucked his chin into his chest. "So the next forty years is just us, getting older, working? That's it?"

My throat tightened and I thought I might start crying right there in the impersonal lobby of the building I'd wanted to live in so badly ten minutes ago. "I'm not enough for you?"

"I never said that."

"You are kind of saying that, though."

"It's not what I meant."

"Okay."

Dan ran a hand over his head, shuffling at his hair. It was one of his endearing moves. He had a full head of hair but was worried that he was losing it, so he'd check it in moments of stress.

"Have you been speaking to your mother?" I asked.

"A little."

"Ah."

"It's not what you think."

"No?"

Dan gave me a half smile. "Well, maybe it's a bit what you think."

"Dan, we can't live our life for her. Or for some idea about the future. Hell, I might not even be able to get pregnant." I pointed to my stomach. "These eggs are old."

"Would you be willing to find out?"

This conversation was getting less casual by the minute. "Honestly? I don't know."

"Okay."

"Is it, though?"

"I'm not sure."

"Fuck."

"Yeah."

"This isn't really the place to have this conversation."

"I know."

"Can we park this for now?" I asked. "With everything at work . . . I need a few weeks to regroup. Let's get settled somewhere and then we can revisit, all right?"

"Sure."

I took his hand. "I love you."

"I love you too."

I breathed out a sigh of relief. "Okay, then. Let's go look at some of the rentals you found."

"It'll be great."

"I know," I said, trying to smile when all I wanted to do was cry.

CHAPTER 18

The Docket

Then—July

Dan and I spent the rest of the day looking at apartments that were perfectly fine but not what I wanted, before collapsing into bed early with a takeout pizza and a bottle of red wine. I woke up on Sunday feeling jittery and hungover—not the best mood for packing.

There was a stack of boxes in the corner of our bedroom that I'd had delivered earlier in the week. We'd accumulated a lot of things while we lived at Penny's, and I hadn't done a triage of the stuff I'd had in my previous place because I was in the middle of a trial when we'd moved in together. There were still boxes I'd never opened in ten years. Even though we hadn't decided where we were going to move, the packing had to begin.

I rose. Dan was out for his usual long run on Sundays with a bunch of guys from his old firm. I'd managed to run for nineteen minutes straight on the treadmill the day before, and I decided to give myself the day off since my legs were stiff.

I shuffled to my closet and pulled out the boxes that were hiding in the back. I opened the first one and dust flew out. It was full of stuff from law school. Papers I'd written, photos, graduation mementoes. I held a picture of myself on graduation day. I looked so young, my ex-boyfriend's arm yoked around my shoulders. We were laughing, and I couldn't remember who took the shot. But that day, I do remember being purely happy. It was a feeling that had become fleeting over the years, as the mountain of work and stress weighed me down and flattened me out.

My phone rang with an incoming FaceTime call. Michelle's face filled the screen when I answered it.

"Where are you?" she asked. Her braid was twisted around her head like a Swedish milkmaid. She was somewhere at the ranch, the mountains framed in the picture window behind her.

"In my closet."

"Interesting choice of location for our call."

I leaned back against the wall. "I had a late night and forgot about our talk. I've been packing."

"Is now still a good time?"

"Yes, definitely." I held my phone out from my face and tried not to focus on the mess that was my hair. "If you don't mind me looking this way."

"I would never judge another woman's appearance."

"I should work on that."

"We certainly can."

I stretched my legs out in front of me, trying not to groan at the pain. I really was going to have to learn to stretch after my runs. "Is that what these talks are? A sort of therapy?"

Michelle laughed. "No, no. I'm not licensed for that. It's more like mentorship in order to help you achieve your goals."

"Seems like most in the group are doing well."

"I'm glad to hear it, but I want to know how *you* are doing."

"Not amazing."

"Why not?"

I filled her in on the apartment saga and what was going on at work. I usually hated FaceTime, always distracted by my own appearance on the screen, but Michelle's soothing voice as she encouraged me to unburden myself made me feel calm.

"You're dealing with a lot. Work. Shelter. Family. These are our building blocks. When even one is on shaky ground, we can feel unsteady."

"It feels like my whole life is coming apart."

"I understand why you feel that way. Now, what are you going to do about it?"

"What can I do?"

Michelle shook her head gently. "I've been where you are. When my marriage ended, and it felt like my career was over . . . My ex, he'd put everything in his name, and I barely had any money. All I had were lawyers who wanted more and more and more from me. You know what I did?"

"You think I should go to Africa?"

"That was just a change in location. What was more important was what I changed in here." She touched her chest. "And here." She touched her forehead. "Up until that moment, I'd been letting life control me. My mantra was 'everything happens for a reason,' which was, to be frank, a cop-out."

I laughed. "Lots of people have made a lot of money off that mantra."

"I might even be one of them. But when I put it aside, when I decided I wasn't going to just toss around in the wake of life, that's when I found my true power."

"And you met Karma?"

"As fate would have it." She waited for me to repeat it, but I resisted.

"What made you decide to work together?"

"After we met, we realized we'd experienced so many of the same disappointments despite our success, and that we both wanted to find a way to try to correct the injustices that still remained for women. We talked about various ways to accomplish that before landing on the fact that it was going to take women in every corner of the corridors of power to change things once and for all."

The lock turned in the front door and Dan thumped it open.

"Babe?"

I turned away from the screen. "I'm in here! Just on a call." I turned back to Michelle. "So what do I do? How do I flip the script for me?"

"Ask for what you need. Don't just wait for it to show up."

The closet door swung open. A very sweaty Dan was standing in the doorway looking at me like I was crazy.

"Hey," I said.

"What are you doing in here?"

"I was in here when Michelle called." I turned the screen toward Dan and angled it up. "Say hi to Michelle, Dan."

He waved to her and then I turned the screen away. "I've got to go."

Michelle nodded. "Think about what I said."

"I will."

I ended the call. I could feel Dan hovering over me. I held out my hand to him. "Help me up." He did as I asked, and I kissed him, tasting the salt on his lips.

"What's all this about?"

"Just getting some advice."

"From Michelle Song?"

"I told you she was one of the founders. Why is it so weird that I'm talking to her?"

"It's not. Forget it."

"Dan."

He pulled away. "I need to take a shower."

"Packing after?"

"Sure."

He walked toward the bathroom. I thought briefly of joining him in the shower, trying to pull back some of the intimacy that we seemed to have lost since the potential kids conversation, but something held me back.

I was the one whose life was imploding. Dan should be trying to make me feel better, not the other way around. I pushed that thought away. None of this was Dan's fault. If I asked for his help, he'd give what he could.

I was the one who was going to have to figure out how to ask for what I needed.

And fast.

. . .

On Monday morning I woke up with a purpose and to some interesting mail on my phone.

The first was a newsletter called *InfoSec* that had been forwarded to me by Athena. As I perused it, I was initially worried that Athena had revealed herself to be an adherent to some kind of end-of-the-world, QAnon conspiracy. It was full of threat assessments and weather reports that were three weeks away. But when I googled the name, I understood what it was. Put together by a group of ex-CIA types, it cost $100,000 to subscribe. Its purpose was to give its readers a heads-up on upcoming events that would affect the market, the world, and the weather. I'd heard more than one story about people who'd fled New York in February 2020 because of it. They'd also been able to time the market and avoid the crash. I'd had my doubts about the veracity of those stories, but now here was proof, in my inbox. Companies that were ripe for a short sale. Places to avoid traveling to. Assessments of the current risk levels for a dozen hate groups and terrorist organizations.

Reading it left me feeling unsettled. One of the reasons I went to law school was because I had an innate sense of justice. Something about the newsletter felt unfair. But it was also revelatory, a partial explanation for all those times when it felt like the higher-ups in my firm were one step ahead of me.

I pulled myself from bed and went downstairs to the gym. We'd packed up half of our stuff the day before, and my whole body hurt from lugging boxes around. We also had a huge pile of things to be donated, which made my heart hurt, too, even though I wasn't generally sentimental.

As usual, I was alone in the gym. I got on the treadmill and started my routine—fast walking for five minutes—when I got a text from Karma in the encrypted app. **I need a favor**, it said. **A young woman will be contacting you about a job at your firm. Please see to it that she's hired.** It was followed by a link to a LinkedIn page, which showed a nondescript woman who'd recently graduated from Harvard Law.

I'm not in charge of recruiting, I wrote back. **And it's not when we usually hire people.**

Be that as it may, I'm certain you can make it work.

Why does she need my help? Harvard Law . . . I'm sure she'll have plenty of offers.

Are you refusing your first request for assistance?

I slowed my treadmill down, my heart already beating fast enough. It wasn't the first request I'd gotten from PL. That had been for donations to Athena's re-election campaign, asking us to give the maximum. Connie's rapid *done!* had been followed by *done!* from Samantha and Heather. I'd scrambled to donate and add my *done!* to the chorus. A few days later, it had been Samantha's turn to ask for donations to a women's shelter that she supported. That was *done*, *done*, and *done* too.

No, I wrote. **It's . . . a big ask. One I'm not sure that I can accomplish.**

I have confidence that you will get it done.

I put my phone down and tried to concentrate on getting the treadmill back up to speed and restarting my run, but that proved futile. After five minutes I gave up and took the elevator back upstairs, my mind cluttered with Karma's request and how I was going to accomplish it.

And also: What would happen to me if I didn't?

* * *

Things didn't improve when I got to the office. Before I could even settle into my chair, I received an email from Thomas noting that I wasn't at my desk when he'd stopped by earlier; he'd attached my dockets for the month, which were low. No shit. Five days away and

Penny dying and the distraction of my career falling apart—what did he expect? Why couldn't I have a minute to be human? I needed some time to collect myself. A moment of fallibility. But nope. Not allowed. Not possible. No quarter. None.

I picked up the phone.

"Hello?"

"Hi, Connie, it's Nicole."

"Oh, hi. How were the apartments?"

"They were wonderful, thank you. Especially the one in Hudson Yards."

"That's my favorite, too."

"It would be a fantastic opportunity to live there. But the thing is—"

"You don't think you can afford it?"

"I know we can't." I tucked the phone under my chin and started to type a response to Thomas. I'm on it. My hours will be up by month's end.

"I'd like you to take it, though."

I hit send on the email and vowed to spend the next week at the office as much as possible. I had enough files that I could churn some hours out of to keep Thomas off my back for a while. It wasn't something I generally condoned doing, but I needed some breathing room.

"That's so nice of you, but—"

"Nicole," Connie said, interrupting me. "I'm offering it to you. I'd rather have someone I know and trust in there right now. So if you liked the one in the Yards, then it's yours."

"For free?"

"We'd work out a reasonable rent. Whatever you're paying now, for instance."

"I can't accept that."

"You can and you will," she said firmly.

Thomas answered me. You should hit 300 this month to show management you're serious about turning this ship around.

I took in a deep breath. Three hundred hours. That meant spending literally all of my time at the office for the rest of the month. Litigation wasn't like corporate; I couldn't bill twelve hours a day on one file unless I was in trial.

"Nicole?"

"Sorry. Are you sure?"

"Yes."

"I have to talk to Dan."

"I understand. But make it a yes, okay? Consider it something you should be doing for the Pride."

"Why?"

"Because it's important for us all to be happy and situated, to work well together."

I emailed Thomas back. It will get done. "True. Speaking of . . . I mean, I feel bad asking for this since you're being so generous."

"What is it?"

"That file you mentioned. Is that going to happen?"

"Oh yes, I'm sorry, I've been tied up with other things. Are you free on . . . Friday at two?"

I didn't even bother checking my calendar. I would make any time work.

"Yes."

"Block two hours, then. I'll bring in Guy and he can fill you in on the file."

"Guy?"

"Guy Mason."

I googled him quickly. "The chairman of SulliVent?"

"That's the one."

"Oh wow. I mean, I wasn't expecting . . ."

Connie made an annoyed growl in her throat. "Nicole, a bit of advice?"

"Please."

"You think too small. You're a good lawyer, right?"

"Yes."

"One of the best?"

"Yes."

"So then you're exactly who SulliVent needs right now."

"Clients like that usually want a senior partner on their file."

"Only because we let them think that way. But trust me, Guy will be there with me on Friday. I'll forward you the basics. Consider it done."

"Thank you."

"No need to thank me. You'll do the same for me. Talk soon." She hung up.

I leaned back in my chair and stretched my hands over my head. It wasn't even nine thirty in the morning yet, and Thomas's three-hundred-hours email felt like a bomb in my inbox.

But maybe now I had the tools to defuse it.

Now—October

I take the emergency stairs from Athena's apartment to the basement two at a time, adrenaline coursing through me. It hasn't been that long since I arrived, but it feels like it's been hours. How much time do I have to get this done? And what am I supposed to do with the gun once I find it, if I do?

That's always been my problem. Asking questions, litigating things. The minutiae. Sometimes I get lost in it and miss the big picture. All I know right now is that I wish Athena didn't live on the twentieth floor.

And, oh God, how am I going to get back up there? My legs are already shaking, my shins screaming from the impact.

There's a grimy door in front of me marked BASEMENT. Through the door the light is dim, and my eyes have trouble adjusting. When they do, I scan the walls methodically. There! The large black garbage bins are lined up along one wall beneath a series of chutes. I approach them cautiously, trying to keep quiet, to not make any noise. There's a clicking sound, and the garage door creaks open slowly. I press myself into a shadow, hoping I'm invisible. A couple enters with a large garbage bag, laughing and drunk. He shoves it into a bin as she tugs on his arm. I pull back further against the wall. I'm grateful for the alcohol fog as they list toward the door to the building and disappear inside.

I let out the breath I was holding and get closer to the bins. A quick glance above me shows that there are cameras trained on them. I cannot worry about that now. I have to trust that the hoodie and the baggy clothing I'm wearing and the darkness will shadow me enough that if anyone ever looks at the footage, I won't be recognizable.

On closer inspection, it appears that each floor delivers to a different bin. How am I supposed to know which one is the right one? I take my phone out, the message for me to get the gun still floating there. I turn on the flashlight and tuck my face further back inside my hoodie as I search the wall for some indication of which bin to look in. It's there—faded numbers that refer to the floors the garbage comes from. Athena's bin is the third one in. I pray the gun is on top, that other tenants didn't decide to throw out several weeks' worth of garbage on the same night.

I haul myself up onto the edge of the bin and scan it with the flashlight, looking for something metal. It's not there. I want to stop and cry, but that's not an option. I have to find the gun. If I don't, I don't know what will happen, but I'm so far into this now I can't even think that far ahead. I should get off this smelly heap and call the police. So far, I haven't done much wrong. A bit of obstruction of justice. I probably won't go to jail for that. I could chalk it up to the shock. I could lose my law license, though.

Fuck, fuck, fuck.

I use the flashlight again. The bin is half-full. The gun probably slipped down to the bottom. If I remove the bags of garbage and put them in the bin next to this one, I can probably find it. I lift the first bag and it splits, spilling coffee grinds and half-eaten pasta all over me. I want to retch, but I toss it aside and keep moving. If I get out of this, I'm going to find a way to tip my local garbage guy. There is no way he's making enough money.

One bag, two, three. The things people throw away.

—A bagful of mothballed clothes.
—What looks like a lifetime of love letters, full of hearts and stars.
—The rotted contents of a fridge.

Oh. Someone died in this building. Not just Jack, but someone old, someone like Penny. It's their life that I'm trampling on in my mad attempt to find a gun someone used to end someone else's life. But I can't stop and think about that.

I toss another bag aside and then another. One more and I hear a clink. I stop and crouch, moving my hands around until I find it. The gun. I hold it gingerly in my gloved hands. Is it loaded? I find the safety and put it on. The gun is heavy, and I have nowhere to put it.

I stand there for a moment, my breath ragged, my heart pounding, my legs shaking.

Now what?

"I'll take that, thank you," a man says, emerging from the dark, and all I want to do is scream.

CHAPTER 19

It All Fit in Two Boxes

Then—July

"**F**igure skates," Dan said that Thursday night. "Keep or toss?"

"Keep."

He poked his head out of one of the hall closets that we used for storage. "You haven't skated since I met you."

"Yeah, but I might."

"I thought the idea was to reduce the amount of stuff we have?"

"Useless stuff." I took the skates from him and put them on my keep pile. I was never a good skater, but that didn't mean I didn't still harbor dreams of taking lessons one day and learning how to do a double axel. I'd need my skates for that. "Like the Rollerblades. Those we can toss."

"I think they're coming back."

"Don't care. Remember what happened the last time we went roller blading?"

Dan looked sheepish. He'd had a bad fall and he'd ended up in the emergency room with nothing broken, but a body full of bruises and a mild concussion. "Okay, you have a point."

I put our Rollerblades and related equipment into the toss pile, which was not as large as it should've been. "Good thing the new place has lots of room."

"Yeah."

"Dan."

"What?" He gave me a look that I understood. He was wearing an old band T-shirt from his college days, and it was a bit tight against his belly. Too many takeout meals for both of us over the last ten years had crept up on him, too, despite his Sunday runs.

He wasn't happy about the new apartment. He hadn't said no, but his "yes" felt like a concession and not an agreement.

"It's going to be a good thing."

"So you keep saying."

"Why don't you think it is?"

"You don't think it's weird that we're getting it so cheap?"

"It's what the group's about. I told you."

"Making bad real estate deals?"

"Ha, ha." I put down the winter coat I'd bought him on a whim a few years before and that he'd never worn, and walked to where Dan stood, at the threshold of the closet. "What's really going on?"

His eyes were on his shoes, an old pair of Stan Smiths that I thought he'd thrown out long ago. "Hudson Yards doesn't seem like a great place to raise kids to me."

And there it was. Dan's casual request that I think about having kids had cemented into something he thought we were doing, despite our agreement to park it.

"We said we'd talk about that, not that it was happening."

"Seems like you decided we aren't going to."

I put my hands on my hips. I felt sweaty and dusty from the packing. I'd spent ten hours at the office that day, billing every second I could, and it was now past eight. I was too tired to fight. "Hey, that's not fair. We *did* decide. Remember? Together?"

He raised his head. "I'm allowed to change my mind, aren't I?"

I knew he wanted me to say yes to this, but it didn't feel like a decision where you could change your mind. Not practically. "I don't know, Dan. This is a big thing. And my career is on a precipice right now."

"You could step back from it."

"What?"

"Forget it."

"No, tell me; what did you mean?"

He sighed. "I know you'd rather be caught dead than working where I do, okay? And don't say you don't feel that way, because you do. You look down on in-house jobs. But you know what? It's not that bad. It's less money, but also fewer hours, and it's not like you're saving the world doing civil litigation. Why are you killing yourself for those assholes?"

"Wow."

"What?"

"How long have you felt this way?"

"Forever?"

"You've never said anything."

He shoved his hands into his pockets. "How could I? You were so into it. You are still."

"I'm sorry."

"Why are you apologizing? It's what it is. But it doesn't have to be, is all I'm saying. When's the last time you were happy? Like truly happy? Not glad you won a case or high on a good distribution, but content."

"Is anybody happy?" I said lightly.

"Yeah, Nic. I think a lot of people are."

My smile dropped. "You think a baby will change things?"

"It will."

"It will change our lives, but you think it's going to, what? Make me care less about my career? And who's going to be taking care of this baby?"

"You're having a baby?" Louise said from behind me.

I closed my eyes and turned away from Dan, my pulse thrumming. Louise walked through our front door with a set of keys in her hand.

Dan plastered on a smile and held his arms out to her for a cheek kiss. "No, Mother, you misunderstood."

"You don't knock?" I said, then shot Dan a dirty look. Sometimes I envied people who were friendly with their in-laws. Especially since my own parents were dead, it would've been nice to have a replacement family to step into. But Penny was right—Dan was the best of the lot by a country mile.

Only now, he wanted things I didn't. I felt lost in our hallway, surrounded by the things we were tossing from our life together.

Was one of us supposed to be on one of the piles?

"We told Dan we were coming," Katherine said, stepping out from behind Louise. They were both dressed in impeccable summer outfits, loose satin skirts with halter tops that skimmed their thin frames. They were fresh from the salon with flawless makeup.

I felt even grungier than I had earlier. "I'm sure he mentioned it, then." He hadn't, but we had to be on the same team where they were concerned. "What can we do for you at eight thirty at night?"

"We're here to measure," Louise said, taking an actual tape measure out of her purse.

I assumed Louise was joking. "For drapes?"

"Drapes, furniture, the works. Our flight leaves tomorrow morning. We wanted to get it done before we go so Katherine can order what she needs."

"This place will be much lighter without all of these old things in it," Katherine said, running her finger along Penny's entrance table as if she was inspecting for dust. "Don't you agree?"

"Obviously not, Katherine," Dan said, more aggressively than I'd ever heard him talk to his sister. "And you said you were coming at six."

Katherine shrugged. "We got held up at the designer's."

I felt a burning rage in my stomach, and I slunk away from the conversation. I went into the living room and decided to tackle packing up my books. There was a full shelf of titles I'd always meant to read but hadn't gotten around to. Was Dan right? Was I wasting my life? What was I supposed to do instead? Read all day and shop, like his mother? No, he didn't want that—I knew he didn't. We'd work through this like we'd worked through everything. We'd be okay. We just had to pack our things and move to our new place and stop seeing his family on a semi-regular basis.

But then I heard the whispered word *baby* float toward me from the hallway, and I couldn't tell whether Dan was telling them to drop it or to hope.

I didn't have the courage to ask.

. . .

On my way to work on Friday, I got a text from Karma asking for a status update on the hiring of one Julia Sanders, the Harvard grad I was supposed to hook up with a job at my firm. I was standing on the subway platform, sweating in the heat, wishing I'd followed through on my plan to leave more clothes at the office so I could arrive in shorts and change there.

I made this plan every year and I never did it.

Julia had reached out to me a few days before and sent me her résumé and transcript. She was in the top third of her class and had all the usual accomplishments you might expect of a Harvard Law graduate except that she didn't have a job. She'd interned at Good Karma when she was in college, which might've been how Karma knew her, though I doubt she had time for interns. She looked presentable, seemed to have friends, and didn't post anything inappropriate online. Why did she need a leg into the firm? Using one didn't help your career, I'd found, watching the trail of sons-and-daughters-of who'd summered at the office or spent a few years there before they realized they were never getting anywhere and left.

I texted the group. **Are we supposed to do favors for each other even when the favor isn't a good idea?**

Like what? Athena answered.

I hesitated. I didn't know the protocol about requests, but I had an instinct Karma wouldn't approve of me broadcasting it.

I switched to a private message with Athena.

Karma wants me to get a job for someone at my firm.

What's the problem?

Well, assuming I can even get it done, which is a big if, it won't be good for this girl. Everyone will know she pulled strings to get in and that's frowned on. Besides, she doesn't even need it. She'd get hired on her own.

Karma asked you though.

Yeah.

I'd do it, personally.

Okay thanks.

The subway car pulled up, blowing its usual hot breeze across my face. It smelled fetid, but walking to work in this heat was a no go. I put my phone away and got on, hoping that a minimal number of bodies would be pressing against me.

Every day seemed to bring a new stress. The fight with Dan after his mother and sister had finally left the night before, in which I made it clear that they weren't going to be invited to our new place. The thick SulliVent file that weighed down the bag slung across my shoulder, which I wanted badly but was anxiety-producing, nonetheless. The need to try to find a moving truck for all our things and the endless exhaustion of packing. And now I had to convince Thomas to give Julia a chance at an open associate position when there were no such positions available.

The subway jolted away from the stop as my phone received a new message from Athena.

Ask for what you need, and you'll make it happen, she'd written. The same advice I'd gotten from Michelle. I'd asked Connie for a file, and now I was about to meet with the biggest client of my career. If I landed it, a lot of things could change for me.

So maybe that was the answer. I was stuck where I was because I didn't ask for the help I needed to get out.

Could it be that easy?

It was time to find out.

CHAPTER 20

New Beginnings

Then—July

My meeting with SulliVent wasn't until the afternoon, so I decided to tackle the Julia problem first.

Thomas, the jack-of-all-trades of our firm, was in charge of recruiting. I figured I could butter him up by telling him about the meeting, and then ask for the job interview. The file Connie had sent me was a doozy—SulliVent had fired their founder, majority shareholder, and CEO, Vic Sullivan, after some vaguer-than-usual allegations of sexual impropriety by a woman named Jennifer Naughton. He'd sued them for millions for wrongful termination and damage to his reputation. Until his ouster, Sullivan had been a Wall Street wunderkind, starting three successful companies in different industries.

Sullivan was fine without SulliVent, but he cared about his reputation, and based on the evidence, he had good reason to fight. Naughton had come forward with accusations of inappropriate language in a few meetings and the feeling that she had to sleep with him to advance in the company, but no one else had backed up her allegations. She'd even gotten a promotion before she made the complaint. I could see why the company wanted new lawyers;

their existing counsel had written a cover-your-ass memo setting out his recommendation to settle, but the company had refused to do so. I was probably going to lose, and I was curious about why Sulli-Vent wouldn't settle, but the file could easily represent a million in billables.

"Well, that's good news," Thomas said after I filled him in. "You're meeting today?"

"Yes, at two."

He smiled. "I notice you've logged more time this week."

"I've been doing what I can."

"Excellent." He folded his hands on his desk. "I'm so glad you took my pep talk to heart."

I gritted my teeth. "Thanks for the mentoring."

"Always happy to help."

"I did have something to ask."

Thomas picked a piece of lint off his suit jacket. "Oh?"

Is that wise? his tone said, but I plowed ahead anyway. "I've received a recommendation for a highly impressive young woman from Harvard who's looking to work at our firm."

"It's not hiring season."

"I know that. However, you've always said it was important not to miss opportunities when they came along, and with this new file, it would be good to have a new associate without anything on her plate to devote herself to it. The trial's only a few months away and I'm going to need someone helping me full-time."

"Why doesn't she have a position already?"

"Sounds like an excellent question for you to ask her in her interview?"

"We'll see."

"I'll schedule something with your assistant." I turned and left without waiting for his answer, so he didn't have a chance to say no.

It's what a man would do.

• • •

That afternoon, my assistant let me know that the clients had arrived, and I went to the boardroom on the fortieth floor. It was our showstopper conference room with mesmerizing panoramic views of Manhattan. I wore my best suit and had taken extra care with my appearance, going for a blowout over my lunch hour. This was as good as it was going to get for me; I was never going to look like Louise or Katherine. But I could do things they couldn't do.

"Good afternoon, gentlemen," I said, reaching out my hand to the nearest suit sitting at the long oak table.

"Ah, Nicole, excellent, so glad you could make it," Thomas said.

I stuttered to a stop, my heart sinking. Thomas was perched at the other end, a notepad in front of him as well as a half-empty cup of coffee. He was settled in and comfortable, and I could almost smell the testosterone in the air. Oh no. I'd misunderstood. They didn't want me, they wanted Thomas. Would I even get the credit for bringing in the file?

But I'd been here before. I knew what to do. I smiled and introduced myself to the men: their new CEO, and then the chairman, Guy Mason, who'd overseen the firing. But where was Connie? I checked my phone quickly. There wasn't any message from her saying she'd be late. Dammit.

I took a seat to the left of Thomas and tried to take control. "First off, I wanted to thank you for trusting me—us—with the file. I understand that it's late in the game to change counsel, but rest assured we will be prepared to proceed to trial as scheduled if that is what you want to do."

"Nicole is the brains of the operation," Thomas said, giving me a paternal smile that made my stomach churn. Men were always saying that like it was a compliment. Like we should be grateful that they identified that we were indispensable to their success.

"Which is why she'll be heading this file," Connie said, coming into the room with an air of authority.

"Pardon me?" Thomas said, swiveling around in his chair.

Connie smiled like a cat with a bowl of warm milk. Her hair was perfect, and her bright red lipstick was intimidating. "We wouldn't want anybody but the brains of the operation handling this file, would we, gentlemen?"

Guy Mason nodded his head. "Stands to reason."

"Thanks for the warm welcome," Connie said, reaching out her hand to Thomas. "We won't be needing you in the rest of the meeting."

"I'm the senior partner on the file."

"We hired Nicole."

Thomas stood, flustered. I don't think he'd been dismissed from a meeting in his entire career. It made me want to laugh, but I did my best to keep my features tight. This probably wasn't the way back into Thomas's good graces, but for the moment I didn't care.

"I'm sure you want to keep your budgets under control," Thomas said, moving toward the door. "Nicole is perfectly competent to handle this file."

"More than, I'm sure."

"As you say."

Connie stared at him, waiting for him to leave. After a moment of indecision, where he couldn't quite believe he was going to have to do it and was clearly waiting for someone to call him back, he left.

Connie turned away from the door as it swung shut on Thomas. "Sorry about that, gentlemen."

"Perfectly all right," Guy Mason said. He was in his late sixties and had a large paunch that stood out from his body almost vertically.

"I almost felt sorry for the poor guy," Mark Fiori said. "He obviously doesn't remember me, but I trained under him, and I have to say, Connie, that was a pleasure to watch."

"Oh," I said. "You're an alum? I didn't see that on your bio."

Mark's mouth twisted into a smile. He was about forty-five and fit, with laugh lines around his eyes and an air of authority that came from being the man in charge early in life. "I don't advertise it. I like to lie in wait for the lawyers and then pounce on them with my knowledge."

"Ha. Love it."

"You been working with Thomas for a long time?"

"Since I was a summer student."

"My condolences."

I kept my features smooth. This was a dangerous conversation. He might be against Thomas, or he might be testing my loyalty. "He's been a big champion for me in the firm."

Mark nodded knowingly. "I'm sure he has."

Connie sat in the chair that had been vacated by Thomas. "Nicole, I'd like your honest assessment of the case. No holds barred, we can take it."

"You should settle."

"Sullivan doesn't want to," Mark said.

"As it stands right now, we're going to lose. Jennifer Naughton was contradicted on some significant details in her timeline. There are no witnesses to the harassment. She got promoted even though she didn't sleep with him. Her allegations are not supported by anyone else."

"What happened to 'believe all women'?" Guy asked.

"That's a slogan for rallies and Twitter. It's not how courtrooms work. The benefit of the doubt, legally, goes to the party that's been accused of wrongdoing. People are assumed to be in good faith. The balance tips toward dismissal, not liability."

"So what are our options?" Mark asked.

"Did you investigate to see if there were other women he'd harassed?"

"We did."

"That's not in the court file."

Connie cleared her throat. "Our previous attorney thought it was better to bury that section of the internal report rather than admit that we found nothing."

"Oh."

"You think that was bad advice?" Mark asked.

I wasn't going to get any points for disparaging their former lawyer, but it was terrible advice. "I'm a fan of being one hundred percent honest with the court. In my view, bad facts always come out. I'd rather control the manner in which they do."

"But if we bring it forward now, we'd lose credibility, right?"

"It's definitely a problem. And a bigger one now that I know about it. I can't lie to the court. But there might be a way to spin it. Since I'm new in the file, I could play the 'this has just come to my attention' card, and let it be understood that you didn't know about the decision to bury it. It's definitely best to bring it out before trial. It could also be a door to opening settlement negotiations again."

"You can't settle with someone who doesn't want to."

"I agree, but everyone will settle. In my experience, it's only a matter of the price."

Guy tapped the table with his fingers. "He's a billionaire. He doesn't care about the money."

Mark leaned forward. "The board has been clear that they don't want to give a dime to Sullivan, so settlement seems unlikely unless he walks away."

"Well, he cares about his reputation, and other things might come out during the trial that he doesn't want people to know."

"Any idea of what?"

"I've done some research, and he's had a lot of departures over the years at Nexia."

"His nanotech company?" Mark said.

"That's right. I bet there's something there."

"But it wasn't at SulliVent. Would that even be relevant in the trial?"

"A pattern is a pattern. And ultimately, a jury has to want to find for someone. If we can show that he's generally distasteful, it can help us. Either to negotiate or win."

"I think I can help you with that," Connie said. "And bravo, Nicole."

"What did I do?"

"You anticipated me. There is, in fact, a woman who's come forward from Nexia." Connie picked up her phone and sent a text. "I brought her with me today." She turned her chair toward the conference room door. There was a knock and then the door opened slowly.

I'd done an okay job, I thought, at keeping my feelings to myself earlier, but it was harder this time.

Because the woman coming into the boardroom was someone I knew.

Samantha.

CHAPTER 21

What Did I Miss?

Then—July

"That was a good meeting," Mark said more than two hours later when we'd been over the file in detail and had put together a game plan.

Samantha was standing at the window, looking at the view. It was quite a story she'd had to tell. She'd been hired by Sullivan early on to be the face of Nexia's advertising campaign, an acting job of sorts that had come with good pay, time for auditions, and then a terrible price.

"Agreed," I said as we stood to go.

"We should have a drink. Swap Thomas stories."

"Sure." I checked his left hand as subtly as I could. He was wearing a wedding band. And so was I.

"How about next Thursday?" he asked.

"Let me check my schedule."

"I'm looking forward to working with you." Mark put his hand on my shoulder and gave it a light squeeze before leaving with Guy.

I waited till the door shut behind them before speaking. "What the hell is going on?" I tried to control the anger in my voice, but I didn't quite make it.

Connie looked up from her phone. "What's the issue?"

"You know what the issue is, Connie. You ambushed me."

"I brought you a great case that you desperately need."

I clamped my jaw shut. "So I'm supposed to ignore the coincidence that you sit on the board of a company that has a legal case where Samantha is an important witness?"

"That's how we met," Samantha said, turning around. Her face was blank, though it had been constricted in pain earlier as she went through the details of what had happened to her. "Connie's been counseling me for months, trying to get me to come forward. That's why I was invited to join PL."

Some of my anger seeped out. "Oh."

Connie cocked her head to the side. "You thought, what? That I'd asked Samantha to make up a story to win a case?"

That was what I'd been thinking, a massive accusation to make. "I don't like coincidences."

Connie put her phone into her sleek black purse. "I'm the head of the litigation committee, and I've been searching for other victims ever since this happened to Naughton because I knew there had to be others. Sullivan is a sleaze. I found Samantha, and she eventually agreed to talk to me. I was impressed with her courage and how she'd turned what happened to her into a passion for helping other women escape abusive relationships. We're always searching for new members for PL, so I suggested to Karma and Michelle that she be invited to join us."

"But not Naughton? She's not in Panthera?"

"No. It's terrible what happened to her, but she's a lower-level employee. Not PL caliber."

"What about me? How did I get invited?"

Connie's eyes met Samantha's briefly. "That wasn't my call."

"Whose was it?"

"You'd have to ask Karma or Michelle." She paused, and her expression made it clear that I should leave it alone.

"I guess it doesn't matter."

"Why so many questions today, Nicole? Is there something you need to say?"

I tried to determine if Samantha had any of the same concerns that I did. Her face was wan and her shoulders were slumped. She wanted the meeting to be over, but her expression didn't register the concern I was feeling.

"No, we just weren't given many instructions on how Panthera works, that's all."

"It's not complicated. We help one another when we need to. But you don't have to take the help. The apartment. The case. Those are your choices. You can say no."

I felt like a chastened child. "Okay."

"I'm sure there are plenty of other lawyers who'd be more than happy to take on this case."

I kicked myself. This is why I wasn't where I was supposed to be in my career. Because I looked a gift horse in the mouth and saw an enemy. "No, thank you. I want the case."

"And the apartment?"

"And that too, thank you."

Connie's features softened. "I understand that you felt left out of the process, and that's my fault. I should've told you that Samantha was a witness when I sent you the file, but until she showed up today, I wasn't entirely sure that she would."

"I was hesitating," Samantha said. "Sullivan is very connected in the entertainment industry."

"How?"

"He funds productions. He doesn't have a traditional production company, but a lot of films have private backers, money men who expect a return on their investment and who aren't going to hire a 'difficult' woman."

"Why come forward, then?"

Samantha's hands fluttered at her sides. "Because, fuck it. Fuck them. He shouldn't get away with this. I read the proceedings, her deposition. Jennifer Naughton just wanted to do her job. She wanted to make a living. And instead, she had to deal with that asshole and his innuendos and everyone in the office thinking that she'd done something wrong when all she did was say no."

"That's a good speech," Connie said.

"It's the truth."

"I believe you," I said.

"Thank you," Samantha said. "Do you think it's going to make a difference?"

"It will help. Now it's a pattern, although we'll have to get permission from the judge to introduce the prior-bad-act evidence." The case had been assigned to Judge Karen Osterlink, a newer appointment I didn't know well but who'd let in this type of evidence in at least one other case. There had been three victims there, though. "Connie, I assume Samantha was the only other person you could find?"

Connie and Samantha shared another glance. I felt left out, and I didn't like it.

"Why?" Connie asked.

"Because the more the better if we're going to get the judge to accept it."

"Don't two people create a pattern?"

"Maybe yes, maybe no. The case law isn't black or white on this issue, and the judge will have a lot of discretion."

"There might be one other victim. But I don't think she'd be willing to testify."

"Can you tell me who it is?"

"No. But it would be explosive."

I gritted my teeth. I was used to clients withholding information no matter how often I told them to tell me everything, but it was always frustrating. "Can you work on her?"

For the first time that day, Connie looked unsure.

"I've been trying, but it's . . . delicate."

"The more I know, the more I can help you."

"I understand. I would tell you if I could."

I wanted to push further, but I suspected the truth would come out eventually. It usually did. "All right, let me know if you make any headway. Samantha, I'm going to need an affidavit from you, which I'll prepare based on my notes from today. I'll send you a draft to review. And then we'll see what the judge has to say." I walked to her and put my hand on her arm. "Thank you for your courage."

Samantha met me with tired eyes. "Just win, okay?"

"I'll do what I can."

They left and I returned to my office and got to work, still unsettled by the connections and Connie's duplicity. Her explanation for them made sense, but something was still bothering me. I thought back, trying to see if this new information changed anything that had happened at the ranch. Nothing came to mind, but I felt as if there was something that was lingering just out of view. I tried to puzzle it out, then let it go. Solutions presented themselves, I found, when I gave my brain enough time to process. So instead, I worked on Samantha's affidavit.

And then, as I packed up my things to go home, it hit me. The first time I'd heard anyone mention SulliVent outside of the news was in Colorado. Something Heather had told me that first day in the gym. That Michelle and Karma had ramped up their efforts with Panthera because of Sullivan's failed attempt to take over Good Karma.

And now members of Panthera might take down Sullivan.

Karma, as they say, was a bitch.

. . .

A week of long hours and packing swept by until it was Thursday, the night I'd agreed to a drink with Mark Fiori. It was a hot, muggy day, and a break from my files and the black mood at home was appealing.

I called Dan to let him know where I was going and with whom. That was the deal we'd made after everything that happened between us five years ago. No lying, no hiding, full disclosure.

Dan was stuck late at work too, but I could tell he was uncomfortable with me going for a drink with another man.

"What are the chances," I said to him in the Uber on the way to the wine bar, "that he's going to hit on me, given the nature of the case I'm representing his company in?"

"Don't be so sure. Guys are always looking for an opportunity to score."

"Including you?" I teased.

"'Course not."

"You checked with the movers?"

"They'll be here bright and early Saturday."

"I won't be late."

We hung up and the Uber pulled up to my destination. The wine bar Mark had picked was a dark, sexy place with a long bar along the right-hand side and mahogany booths with soft red leather seats that were meant for two people. Soft jazz was playing, and the price per glass was what I used to spend on food for a week when I was in law school.

"Thanks for meeting me," Mark said, standing as I approached his table. He didn't have his phone out, something I appreciated and admired. I couldn't think of the last time I'd waited for someone without taking my phone out and doomscrolling. When I got close enough, he put his hand on the small of my back and kissed me briefly on the cheek before I had a chance to get my hand out. His cologne was unfamiliar, but appealing. "I know it's an unusual request."

"Is it?"

"Can't be too careful these days," he said as I sat down. He'd taken off his tie and his five-o'clock shadow had come in. He was an attractive, confident man. "And that's good, don't get me wrong. The things we've all seen . . ." He rolled his eyes. "I'm sure you have many stories."

"Everyone has stories."

"That's sad."

"It is." I picked up the wine menu. "What do you recommend?"

"If you like Montepulciano, they have one that's delicious. And the charcuterie plate is great."

"That's a red wine?"

He chuckled. "You're joking, I assume."

"It sounds good." We put our menus down and he called over a server and got the ordering out of the way. Our drinks came quickly, followed by the charcuterie plate moments later. Did this bar not want people to linger?

"Good?" Mark asked as I took a sip.

"Delicious." I eyed the charcuterie plate. I didn't want to eat sloppily in front of a client, so I went for a piece of cheese that was already cut. "Wow, this is really good too."

"Yeah, I love this place. I come here a lot since the separation."

I felt a sliver of unease. "How long have you been separated?"

"Couple of months." He played with his wedding band. "Can't quite bring myself to take this off yet. That would make it permanent."

"You don't want that?"

"Ending things wasn't my choice."

"I'm sorry."

"Thank you. What about you? Happily married?"

I took a large sip of my wine, thinking of the word that hung in the air every time Dan and I spoke now. *Baby, baby, baby.* "Dan is great," I said, because he was. Whatever happened between us, that never changed.

"What does he do?"

"He's also a lawyer. In-house at a bank."

"He get sick of Thomas?"

"Oh, ha, no. He was at Ogilvie's. We never worked together."

"Smart."

"You?"

He raised his eyebrows. "I was not that smart."

"Ah."

"Yes, well, when we get through this case, I'm going to need you to negotiate a large severance package for her. She's the head of finance."

"Got it. Should be doable."

"What did you say during our meeting? Anything's doable if you're willing to spend enough money."

I smiled. "I did say that."

"Amanda can be very stubborn."

I leaned back in the booth with a second piece of cheese. The wine made me feel warm on the inside and more relaxed than I had in a while. "Tell me about Sullivan. You worked with him?"

Mark's face clouded over. "I did."

"And what's he like? What do I need to know about him?"

"He likes to think he's the smartest person in the room."

"Don't we all?"

Mark smiled. "Sure, right. But the thing is, he is. He'll see anything coming a mile away. He has this ability to laser focus. Have you read the depositions?"

"Not yet."

"I'll save you the trouble. We got nothing."

I held my wineglass in my hands. It was almost empty, and I would've loved to have another. But I told Dan I'd be home early, and I could already feel my defenses weakening. Mark was charming and smart. He spoke with a directness I liked.

What was I thinking? Not clearly, obviously.

"There probably never was any point in cross-examining Sullivan at trial anyway."

"Cases are not made through cross-examination," Mark said.

"If you need to cross-examine your opponent successfully to win, you should settle," I complete. "Oh, Thomas."

"He never . . ."

I shuddered. "What? No, never. He wasn't like that with me."

Mark finished his glass of wine and signaled to the waitress to bring another. He nodded toward me to ask if I'd join him, and after a moment's hesitation I nodded back.

"What have you heard?" he asked.

"Nothing much. Maybe he was looser before he married Sandy?"

"Well, you know that she was his protégée."

Sandy was his second wife, and fifteen years younger. She'd left the firm after they'd become a couple and was now a senior partner at one of our competitors. But that was so long ago it didn't matter anymore. "I wasn't lying in the meeting. Thomas has been good to me."

"I'll bet he could have been better."

"Well, sure," I said, raising what was left of my glass to him. "Who doesn't want more?"

He put his glass down slowly. "Do you?"

The tone had shifted beneath me without warning. My face felt hot, my hands unsteady. Never again, I'd promised myself. And yet, all it took was one fight with Dan and one semi-decent man and here I was again. I looked away from Mark, desperate for a way to get out, an escape route. And then I saw it.

Athena.

CHAPTER 22

If the World Was Ending

Then—August

"How do you know Mark Fiori?" Athena asked me when we were ensconced in her living room an hour later. She'd been having a glass of wine at the bar with the woman who oversaw fundraising for her campaign when I'd clung to her like a life raft and begged her to get me out of there. I'd made my excuses to Mark, then texted Dan in the cab to let him know where I was going, while Athena ordered Lebanese takeout that I *just had to try*.

"He's a new client."

"Ah." Athena tucked her feet up underneath her on the chenille sofa. She'd changed out of her suit into a pair of expensive sweatpants and a loose T-shirt. She kept the temperature winter cool, and she'd turned on the gas fire, which was now dancing cheerily. A bottle of wine sat on the coffee table, two glasses emptied and refilled. The Lebanese food had been incredible, and I felt full and sleepy from having eaten too much.

"How do you know him?" I asked.

"I worked there. At SulliVent."

I felt a thud in my stomach. "You did?"

"After Harvard. I was in their marketing department for a few years. Mark joined a year or so after I did."

"When he left my firm."

"Do you know him from there?"

"No, he left before I started." I took a large sip of wine. Another connection between Panthera and the SulliVent file. I felt uneasy. "Did you work with Sullivan?"

Athena shuddered. "Yes."

"And?"

"That guy's an asshole, and I hope he loses his stupid case. But I don't want to talk about him. What's going on with you and Mark?"

"Nothing."

She raised an eyebrow. "You seemed pretty cozy. And you did ask me to rescue you."

I swirled my wine around. "Dan wants a baby."

"And that's bad news?"

"We'd agreed no children."

"Ah."

"You should ask why," I said.

"Why, then?"

I felt ashamed. I'd never told anyone about what had happened. "Because five years ago, both of us almost cheated on the same night."

Athena sipped at her wine. "That's interesting."

"Is it?"

"A certain synchronicity, anyway."

"I guess."

"How did you find out?"

"We confessed."

"Also interesting."

I wouldn't have called it *interesting* at the time. Our life was a catastrophe. Dan had just found out he wasn't making partner. I'd been working insane hours on a yearlong trial that sucked up every ounce of my life. We'd been fighting about stupid things: who was going to stay home for the plumber, the groceries one of us forgot to buy. We were life-plan people, and it was when we'd long-ago agreed that we were supposed to be trying for a baby. But I didn't want to. Bringing another human into our life seemed impossible. Dan said he was okay with that, but he was always pointing out kids at the store, talking about how cute they were. Is that what men who didn't want to have kids did?

"We were in a bad place," I said. "And we both had work events to go to one night. Some accounting firm was having a cocktail party. I ran into an old boyfriend from law school, the kind who felt like he could've been the one until he turned into a jerk. I had too much to drink and followed him to a dinner at a restaurant uptown."

"And Dan?"

"He didn't make partner and he'd ended up with the other associate who hadn't made it, a woman named Wendy, out commiserating."

"The universe was conspiring against you."

"We were conspiring against ourselves. Our lives were off plan and so we were blowing them up. A week earlier, if I'd run into Law School Guy, I would've talked to him for two minutes and then ignored him for the rest of the night because he's an asshole. That girl, Wendy, had been flirting with Dan for years. We used to laugh about it, but that was the night he went to dinner with her."

"What happened?"

"Asshole tried to kiss me, and I avoided it, threw up in some bushes, and took a cab home. Wendy succeeded in kissing Dan, but then he came to his senses and left."

Our cabs had arrived home almost simultaneously, like some romantic comedy in reverse, and after a second bout of vomiting in the bathroom for me, we'd each confessed what had happened. It had almost been funny, how quickly we wanted to unburden ourselves. The words had tumbled out, tearful in my case. We'd stayed up all night talking, nursing our hangovers, dissecting where we'd gone wrong, if we should break up. When dawn broke, we had a plan.

—We'd go to therapy for six months.
—We'd make sure to let the other know where we were at all
  times.
—No kids.

The last one had seemed like the obvious result of the evening.
If we almost couldn't keep it in our pants for one night, then we
shouldn't bring kids into our mess. Our therapist agreed with us.
Too many people tried to save their troubled relationships by having
children, with disastrous results. Kids are a test, he'd said, not a balm.
We agreed with him, and we worked on our shit. Dan got his new
job, my trial ended. We checked in more, made time for us. We got
better. But in our yearly check-ins we remained vigilant about no
kids. Until Dan's stupid family had stolen our home and our peace.

"Anyway, we worked through it and we were doing good."

"And now?"

"Dan suddenly says he wants kids. That's a nonstarter for me. I
mean, I'm thirty-nine."

"Lots of people have babies older."

"Right. Last-minute babies. All my college friends are doing it.
But they want them. I'm already tired. I don't sleep enough. I just
started exercising recently, I don't—"

Athena held up her hand. "You don't have to explain yourself to
me. Trust me, I get it."

"No kids for you?"

"You need a partner to have kids. I guess I could do it alone, but
it's not a good look for someone in Congress."

Especially if you aspire to higher office, I thought, which Athena
clearly did.

I drained my glass of wine and considered pouring another. "I
should go."

"Stay. I have a spare room and pajamas. I could . . . I could use
the company."

I put my glass down and focused on her. Her hair was pulled back and there were dark circles under her eyes. I felt like a bad friend for not realizing earlier that she was struggling too. "You okay?"

She smiled briefly. "In the grand scheme, sure. But I get lonely sometimes."

"And here I've been rattling on about my own problems."

"I asked."

"Still." I stood. "Hold on, let me go and tell Dan."

"Sure."

I went into the hall bathroom and pulled out my phone. I saw what I'd texted him earlier. **I ran into Athena, we're getting some dinner. Will check in later.**

Dan had written back with a thumbs-up emoji. I started to type that I was staying over at Athena's, and then stopped. Something about it felt childish, having a sleepover. And something in *me* felt childish. I was mad at Dan for changing the rules. That's the only explanation I could give for what I wrote.

Got called back to the office. That new file. I'll be here for the night prepping a motion.

I waited till Dan's bubble of reply appeared.

Make sure to get some sleep, he wrote. **Love you.**

Love you, I wrote back, then forwarded my work phone to my cell on the off chance Dan called.

I used the bathroom, then went back into the living room. Athena had refilled my glass and was working her way through her own. I'd lost count of how much I'd had to drink. Tomorrow was going to be rough.

"So tell me," I said as I sat back down. "What's going on with you?"

"I have a much better idea," Athena said, reaching for her phone. "We should look for guys on Radius."

"What's that?"

"The celebrity dating app? It's like this private dating site for people who don't want their profiles everywhere."

"Oh, interesting."

"You would not believe some of the guys I've seen on there."

"Famous?"

"Married."

"Jeez."

"Yep. But you can't screenshot or anything so there's no evidence."

"We should find you a non-married guy."

"I agree." She put the phone on the couch between us and opened the app. We scrolled and laughed at some of the photo choices of the men she'd matched with.

And holy shit, *Thomas* was showing as a potential match. Thomas, the married senior partner of my firm. What the hell?

After a few adjustments, the app started matching Athena with people more in her age range, and she indicated her interest in a few of them. Then she got a message from an investment banker in his early forties with movie-star good looks.

"What do you think?" she asked, holding the photo toward me.

I took the phone and studied his face through the fog of wine.

Dark hair, light eyes, Italian coloring. "Hello, Jack."

Now—October

"**W**here did you come from?" I demand, when I can get the words out. I peer into the darkness at Gary. He's dressed in black—dark pants, a dark sweater, a hat without a logo. Without his cowboy outfit, I barely recognize him.

"Same place as you," he says. "Hand it over." He reaches out with a gloved hand, and I give him the gun. I feel lighter letting it go, but Gary being here raises a whole new set of questions. I climb out of the dumpster and brush off the trash that's accumulated on me. The smell of rotting food is thick in my nose.

Gary slips a backpack off and puts the gun inside. He's about to say something when the garage door starts to click. He grabs my arm and hauls me toward the door to the stairs.

"Let go," I say in a harsh whisper.

"We need to move quickly. We can't be seen."

He opens the door to the stairs. Another yank, and he's pulled me into the stairwell, the door clanging behind us.

I pull my arm away and rub it. "What about the cameras?"

"I took care of those."

"So what's the plan?"

"How's Athena?"

I give him a look. "How do you think she is?"

"We need to get the body out of there."

"We should call the police."

"No, that's not an option."

My actions could be explained by shock, but Gary's being here makes it conspiracy to obstruct justice and makes us accessories to whatever it was that Athena did to Jack. I want to give her the benefit of the doubt that the shooting was self-defense, but that doesn't mean anyone else will. Either way, if this gets out, her career is over. Mine, too.

"So what do we do?"

"Like I said, we need to get rid of the body."

An image of us dismembering Jack like the deer back at the ranch springs unbidden into my mind. "No, I meant, how?"

"We're going to put him down the chute," Gary says.

"Into the garbage?"

"Yes. We get the body in, then the bin will be relocated to a place where it can't be traced to us."

"Who's doing that?"

"It doesn't matter. But we need to get a move on. Let's go."

I can see a million things wrong with this plan as I follow Gary up the stairs, but I don't have my own plan, so there's nothing I can do about it. That's what this whole night has felt like. A series of events that I have no control over.

We climb the stairs quickly, adrenaline pushing us. My calves start to protest halfway up, but I ignore it. Up, up, up, until we're finally at Athena's floor. Gary makes sure there's no one in the hallway, and we slip into Athena's apartment. She's sitting on the couch, watching the fire. She probably needs medical attention—who knows what Jack did to her—but there isn't any time for that. I point Gary to the stairs, and we walk up to Athena's bedroom.

He enters first, and I steel myself and follow him. Gary walks gingerly around the body, taking it in. I try not to look too closely. Once was enough.

Gary slips the backpack off again and pulls out a folded-up tarp and some duct tape. He spreads the tarp out on the floor and crouches down near Jack's head. "Let's go, Nicole. We haven't got much time."

Once again I want to bolt, but there's nowhere for me to go. So

I put my hands on Jack's legs, still warm to the touch, and when Gary says so, we lift him onto the tarp. A low groan escapes me, my back straining, and Gary shoots me a look, but then I realize it wasn't me.

It was Jack.

CHAPTER 23

Stranger in a Strange Land

Then—August

It was odd to wake up in a strange bed without Dan, though it wasn't so long ago that I did it at the ranch. Situational habits, I guess. At Athena's I felt like I was at a hotel, traveling for business. Everything was set up that way, Athena explained, because she often had her chief of staff staying with her when they were in town for constituency business.

She spent a lot of time in New York when Congress wasn't sitting. It kept her in touch with her voters, she said, which she liked better than committee work and the daily grind of passing legislation.

So there I was in what felt like a hotel room, showering under a rain head with the water as hot as I could stand it. The hangover was as bad as I'd feared, and I thought about asking Athena for a Xanax to fend it off. Instead, I brushed my teeth and took three aspirin from the bottle I found in the medicine cabinet. Some food would help, too, and I could already smell the coffee brewing downstairs.

When I got back to my room, Athena had laid out an outfit for me. I dried my hair and dressed quickly, then checked my messages. A text from Dan that I answered quickly, shoving down the persistent guilt, and the usual slew of work emails that always accumulated overnight. Buried among them was a message from Mark, asking if everything was okay and expressing his wish that I hadn't had to leave so quickly. Not good. I wrote back quickly, assuring him that everything was under control, the family emergency I'd claimed the night before was now resolved. I'd catch up with him about the file next week. I hoped that this would send the right signal—that I wanted us to have a good working relationship but nothing more.

"That suits you," Athena said when I found her in the kitchen over a large coffee and a plate of fruit.

"Thank you." I patted my hands over the lush material. "I think it's nicer than my wedding dress."

Athena laughed. She was wearing one of her signature dresses with a blazer over it. She was still as lithe as she'd been as a model, and clothes fit her in a way they'd never fit me no matter how much running I did. "Tricks of the trade. And I still have connections in the industry, so I get good discounts and samples."

"From others in PL?"

"More from my life before. I do have Connie to thank for this place, though."

I was surprised she hadn't mentioned it before. "Oh, I thought it was yours."

"I wish. No way I could afford this place on my salary. But Connie likes having people she knows in her properties. So I get to live here."

I took a seat at the counter as Athena poured me a cup of coffee. "How did you end up in Panthera?"

"I was invited, same as you."

"By who?"

Athena hovered with the milk jug above my cup. I nodded and she added some. "No one ever knows who invited them."

"Connie invited Samantha. Or suggested her, anyway."

Athena put the jug down slowly. "She told you that?"

"Yeah, I, uh, can't get into the details because of confidentiality, but she and Samantha are involved in a case Connie referred to me."

Athena sucked in a deep breath then let it out slowly. "Can I give you some advice, Nicole? You shouldn't litigate this."

"The case Connie sent me?"

"Panthera Leo. Asking so many questions. Who brought you in, or why I joined. That sort of thing is . . . discouraged."

"Why?"

"Another question."

"Okay, okay. But it's the way I am. I can't just turn it off."

"You accepted the invitation without question, didn't you?"

"Well, yes, but . . ."

"Go with that instinct." She popped a strawberry into her mouth. "Let me put it this way—Do you think men go around questioning how they got the job they weren't quite qualified for or the promotion that should've gone to someone else?"

"I doubt it."

"Well, that's part of what we're about. Creating an environment where you don't have to think like a woman. You don't have to query why you got something or whether you deserve it. You can just be a man about it."

"A white man?"

Athena smiled. "Even better. The only question you should be asking yourself is: How would Dan react to whatever's happening?"

I took a sip of my coffee. I got her point, but she'd chosen the wrong example. Because Dan was a questioner too. It was one of the things we had in common. We liked debating and figuring out puzzles. One of the reasons Dan was so disappointed when he left his firm was because he wasn't going to get to litigate anymore. He wasn't going to be the one to convince another person to do what he wanted. There was a power in that, in persuasion. When you were good at it, it was like a drug.

"You're telling me to be grateful," I said.

"Aren't you? A new file, an apartment. The support of the Pride."

"Yes, I am."

"Well, good then."

Athena's phone *ding*ed. She picked it up and a smile lit up her face. "Finally, some good news."

"Oh?"

"That guy, Jack. He wants to meet."

"That's great."

"You don't sound convinced."

"Sorry. I've never internet dated. How do you make sure he's not a psycho?"

"That's one of the good things about Radius. There's a filter built in because you have to be recommended to join. Then you meet in a public place and trust your instincts."

"And that works?"

"I'd say one good date for every four that are a disaster."

"Not amazing odds."

"You've got to break some eggs . . ."

"True." I glanced at the clock on the microwave. "Shit, I should get going."

"Thank you for staying."

"Thank you for having me, and for rescuing me last night."

Athena pulled me into a hug. I was surprised at the gesture, but I accepted it. She smelled like the shampoo I used that morning, spicy and fresh.

She held me away from her like my mother used to do sometimes when I was young to check that my school uniform was on properly. "You're not wearing your pin." She tapped the one on her lapel.

I reached up reflexively to my collar. I had been wearing it, though I still felt self-conscious about it. "It's on my other dress. I'll put it on when I get my stuff upstairs."

"Good."

"Why's it so important?"

Athena shook her head.

"Okay, okay, no more questions."

"That's the right attitude." Athena's phone *ding*ed again, and she moved toward it. I gave her a small wave, then walked upstairs to collect my things. I found the pin on my suit jacket and moved it to the dress's collar, feeling bad about putting a hole through the luxurious fabric. I checked myself in the mirror to make sure it was on straight, and it felt like a stranger was staring back at me. A thinner, more sophisticated version of me. Someone who was already on her way to being more successful.

That's what the pin symbolized: not only a way to recognize one another but also a way to remind us of who we were. What we were.

I smiled at this new me. Athena, Connie, Samantha, Heather. We were a unit, and together we could take on the world. It was exhilarating until it struck me.

Connie. Samantha.

They hadn't been wearing their pins in the meeting the other day. I was almost sure of it.

But why?

.   .   .

I spent the day reading depositions in the SulliVent file and prepping for the very real motion that I had to present to the court to get Samantha's evidence admitted. As the sunlight streamed through my office window, the doubts I had that morning at Athena's began to fade. I was being silly. Reading things that weren't there into a situation. They probably were wearing their pins and I didn't even notice. It wasn't significant either way. I filed it away like I had to file so many things in my job. The clients who you knew were lying, sometimes about small things, sometimes about significant facts. The sexist and sometimes racist comments made by senior counsel, all said with an innocent wink. The way you highlighted or downplayed certain facts, depending on how they helped or hindered your file.

Maybe Dan was right. What was it that I loved about this job again?

The ennui slipped away as I worked through the evidence. Cases were puzzles and I liked puzzles. I enjoyed being able to figure out how to get what I wanted out of a witness. For them to underestimate me and then wonder what happened when it was over. The tight expression on the face of opposing counsel when I'd scored points in cross-examination. That was why I did this. Because I was good at it. Because it was fun.

As the day waned into night, I made some calls and texted Dan to meet me at Hudson Yards. Then I collected my things and went to wait for an elevator. John, the managing partner, was waiting too. He was the benevolent ghost of the office—sometimes he felt more mythical than real, with many people, including Thomas, attributing things to him that he might not have been behind. "John was saying . . ." "John asked me to tell you . . ." John, John, John. People invoked his name like the Bible, both for good and evil. The real man was sixty, unassuming, and sometimes seemed to wear the power that he wielded as a burden.

"Nicole, just the woman I was looking for," he said with a smile and tired eyes.

"Here I am," I said, though I'd been in my office all day, easily findable.

"I've been hearing things about you from Thomas."

I shrunk in my heels. Fucking Thomas. He couldn't stand to be anything other than the center of attention for five minutes.

"He says you've landed a new file from SulliVent?"

"Yes, that's right."

"That's great. And might there be other work from them?"

"I had drinks with the CEO yesterday. He mentioned at least one other file. Nothing guaranteed."

"Understood. But that's fabulous news, all around. Thomas is very proud of you. And so am I."

"Thank you," I said, though part of me wanted to tell him to get lost. I wasn't his ten-year-old daughter with a good grade on a book report. I was old enough to be his third wife. But maybe I could use this to my advantage. I hadn't heard back from Thomas after he'd interviewed Julia, and I'd already received two follow-ups from Karma about what was happening. "I could use a junior associate dedicated to the file."

"Do you not have an associate assigned?"

"Not yet. We've lost a few recently, and everyone is swamped. But there is a promising Harvard grad who Thomas interviewed a few days ago."

John gave me an appraising look. He probably saw one of me a day—someone going around the usual protocols to get what they wanted. I'd never done it before, but I'd seen plenty of others do it.

"The file will support the billables?"

"One hundred percent. We don't have to make a long-term commitment—if she doesn't work out, we can always let her go."

"Consider it done."

The elevator arrived and we got on, riding downstairs in silence. John was like that. He said what he had to say, then moved on. When we got to the lobby, I thanked him, and he gave me a tired nod then walked to the car that was waiting for him.

I texted Karma to let her know that Julia was going to be hired and sent myself an email as a reminder to follow up with Thomas in the morning. He was going to be pissed, but I was trying to have a post-Thomas view of the world.

The day had cooled off finally, and I decided to walk. I opened my Uber Eats app and ordered from a place near the new apartment, telling the driver to meet me in the lobby.

I walked through Bryant Park, unpacking the day, unpacking myself. I'd lied to Dan the night before about where I was. That was stupid. I wasn't going to do that anymore, I promised myself, like I'd promised him five years ago.

It was a nice walk from the office to Hudson Yards. I decided that I'd add it to my daily routine; half an hour there and back was a good buffer between the stress of the office and the peace I should have at home.

The delivery guy was in the lobby when I got there, and so was Dan.

He waited while I retrieved our dinner. "What's all this?"

"I got the keys today and I thought we'd have dinner here. Celebrate." The real estate agent had messengered the keys over earlier that afternoon.

"Good idea," he said. His tie poked out of his suit jacket pocket. He was wearing a black backpack like he always did to the office, not caring if it was cool or not. It was convenient for carrying what he needed. Another thing to love about Dan, the fact that he didn't care what people thought about him.

But why was I tallying up the things to love about Dan?

We rode the elevator up as it filled with the delicious smells of the food I'd ordered. Then I opened the door where I had another surprise waiting.

"It's furnished. Wow."

"It's mostly the stuff that was here for the staging. I asked if we could keep it and Connie said yes."

Dan turned to look at me, trepidation in his eyes.

"What?"

"It's just . . . a lot has changed in a really short time frame. Two months ago, we'd never even heard of this Panthera thing, and now here we're living in one of their apartments and you've gotten the biggest file of your career from someone in the group and you're hanging out with them all the time."

"Those are good things."

"You sure?"

"Are you upset that I have new friends?"

"No, I . . . Look, I'm grateful for this place. And it's good that you're getting work. I just . . . I don't know. You seem different these days. You even look different."

"It's the dress."

"Is it new? I've never seen it before."

"Oh." I looked down. "Athena gave it to me. She gets all these samples because she used to be a model."

"See? You're even being dressed by Panthera."

"No, I—" This is not how I wanted this evening to go. "I promise you they're the most benign group of women you've ever met. They take on the world, sure, but in a good way."

"If you say so."

"I do. But why don't you find out for yourself? I'll organize a drink for all of us, okay? You can meet them and then you'll see."

He still looked dubious. "All right."

"Can we eat now? I'm starving."

We spread the food out on the dining room table. It was made of reclaimed wood and concrete. So much more modern and trendier than the furniture at Penny's, which we decided to leave for Katherine despite her disparaging comments about the furnishings.

I'd ordered all our favorites, and a double order of sesame noodles. Dan sat across from me and dug into the container of noodles. He made a face.

"Not good?" I asked.

"Fine, I guess. Just doesn't taste the same."

I reached out to take the container from him, ready to chide him for seeing differences where there weren't any. But he was right. The noodles were good, but not as good as the ones from our usual place, so I couldn't correct him.

Instead, we ate and made polite conversation, and then we packed up and went back to Penny's, trying not to focus on how we were about to move to a place where even the same food tasted different.

CHAPTER 24

The Dust Settles

Then—September

As the days went on, things settled down. Between me and Dan. Between me and Thomas.

—Dan and I had a tearful moment alone thinking of Penny before Katherine and Louise swept in.

—Julia was hired and began to work with me on the Sulli-Vent file.

—We moved into Hudson Yards and quickly settled in despite the new surroundings and furniture, Penny's portrait the only familiar item on the mantelpiece.

Work was crushing, but manageable. Julia was smart and efficient, but I could tell immediately why she hadn't gotten a job on her own—she had a blunt way of talking and seemed incapable of small talk or jokes. She was probably somewhere on the spectrum, but it wasn't something I cared about. Law firms might pretend that they were into diversity hiring, but it was a facade. She probably never made it past the first interview at most places, despite her stellar grades, which was ridiculous because she was more than competent.

Most firms had at least one senior male partner who was obviously on the spectrum but had never been diagnosed.

I met with the Pride once a week and did my check-ins with Michelle. They brought a certain structure to my life that had been missing, something to look forward to outside the daily routine of work. In the between times, our *Women Killing It* thread remained active with encouragement, complaints, and small but frequent requests for favors. Sign up for a voter registration drive (Athena), come to a fundraiser for a women's shelter (Samantha), and consider investing in an IPO (Heather). The expected *done, done, done, done* always followed quickly, an endorphin rush of accomplishment.

Heather's office wasn't far from mine, and we took to eating lunch together a couple of times a week, sitting outside of Pret when we could find a table, sweating in the sunshine.

"You never said how your bosses reacted when you 'came back from rehab,'" I said to Heather at one of them. We were working our way through enormous salads that she'd picked up at Sweetgreen.

A moment of confusion crossed her face, then passed. "I forgot I told you that. No one said a thing. Though I'm pretty sure I caught my boss checking my face for traces of coke the other day after he remarked on how long I'd been in the bathroom."

"Why is he even paying attention to that? Do you work at an Amazon factory?"

Heather threw her head back and laughed. "Honestly? Sometimes it feels like it. But Greg is okay most of the time."

I put a piece of tempeh in my mouth. Running plus salad every day for lunch was shaving off the pounds, but it made for boring eating. "And the rest of the time?"

Heather shuddered. "Best not to talk about that."

"I'm sorry."

"It's fine. Comes with the male territory."

"Wouldn't it be nice if it didn't?"

Heather lifted her fork and I tapped mine against hers. "Amen."

• • •

Pages flicked by on the calendar and then it was the Thursday before Labor Day, the city empty as everyone enjoyed the last of the good weather in the Hamptons, Dan and I staying behind because we've never liked that scene.

"We should have rented something on Lake Champlain," Dan said. We were getting ready to meet the Pride, who were likewise all in town for one reason or another. Neither of us relished leaving the cool boundaries of our apartment to face the unrelenting heat that had settled over the city two weeks ago and hadn't let up, even at night.

"I could look on Airbnb. Maybe for a couple weeks from now?"

"You'd take vacation?"

"I have a window before the trial. We could do a long weekend."

Dan kissed me. "That'd be great. We should go or we'll be late."

I agreed and we left. It was beautiful, our new place, but if I was being honest, it often felt temporary and soulless. I hadn't told Dan I was regretting the choice, but I'd started checking listings online at night when I couldn't sleep. Anything as nice as what we'd had was out of our price range, though, as I already knew, so it was fantasy shopping for when I'd regained my footing in the partnership.

We were meeting the Pride at a bar nearby, rather than having them over. Neutral territory that would be easy to retreat from, Dan said, and then he chucked me under the chin and told me not to be so serious. He wasn't going to embarrass me in front of my "lady friends."

"They might not appreciate your sense of humor," I said to him as we approached the upscale wine bar. There were so many of them springing up all over; it was hard to tell them apart. This one was called In Vino Veritas.

"Who doesn't appreciate my sense of humor?"

"Um . . ."

"Don't worry, I'll behave. I know it's important to you."

"Thank you."

We went inside and found our table. Athena, Samantha, and Heather were already there, large glasses of red wine glowing on the burnished table in front of them. I made introductions and Dan shook hands seriously, then followed up with his boyish grin.

"Where's Connie?" I asked.

"Work emergency."

"Oh well," Dan said, sitting down and rubbing his hands together. "We'll just have to make do."

"Dan . . ."

"Is she always this worried that I'm offending people?" Dan said.

Athena smiled. "She speaks very well of you, actually."

"I'm glad to hear it. You're her favorite."

"Dan!"

He laughed, and Samantha and Heather joined him, but it was true. Though I saw Heather more often, I'd formed a closer bond with Athena. Heather and I discussed surface things, but with Athena I felt like I could get to the heart of the matter.

We ordered wine and Dan began regaling them with stories. Dan is at his best in social situations. He's an extrovert and has an ability to make people feel as if they've always known him. I sat back and enjoyed my good glass of wine and listened to him retell the story of our almost disastrous first date. We'd agreed on an Asian place and ended up at different restaurants with almost identical names two blocks apart. It was the opposite of a meet-cute. Dan had almost given up on me when I'd realized what happened after waiting for him for thirty minutes, and rushed to the right location.

"So she comes in," Dan said, "and she looks a little crazy because it's misting out and she's been running, and she just plops down in the chair across from me and says, 'You should give better directions.'"

"Well," I said. "I was right. I mean, we were minutes away from never getting together."

"Like in *Sliding Doors*," Samantha said.

"I hate that movie," Heather said. "Magical realism sucks."

"Well, this would've been reality," Dan said. "No magic."

"It is weird," Samantha said, "how close you ended up to not being together at all."

"It is," I said. "Life is like that though, right? So many things turn on tiny decisions you make along the way."

"Sounds like something Michelle would say."

"Michelle?" Dan asked.

"One of our fearless leaders," I said. "I've told you about her."

"Oh, right, the singer." Dan turned his head to look for the waitress, and I saw a frown form on Athena's face.

Something wrong? I mouthed.

She shook her head.

"What's up with that Jack guy, Athena?" Heather asked. "How's that going?"

Dan rubbed his hands together. "And that's my cue to leave."

"Oh, no," Samantha said. "Stay."

"Nah, I've got a presentation to work on for tomorrow. It was great to meet you guys." He stood and I followed him to the door.

"You don't have to leave."

He hugged me quickly. "It's fine. I'm glad we did this."

"Me too. Thank you."

"What for?"

"For being you."

"That's a Hallmark card."

"Well, it's also true." I kissed him.

"Will you be out late?" he asked.

"Don't think so, but potentially."

"Have fun."

We kissed again, and when we broke apart, Connie was there.

"You must be Dan," she said, holding out her hand, cool and poised like always.

"Dan is me," he said, and shook her hand.

"And I'm Connie. Nice to meet you. You're leaving?"

"I thought I would. Boy talk is starting."

Connie chuckled. "Can't blame you, then. I'm sorry I'm so late."

"It happens. Next time?" Dan said.

Connie nodded.

Dan kissed me on the cheek, then left. I felt bad that we hadn't discussed when he should cut out or if I should go with him, but I was just overthinking as usual. Things were still strained between us, but it was changing slowly. We'd get past this.

Connie and I walked back to the table, and she repeated her excuses for being late as we slid into the booth.

"Are we getting another round?" Heather asked.

Samantha smiled. "Do you even need to ask?"

. . .

Several drinks later, we were trying to decide whether to order another charcuterie plate or call it a night. I was all for more food; whenever I drank, I ate all the food. It was a problem, particularly with my new health kick, that I mostly avoided by not drinking unless I was in social situations. Problem was, I was in social situations more and more often. Self-control. That was something I could learn. Something I should learn.

"I should head out," I said. "I've got a big motion next week and I'm still not ready."

"For the case?" Connie asked.

"To get Samantha's evidence admitted."

"What?" Athena said as Connie shot me a warning look. "Samantha's evidence of what?"

Samantha was staring at her empty plate, which had never held much food.

"I can't say," I said. "I shouldn't have said anything. It's confidential."

"But I can say, right?" Samantha said.

"It's your story to tell," I said gently.

She lifted her chin. "I want to do it. I need the practice."

"I'll prepare you before you have to do it in court."

"I know. But it will be easier here first, among friends."

"Can someone fill me in, please?" Heather said. She was on her third glass of wine and her teeth were stained purple.

I played with the coaster in front of me. "I'm defending SulliVent in a case where they're being sued by their former CEO. He was fired because of some #MeToo allegations."

Heather put her wineglass down. "Vic Sullivan. My office has done work for him."

"Right. You mentioned when we were at the ranch. He tried to take over Karma's company.

"Karma outwitted him," Connie said.

Athena was pale. "What's all this have to do with the case?"

"Early in my career, I was hired to do a series of advertising campaigns for his other company—Nexia. I was the face of the business," Samantha said. "So, he started coming to the video shoots. Sullivan. Everyone said, it's great, he's taking an interest, he's a hands-on guy and he knows a lot of people. He finances films. He can help you out."

"I've heard this story before," Athena said, reaching for the bottle and refilling her glass.

"We all have," Heather said. "Ugh."

"Yeah, well, it's such a fine line, right? Sometimes people *do* want to help you out. And other times they want something more. There's a price to pay for their generosity."

"There is always a price to pay," Connie said fiercely.

"All things I wish I'd known then, but I didn't. I'd heard stories, sure, casting couch or whatever, but I didn't think it would happen to me."

"What happened?" Heather asked.

Samantha checked our surroundings. The wine bar crowd was loud and self-absorbed. No one was listening to us. "One night the shoot went late, and Sullivan kept hanging around. He stayed to the end. I thought it was weird, and I had a bad feeling about it, but there were others there, so I tried to put it out of my mind. I was tired and hungry, and when the shoot was finally over, I went into the room that was being used as my dressing room to get changed and when I came out, everyone was gone."

Athena started rubbing her hand up and down her left arm. "Everyone but him, you mean."

"That's right. He was there. Said he'd got caught on a phone call and when he got off everyone had left. He was checking that they'd locked everything up tight when he found me."

"A likely story," I said.

Samantha shrugged but her shoulders were shaking. "It could've been true. I didn't like it, I didn't feel safe, but he hadn't done anything so what could I do? He offered me a ride home. I tried to decline, but then I felt silly. He had a car, a driver. There'd be another person with us. We were shooting in a warehouse in the middle of nowhere. Somehow it felt safer to go with him." Samantha shook her head. "That's what haunts me. That I thought it would be safer to go with him."

"Where did it happen?" Heather asked.

"In the car. It didn't matter that the driver was there. He put up that window dividing us, and it was like we were alone. Sullivan made a point of telling me it was soundproof. That no one could hear anything." Samantha shuddered.

Connie put her hand on Samantha's arm. "You're brave."

Samantha was uncertain. "I don't know if I can do this."

"You can."

"But what's the point? Nicole said herself that one more person might not even make a difference. That the judge might not let the evidence in. So I'll have gone through all of this for nothing. Dredging this up again. I'd put it behind me, but now I can't sleep, I'm not eating . . . Unless others come forward . . . and there aren't any others. No one can find them. They're going to call me a liar and make every decision I made look like some calculated plot, and for what? So some rich company can avoid giving another rich man a payday?"

"What about Jennifer Naughton?" I said. "She's the woman who filed the complaint against Sullivan. That's who I think about. Her having someone else to stand up for her. Someone who can say 'I believe you. I know it happened to you because it happened to me too.'"

"That helped her?"

I'd met Jennifer a couple of weeks earlier. She didn't believe it at first that there was finally someone else to support her. When it penetrated, the fear had seeped from her body. "It did. When I told her, she cried in relief."

Samantha drained half a glass of wine. "I cry in dread."

"I'm sorry," I said.

"Would it help you?" Athena asked Samantha. "If someone else came forward?"

"Yeah, I guess. There's power in numbers, right, Nicole?"

"Definitely. From a legal perspective, but also from a persuasion one. The more people who come forward, the more people will come forward. It's a domino effect."

"You okay, Athena?" Heather asked, her words slurring slightly. "You don't look so hot. No offense."

Athena was gripping her wineglass tightly. She was staring across the table at Samantha, her lips pursed, clearly wanting to say something.

"Athena?" I said.

"I believe you, Samantha," she said. "I know it happened to you because it happened to me too."

CHAPTER 25

Pride Goes Before the Fall

Then—September

That made four points of connection.

—Connie on the SulliVent board.
—Samantha, the victim they needed to save their case.
—Heather, who worked at the firm that Sullivan had used to try to take over Good Karma.
—Athena, who'd worked at SulliVent and was also his victim.

Too many. Too many coincidences.

That's what was swirling through my head as I listened to Athena tell her story. How she'd been working late. How she'd been cornered by Sullivan. The offer of the ride home, the car parked off a side road, the driver who did nothing. It was all the same except for the woman telling it. It was shocking and horrifying.

Only Connie didn't seem surprised.

"Will you testify?" she asked.

"I can't. You know I can't."

"So everything you said about being with Samantha, that was what? Smoke? Nothing?"

"I am with Samantha. I just can't be with her publicly."

"Why tell us, then?" I asked.

"Because I want to support her. But I can't testify. I'd never get re-elected."

Heather twisted a piece of hair through her fingers. "Don't you think people would find it courageous? That you came forward in a situation like this?"

"Please. Have you been paying attention? A Black woman accuses a powerful man of a sexual assault that happened a decade ago? I never came forward at the time. And to come out now, in the middle of a civil lawsuit? I already had to learn to shoot because of all the hate mail I get. I have a gun in my home, for Christ's sake, something I thought I'd never say. Please. If I did this, Fox News would be running hourly countdowns to my lynching."

I couldn't help but agree with her. If I were Sullivan's lawyer, I'd be thinking of all the ways I could destroy Athena, an easier target than Samantha, who had a certain insulation as a B-list actress and, frankly, as a white woman. Samantha was popular enough to be believed and benign enough to be ignored. But Athena was another matter. I couldn't begin to imagine what extra scrutiny and anguish she'd already gone through, and any woman in her position would bring on a tsunami of media coverage if she came forward with this kind of allegation.

But also: the connections, the web. They were making me doubt Athena. Samantha, too.

"I have to go," I said, standing up, unsteady on my feet.

"We should talk this out," Connie said.

"I don't feel well. I have to go." Her hand reached out to grab me, but I swept my arm away. "I'll speak to you tomorrow, okay? I need to go home right now."

Connie and I locked eyes, a tug of war. Maybe she saw my desperation, or simply knew that tonight was not the time.

She let it go.

I left without looking back.

• • •

It felt like I spent the next two weeks in hiding.

On the outside, everything was normal. Dan and I unpacked our things and tried to make the apartment feel more like home by putting up pictures and paintings, driving anchors into the concrete walls, marrying our old life to the new. We didn't talk about babies or my quitting the law. We found a better place to order sesame noodles. We were good enough at pretending that our old life had followed us to the new location that it began to feel as if it had.

In the mornings, I did my time on the treadmill then walked to work. I woke earlier and earlier, a tight feeling in my chest. At work, I was laser focused on the SulliVent file. I read every scrap of paper, put together timelines, knew Sullivan's life better than my own.

I applied the same scrutiny to Samantha and Athena. There were objective facts that supported their version of events. They'd both left the companies they worked for shortly after the alleged assaults. Samantha had been supporting abused women's organizations since then. She'd spoken out during #MeToo, not naming her abuser but giving many of the details on Twitter and Instagram. I assumed that's how Connie found her.

Athena hadn't done that, but the start of her lost years coincided with when she left SulliVent. Her campaign videos were vague about that time, showing a collage of photos of her in exotic locations, but some digging showed that she'd spent time at an ashram in India, had volunteered for a while in Africa, and had also had a hard-partying phase in New York. It was the kind of life you might lead if you'd been assaulted and spun off course in the aftermath.

But still my suspicions lingered. The day after the drinks at the bar, I realized that Julia was another point of connection, that she'd been sent to me by Karma, so I kept her focused exclusively on the menial tasks of the case, doing legal research, gathering documents, preparing summaries of depositions. I didn't tell her I was fact-checking Samantha and I didn't tell her about Athena at all.

Was she a plant? What would be the point of that? my rational brain countered. But there had to be a reason Karma had pushed so hard for me to hire her.

So I held my counsel close as we finalized and argued the motion to admit Samantha's evidence. It was a hard-fought hour in court, and the judge told us she'd render judgment in a week or two, with plenty of advance notice before the trial. Connie and Mark, who'd attended the hearing, were convinced that we'd prevail, but I wasn't so sure. I tried to manage their expectations, treat them like any other client.

To the extent possible, I kept the rest of Panthera at a distance. I monitored the group thread, but I didn't answer unless someone asked me a direct question. I didn't always add my *done* to the chorus of requests. I skipped my weekly check-in with Michelle, and then the one after that. Her tone remained friendly but firm. I needed to check in. I couldn't abandon my Pride. I told her I was busy doing what they wanted me to do. I asked for a bit of time, and she relented, but I could sense I was running out the clock on her patience.

Heather kept asking me to go to lunch. When I blew her off one too many times, she showed up at the office with a to-go salad. We sat in one of the conference rooms and made small talk while we ate our meals. I babbled about how stressed I was with work and how guilty I felt letting everyone down, that I'd be back to normal once the trial was over. She listened and made her usual wisecracks about the patriarchy, but it felt like she was there on a reconnaissance mission. She mentioned that the Pride had held a few dinners without me, and for a moment I had that same left-out feeling I'd had on and off since high school, a weird beat of insecurity. But then I told myself that I was leaving myself out, that I could rejoin them any time I wanted.

Athena also reached out, and I answered her as briefly as I could, giving work as the excuse it always was. She was back in DC and busy herself, but I was sure she could sense the shift between us. I only hoped she didn't think it was because of what she'd told me.

After days of silence, I told the group I needed to get away with Dan for a long weekend to relax before the true trial prep began and that I was going dark for forty-eight hours. They told me to *have a good time* and *enjoy yourself!!!* Athena sent me a few messages in our private thread about the couple of good dates that she'd had with Jack, and then a more serious message where she told me she understood why I was pulling away, but there was a good explanation for everything if I wanted to hear it.

I didn't want to. I wanted to think about it on my own, to gather my evidence, to come to my preliminary judgment about what was happening and whether I was going to participate in it. But I also didn't want to think about it. I wanted to go away with Dan and stare at the lake and turn off my brain, if I could.

We packed a rental car and drove upstate until we reached a house with a spectacular view of the Green Mountains and a fire pit in the backyard. We drank too much wine and roasted marshmallows, and I slept every night without dreaming. And when the weekend was over, one thing was clear.

I didn't know what the web meant, but I didn't want to be caught in it anymore. I was out. I was going to tell Michelle on Monday. I didn't know what that was going to mean for me, but the path was clear, even if the consequences weren't.

The hardest part of it all was keeping it from Dan. Dan who'd joked about Panthera from the start, but who'd supported me joining the group despite his misgivings. Dan who wanted our life to change, but not in the way it was changing. Dan who knew me so well, who could sense the danger around me. He was right to point out that everything had changed in our lives so quickly, and he didn't even know the worst part, how close I'd come to temptation with Mark at the wine bar, how too much of me wanted to simply give in to whatever it was that Panthera wanted me to do and take the easy path.

I wanted to tell him all of it, but I couldn't tell him any of it. When he asked me what was wrong, was it the baby discussion, was it *something he'd done*, I told him no, no, I was just in a funk and *I'd be fine, we'd be fine, we* were *fine.* I couldn't tell if he believed me, and that scared me.

On our last night at the lake house, Dan wrapped his arms around me in bed and whispered that he was on my side, no matter what. I didn't ask him what he meant. Maybe he didn't even know. He only knew what I needed. He wanted to make this work and he knew, like I did, that despite everything, we might not make it. We hadn't resolved the baby issue, only pushed it to the side. But in that moment, his words brought me comfort, and eventually I fell asleep.

On Monday morning, we rose early and drove back to the city before the sun rose. I felt good about my decision. Resolute.

I should've known that it wasn't only up to me.

Because when Dan dropped me off at my office and left to return the car, Karma was waiting for me.

CHAPTER 26

Woman without Pride

Then—September

"What are you doing here?" I asked Karma as I walked into my office. She was sitting in one of the visitor's chairs in front of my desk, her hands folded in her lap, her hair blown out, and dressed in a pantsuit that accentuated her power. I stopped short when I saw her, my throat dry.

"We have to talk," Karma said as she rose. She waved to me to sit down, and though this was my office, I felt like the intruder.

She waited for me to take my chair, then closed the door.

I folded my hands on my desk and tried to still my heart. I was always nervous before I went to court, but this wasn't that. My hands felt clammy, and I could smell my own sweat. But what did I think that Karma could do to me here, in a law office in Midtown?

"I have to say, Nicole, I had my doubts about you from the beginning." Karma's eyes challenged me and she spoke in a clipped tone. Her usually wild hair was slicked back into a chignon, and her makeup was professionally applied. This was CEO Karma, the Instagram version, the woman who'd taken Wall Street by storm with her organic and ancestral products. If I'd passed her on the street, I might not have recognized her.

It was the same thought I'd had in a fleeting moment in Colorado when Heather told me who she was.

Who was the real Karma?

"The beginning of what?"

"You joining Panthera. We had a debate, Michelle and I. She thought you'd be an asset, but I wasn't so sure. You lawyers, questioning everything."

I kept my gaze steady, my face impassive. My Court Face, I called it, where it was important to mask all emotions. "Are you going somewhere with this?"

"You've stopped participating in your Pride. You missed your meetings with Michelle."

"I've been busy."

"Do not lie to me." She didn't yell or even raise her voice, but it was full of menace.

"All right, then. I don't want to do this anymore. I want out."

Karma nodded as if this is what she was expecting. "I'm afraid we can't agree to that right now."

"It's not about your agreement. This is about my life."

"That's where you're mistaken. You made a commitment. A Pride is not something you can simply abandon when it suits you."

"Sure, in a jungle, when your life is on the line. But this is the real world."

"You think the real world is different than the wild? No. Not for us. And not for you."

"Why do you care so much, Karma? What do you need me for?"

"Questions, questions, always questions."

"Can I get some answers?"

"You may not."

"So what happens if I don't do what you want?"

Karma smiled grimly. "Tell me, Nicole, when you accepted our invitation, the apartment, the file that Connie brought you, did you not think that there'd be a cost?"

It came down on me like a weight. All the points of connection, the web they formed. I was caught in it. Karma didn't have to say it out loud to remind me—I already knew it.

"Are you threatening me?"

"I'm merely doing what is necessary to attain the goal I've set."

"And what is that goal? Winning the lawsuit against Sullivan? Why do you care so much? Because he tried to take over your company? Revenge?"

She hated my questions, and I was doubling down on them. I had a million more, but these would do for a start.

"I don't owe you any explanations."

"So it's just supposed to be blind obedience? Take this case, bring these witnesses? Court cases don't work like that. There's only so much I can do. The decision is out of my hands. Literally. The judge might not even let Samantha's evidence in."

Karma watched me impassively, and it occurred to me that I truly didn't know what I was talking about. It wasn't just about me. Karma and Michelle could be controlling the judge, too. *Every successful woman you know is probably one of us.* That's what they'd promised me in the invitation.

"Is Judge Osterlink in Panthera?"

Karma raised her shoulders slightly, not a confirmation or a denial. "Let me make a few things clear for you, Nicole, since you seem so focused on questions and won't work for the answers. I do not leave things to chance. When I ask a question, I already know the answer. Which is how I'd always assumed that lawyers operated too." She leaned forward. "But since you seem to need things to be spelled out for you clearly, here it is. Athena will testify. You will bring the evidence against Sullivan, and you will win the case. Once this is done, if you wish to leave the Pride, we will discuss the terms."

"And if I don't do what you say?"

"Then all this"—Karma raised her arm and swept it around the room—"goes away. Your home, your career, your marriage."

"My marriage?"

Karma wordlessly pulled out her phone and flashed a picture at me. It was me and Mark from the wine bar when he kissed me hello. It was innocent when it happened, but the picture makes us look intimate. His hand on my waist, his lips on my cheek near my neck, my eyes closed.

I felt sick. Who took this picture? And why?

"None of it will survive," Karma said. I opened my mouth to protest, but she cut me off. "You don't think we have this power? You are mistaken. Everything you have right now is because we have allowed it, because we have offered it, because we have sustained it. If you comply with what we want, then all will proceed smoothly." She didn't have to say again what would happen if I didn't.

She smiled and for a moment she was back to being the strong but flowy earth mother from the ranch. "But look, now, Nicole. Don't be so glum. Sullivan is a terrible man. He assaulted these women and likely many more. I would've thought that you'd jump at the chance to take down such an evil presence. Isn't that why you became a lawyer?"

She was quoting from my law school application essay. For the first time, I felt scared. "I still believe in that."

"Then this should be easy. Prepare the trial, call the witnesses, right the wrong."

"But that's not the end of it, is it?"

"Why do you assume that?"

"Because if it was as simple as winning a trial, you would've told me what was going on."

Karma appraised me again. Maybe it was respect. Maybe that was wishful thinking.

"You don't expect me to answer that question, do you?"

I took a moment, but I knew what I had to say. I couldn't risk everything I'd built over the last fifteen years because of one case. Karma was right. Sullivan was a bad man and he deserved to lose. He wasn't worth throwing away everything I'd worked for.

"I'll do the case. But then I want out."

Karma nodded and rose. "Stay in touch in the meantime."

She turned and walked to the door to my office. It opened with an ominous creak.

"Karma," I blurted. "Why me?"

She glanced at me over her shoulder. "Another question. Let us just say that you were in the right place at the right time."

"As fate would have it."

She smiled. "As fate would have it."

CHAPTER 27

Swallow My Pride

Then—October

Suddenly it was October.

I answered the text thread as best I could. I added my *done* to the choir of demands. I worked the case, spending some time with Athena. She was holding firm on not wanting to testify, in some contest of wills with Karma. The thing that made it impossible for her to come forward was also the thing that insulated her from the pressure being exerted on me, which we did not discuss. Instead, we kept our conversations light. She told me about her latest date with Jack and their plans to see each other again. They were taking it slow, but Athena seemed optimistic.

Judge Osterlink ruled in my favor. During the hearing where she read us her judgment, I searched her face for any evidence of bias, but I found nothing. It was a decision within the case law, and judges aren't allowed to wear symbols on their robes. I wore my pin, though, showing outward obedience while I plotted my escape. I needed to get through the trial and then I'd leave it all behind me.

—I ran on the treadmill every morning, my heart pounding
even long after I stopped.

—I worked all the hours I could, because in work I could still
   convince myself that I was on the right side of the equation.
—I didn't tell Dan what I was facing.

I was exhausted, barely sleeping, eating by rote. But there was a
light at the end of the tunnel. The trial was two weeks away. I was,
perversely, already feeling the positive effects of the SulliVent file on
my standing in the firm. Julia was a billing machine, and Thomas
and John were happy with the hire. Thomas emailed me my hours
for September with exclamation marks in the subject line because,
even with my time away with Dan, I'd billed an insane amount. I was
on track to have one of the best years of my career if I kept this up.

But I was fantasizing about going in another direction. A small
house in Jersey wouldn't be so bad. I could step away from my career,
this career at least, and not look back. I'd find something else to do,
something that didn't feel like it was aging me by the day. By the hour.

Each night I fell into bed like I was swan diving into a pool, hoping for an easy sleep. And the last thing I did was mentally check off
another day.

One day, two, three. When I got to thirty, I'd be free.

And then right before I was about to fall asleep on a frigid October
night, my phone buzzed with a message from Athena.

SOS, she wrote. **Please come as fast as you can.**

I held my phone in my dark bedroom, Dan snoring beside me,
wondering if I should call her or just go. Before I had a chance to
decide, I received a message from Karma.

Go, it said. **Instructions to follow.**

I cursed myself as I climbed out of bed and made my excuses to
Dan when he woke briefly. I blamed work, my perennial excuse that
I couldn't believe Dan was still buying.

—I dressed in dark clothing and grabbed my phone.
—I found a box of surgical gloves and shoved a pair into my
   pocket.

—I took an Uber to Athena's and read the instructions I
   received from Karma.

I didn't call the police. That was the main direction: whatever I
found, they were not to be contacted.

—I entered Athena's apartment.
—I found her in the bathroom, Jack in the bedroom, dead.
   The gun in the basement.
—I followed Gary's instructions. I was going to help hide a
   body.

I was lost in a nightmare I didn't seem to be able to wake from.
And then Jack made a sound.

"He's still alive," I say to Gary. I bend down to check, and Gary pulls me away, his hands a vise on my shoulders.

"Dead bodies make sounds. He has a bullet through his chest. He's not alive."

"We need to make sure."

"We do not," Gary says, his eyes dark and frightening. "We need to get him out of here as soon as possible."

"But if he's still alive—"

"It won't make a difference."

I move away in horror. "No. No, I'm not going to be a party to this."

"You already are. What do you think is happening here? It doesn't matter if he's dead yet or not. But you can save your horror. He's moved on."

"How do you know?"

"I was a medic in the army. Trust me. He's no longer with us."

I don't feel reassured, but Gary has one thing right. I'm already too deep into this. I can't save Jack if he's still alive. If I try to call the police, it will only get worse for me. Worse for Athena. Worse for anyone I care about. The only thing I can hope for is to get out of this without further endangering my life.

Because Gary is dangerous. I can sense it. It's not just the muscles bulging under his shirt, or his pungent sweat. He's not afraid of death.

"Let's get a move on," he says.

My hands and legs are shaking uncontrollably. I'm in shock, like

Athena, and I remember enough from my distant lifeguard training to know that I need to do something about it soon. Shock left untreated can be fatal. I force myself to focus and help Gary roll Jack into the tarp. Once that's done, Gary pulls him up into a fireman's lift and brings him down to the first floor.

"I've got it from here. Go check on Athena," Gary says as he heads toward the kitchen.

I follow his instructions gratefully. Athena is still in the living room, sitting on the couch, watching the fire, wrapped in a wooly shawl. I sit down next to her and pull another blanket off the back of the couch and wrap myself in it. I'm cold and scared. I feel like my body is out of my control. This entire situation is out of my control.

I check Athena. There are tears running down her cheeks, but she seems otherwise calm.

"What happened? Can you talk about it?"

"He was bad."

"Jack?"

Athena nods. "I thought he was good. Fun. We had fun together."

"How many times have you seen him?" I'd lost track of how many dates they'd been on.

"Four, five. We'd go to dinner and talk. He was polite. A gentleman. So different from so many men. That's what I thought." Athena laughs bitterly. "I was used to this. When I was a model, when I went to Europe for the first time when I was fifteen . . . The agency had a chaperone, but she was useless. We were bait."

"I'm sorry."

"Yeah, well, turned out it was just the first in a long series of assholes I'd encounter."

I feel sick. I've had my share of unwanted attention like every woman has, but not this. Not what Athena and Samantha have gone through. That's why I went along with this, I realize. Why I didn't tell Karma to go fuck herself. Because Sullivan is a terrible person who needs to be taken down—she's right about that. Maybe the methods aren't kosher, but sometimes working outside the box is necessary.

Is that true, though? Or am I only trying to come up with an excuse for acting in my own self-interest? And what about the consequences? How are we going to get away with any of this?

"After Sullivan," Athena says, "I was lost for a long time, but then I pulled myself together. I had my walls up and I made damn sure I wasn't ever going to be in a situation again where I could be taken advantage of. Not that it was my fault, I know it wasn't, but I had to take control of my life. I had to feel like I was the master of my fate."

"I get that."

She pulls the shawl tighter. "I didn't let anyone in. If I kept everyone away, then I couldn't be hurt."

"I'm not sure that's how life works."

"But it did. I was lonely, but I was safe. I rebuilt my life, got the things I wanted. And then I let my guard down."

"It's not your fault, Athena."

"Isn't it? Ten years ago, I would've made that guy from the first minute. And now, he got all the way into my bedroom before . . . before . . ."

I put my arm around her shoulders, holding her to me. "It's going to be okay."

"How can you say that?"

This silences me. She's right. I'm feeding her platitudes I don't believe in.

Gary enters from the kitchen. He's carrying a large garbage bag that's half-full. "I've got everything from your room. I'm going to go out the back way. I'll take care of the cameras."

I shiver under my blanket. I don't ask if he only means the cameras downstairs or the ones in the apartment, too.

"Did anyone see him arrive, Athena?"

"Just the doorman."

Gary nods. "I'll take care of him."

"Thank you, Gary."

Gary nods again and walks out.

I wait until I hear the door in the kitchen click. "Was it self-defense?"

"He tried to . . . he was going to . . . But I got to the gun in my nightstand and stopped him."

I watch the fire for a moment, trying to calm my heart. What Athena went through was harrowing, awful, and I couldn't imagine being in that position.

I stand and approach the fire, then turn to let it warm my back.

It's then that I notice. Jack's coat is still slung over the end of the couch. Shit.

And what about the blood that must be in Athena's bedroom, seeped into the carpet? What about his DNA that must be all over this place? Or his cell phone data that will place him in this apartment?

"This isn't going to work," I say.

"What?"

"Someone's going to report Jack missing at some point. And the evidence is going to lead them here. When it does, you aren't going to be able to give them a satisfactory explanation. If they look closely, if they look at all, they're going to know that Jack was here. They'll figure out what happened."

Despite all the things I've done tonight, we are royally fucked. I'm going to lose everything anyway, everything Karma threatened.

"You're right."

"Why do you seem so calm about it? Are you still in shock?"

Athena turns toward me. "I'm sure I am, but it's not that."

"Aren't you scared of going to jail? Of losing everything that you've worked to build? Isn't that why you called Karma instead of the police?"

"Yes."

"So what's changed?"

"The police aren't going to come."

"Someone will notice Jack's missing and they'll file a missing person's report, and the police *will* investigate."

"They won't."

"People don't just go missing."

"He's not a child. There's not going to be an Amber Alert."

"But his job. When he doesn't show up?"

Athena stares into the fire. "You don't get it. Karma, Michelle, Gary—they're going to take care of all of this."

"They can't make a police investigation disappear."

"They can."

"How?"

Athena shrugged. "I know you're one of those people who believes in justice, but things don't work like that."

"Work like what?"

Athena pulls her feet up onto the couch, tucking them under her. "Like you think it does. Like you go to court, and witnesses testify, and you make arguments, and justice prevails. That truth matters. That the weak have a chance in this system."

"I know it doesn't always work out like that, but—"

"But nothing. Come on. You saw that newsletter I forwarded to you? The one with all that insider info in it? News organizations tracked the cell phone data of people in rich neighborhoods in New York during the pandemic and they emptied out before the first lockdown. How do you think that happened?"

"I'm sure people who had means figured they should get out by paying attention."

"Don't be naïve. They had advance warnings. Trust me. I received them."

"Okay, but that was a once-in-a-lifetime thing."

"Please. How many cases have you lost? Cases you were sure you were going to win?"

"It happens."

"But why, though? Have you ever thought about it?"

I rub my hands together. They're ice cold. "I have, but judges aren't computers, and things don't go to court unless the law is gray, or the facts are."

Athena laughs bitterly. "Amazing platitudes."

"I don't want to fight."

"We're not fighting. You're telling me a fantasy and I'm telling you the truth."

"What's the point of this, Athena? What does this have to do with what happened tonight?"

"Because it's how I know the police aren't going to get involved, that we'll never hear about Jack again. You'll see—the police won't come."

"How can you be so sure?"

Her face is calm and certain. "Because this is the Test."

PART III

CHAPTER 28

No Show

Now—October

Athena's right. The police never come. We sit there all night, eventually falling asleep on the couch, curled up like children waiting for our parents to return.

In the morning, I go to work, showering in the office gym. I drink multiple cups of coffee and try to concentrate at my desk. Dan texts me, wondering where I am. I tell him I'm at the office, he must have forgotten, *silly*, and apologize for waking him in the night. Then I say I'm in a meeting and I'll call him later, because I can't risk speaking to him.

Dan will know that something's wrong. And what would I say? How can I go home tonight? How can I ever face him again? I need to manufacture another excuse, something that will keep me at the office overnight. Maybe after a day's distance I'll be able to face my husband again.

Then Athena provides an excuse for me. She messages me that she's going to testify, and that she wants to get her evidence down today before she loses her nerve.

Did Karma tell you to do it? I type, hoping that the app Connie invented and which we're using is as secure as it's supposed to be.

What do you think? she answers. **Will you help me?**

I agree, and she says that she's not comfortable at her apartment; she's not sure she can ever stay there again. We arrange to meet at a hotel, because this conversation is too sensitive for a public space like a coffee shop or even my office, and I let Dan know I have a late-breaking witness whose testimony I need to take immediately. I find the strength to call him briefly, a rapid-fire conversation, because I feel manic after the caffeine and lack of sleep. I watch the clock and after two minutes, I tell him Thomas needs me and that I'll see him tomorrow.

I love you, I say, then I hang up and put my head down on the desk and cry. I give myself five minutes to do that, then I wipe my tears away and leave to meet Athena.

We work together for several hours, getting her story down into affidavit form. Karma texts me frequently for updates, and I almost send her the draft affidavit, but then think better of it. I promise instead that I'll send her a polished document tomorrow, and turn off my phone.

At the end of the day, Athena and I check into a hotel. I order pajamas and underwear and clothes for tomorrow from Amazon, which get delivered two hours later. We decide on room service and wine, but it's not festive, just harrowing.

"I'm so sorry about all of this," I say to Athena after we've eaten.

"It's not your fault."

"I know, but I can still be sorry."

She gives me a wan smile. She's wearing a pair of pajamas and her hair is pulled back. She looks vulnerable and young, but her eyes are ancient. "I wish there was a way we could stop all this, you know?"

"I do."

She thanks me and gives me a hug, then we separate to sleep, if we can. I tumble into my room and sleep for twelve hours, my dreams a kaleidoscope of all the terrible things that have happened in the last twenty-four hours.

In the morning, I check on Athena. She's still asleep, the blanket pulled up over her head. I leave her a note and change into the new clothes I ordered.

I don't look at myself in the mirror.

I don't put on my pin.

I've realized that it must be a tracker and maybe also a microphone. I'm not technically equipped to tell, so I tuck it into the inner pocket of my purse, wrapped in Kleenex to muffle it.

I check my phone and give short answers to the group thread. Heather's bored with the takeover file she's working on. Samantha's reading the script she received for her new show and she's worried it's bad.

Women Killing It.

I didn't think that was going to be anything more than hyperbole.

At the office, I sit at my desk, unable to concentrate. I flick through the internet, reading stupid celebrity stories, a book review for a book I'll never read. I have work to do, I need to get my shit together, but I can't.

I wait, wait, wait, but my time is almost up.

"I've done a draft of the motion," Julia says, waltzing into my office without knocking. She has white-blond hair and pale-blue eyes, and she's wearing a suit that's a size too big. But I know when I read the motion that I asked her to draft to introduce Athena's evidence: it will be flawless. "It's good that someone else came forward. We can win the case now."

Impatience rises within me. "These are people, Julia. Women whose lives were destroyed by this monster. It's not something to relish."

Julia frowns. "You think I'm unfeeling."

"I didn't say that."

"You just did."

A wave of tiredness descends. I speak as calmly as I can. "I was only trying to give you a bit of advice. Not everything is about whether it's better to win the case."

"But that's our job."

"Not at any cost. Not at the price of your reputation."

Julia cocks her head to the side. "Sure, I get that, but that's not going to happen here. This guy is a scumbag. Bringing in more witnesses will help us prove that."

"It will."

"So, it's good."

Our eyes meet briefly and then hers slide away. I get her frustration with me, the position I'm taking. I can't tell her everything that's going on, that there's something else afoot. What I need is some time to figure out what's going on myself. Time and space to sit down and examine all the possibilities. But I don't have time. My watch is buzzing on my wrist with message alerts. When I check, I know it will be filled with instructions, orders, more things I don't want to do.

"Yes, it's good for the client."

"Isn't that all that matters?"

I sigh with a weariness that makes me feel double my age. "If you're SulliVent, sure. But if you're the witness, if your life is about to get ripped apart in public, then no."

She considers what I'm saying. "We could always ask for a sealing order."

Hope beats in my chest. I'd considered this for Samantha then discarded it, though I had gotten permission to use only her initials in court documents so that the media wouldn't find out who she was before she testified. When she did, there was going to be a media firestorm, which would be made even worse if Athena was added into the mix. A total media ban is a very high bar to meet, and rarely granted, but based on what had happened to others in these situations, a judge would consider it.

"That's a good idea. Can you do the research today?"

"Sure. What's the angle, though? Basic privacy?"

I haven't told her who the new potential witness is—just a basic outline of Athena's testimony. I need to keep that circle as tight as possible for as long as I can, and I don't know if I can trust her. "The new witness is a public figure. It could have . . . let's just say career ramifications. Look for precedents for government officials, whistle-blowers, that sort of thing."

"You really can't tell me who it is?"

"Not yet. Cast a wide net, all right?"

"We're going to need her affidavit soon. We have to give proper notice to the other side."

"I know, Julia, I'm working on it. I have a draft. That's what I was doing yesterday."

"Okay, I'll get on that, then." Julia nods to herself. "You know, if the evidence is sealed, maybe we can get them to settle. To keep it from coming out. If they know they aren't going to be able to drag the witness through the mud in the media and the evidence is going to be admitted because Samantha's was . . ."

"That's a good idea. I'll explore it."

"Okay." She turns to leave, then hesitates in the doorway. "I, uh, wanted to thank you."

"For what?"

"For making this job happen for me. I know you got me hired."

"You're doing great work, and you have some friends in high places."

"I do?"

If it were any other day, if I hadn't been through what had happened at Athena's, then I might never have said it. But *fuck it*, my brain's saying. Karma thinks I ask too many questions, but I'm only just getting started. It's time I ask the questions I should've been asking all along.

"Karma Rosen. She put in a good word for you."

"Oh, I told her not to do that. I wanted to get this on my own."

"People rarely do."

Julia lifts her chin. "You sound like her."

"Who, Karma?"

"No, my mom. You know her, too, right?"

"No, I don't think . . ." Oh. Oh shit. Julia's last name is *Sanders*. Michelle's ex-husband is Jim Sanders, the hippie-dippie singer who'd broken her heart and her spirit. Sanders is such a common name I'd never made the connection.

"Michelle Song is your mom?"

"You didn't know?"

"No." My mind is spinning so fast I feel dizzy. What does this mean? Why is she here? "But Julia, can we keep this to ourselves?"

"I have no interest in others knowing."

"No, I mean . . . Don't tell Karma I told you about her helping you get your job. Or your mom. And you can't tell them what you're working on. Confidentiality is important."

"I wouldn't do that," she says, her face red, her chin high.

I want to believe her, but it feels like everything and everyone around me is a trap.

One I walked right into.

* * *

When I check my messages after Julia leaves my office, it's as expected—more orders from Karma. A plea from Michelle to contact her. Chatter in the group thread that seems so normal it almost makes me cry. Silence from Athena. I send her a message.

You okay?

Fine, she answers quickly. **I'm at my office.**

Any visitors?

No.

I put down my phone. How is that possible? It's Friday afternoon—the events with Jack happened Wednesday night. If I hadn't shown up at work two days in a row, someone would notice. My assistant, for one—she is used to receiving a barrage of emails from me as I forward her things to file and letters and emails to write whether I'm in the office or not. If I went silent, would she reach out to Dan? No. She'd email me first. But by now she'd be worried, especially if I didn't answer. But what would she do about it? She'd wait till Monday, I think, but not longer than that.

But what about Jack? I don't know much about him other than he works in finance. Is Jack the sort of person who has someone in his life that would notice if he is missing? Or is Panthera so powerful that they can make someone disappear without anyone noticing?

I open a private browser and search my memory for his last name. I think back to when Athena showed me his profile on Radius. I try to remember what he looked like. I didn't look at his picture long enough to remember. His name is Jack, but Jack what? I start through the letters of the alphabet, a trick I learned long ago to help me remember names. *A, B, C, D*—Oh. Jack Dansen. That's it.

I google him and get a long list of hits, none of which seem immediately relevant. I try *Jack Dansen investment banker*. Nothing. *Jack Dansen money manager*. Nothing again.

I need his photo, to do a reverse image search.

Can you send me Jack's picture? I text to Athena.

Why?

I'm trying to find out who he is.

What do you mean?

I can't find him online. I'll explain when we meet. Can you send me his photo?

I can't do that—no screenshots.

I think about it. **Use your iPad to take a photo of your phone?**

Hold on.

I tap my foot impatiently. We shouldn't even be communicating on this app, now that I think about it. Gary installed it on my phone, and Connie invented it.

While I'm waiting for Athena, I download Signal and send Athena a link request.

Answer me here, I write, hoping she sees the message.

Another minute and I get an alert. She's answered me in Signal.

Why the app change?

I don't trust Gary. *Or Connie for that matter*, I think but do not write.

K, good point. Hold on a sec.

I wait and then it appears. A picture of Jack in his Radius profile.

I save the picture, then put it into a reverse image search. An Instagram page where Jack identifies himself as a "working actor" comes up, but nothing else.

What the hell?

What firm did he work at?

KPW.

I go to their website and search through their directory. He's not there.

Did you check it?

A pause, and then she writes, **Like I told you, I let my guard down. You have to be referred on Radius. They check you out before letting you in.**

K.

Don't judge.

I'm not, I promise.

I scroll back to Jack's Instagram. He posts a shot at least once a day. Shots of his gym. Shots of his food. Shots of the wine he's about to drink, living the life of a quintessential New York bachelor. Nothing to indicate that he'd turn violent. He's even posed in front of a few places I recognize, bars and restaurants I've been to.

I plug his name into IMDb. He's had some bit parts over the years, a once-a-year guest spot on *CSI* or one of the *Chicago* shows. More than once he's played the victim.

Oh, oh shit.

This is the Test, Athena had said.

They hired him. They hired him to date Athena. Just like they took those pictures of me and Mark. They wanted something on Athena. Maybe not this, not what happened, but something.

I sit there shaking, thinking of the implications.

He was an actor, I tell Athena. **Not a banker.**

There's a long pause before I hear from her again.

I must testify, Athena writes. **Karma is insisting.**

And I'm sure she'll use this, but . . . my thoughts trail off. I don't want to do what Karma wants. I don't want to be caught in her plan, her test. I'll bet Athena doesn't want to either. **Can you meet me to-morrow morning? When do you go back to Washington?**

On Sunday night. So, yes, but why?

Can you bring Samantha?

What about the others?

Let's keep the circle smaller for now, okay?

All right. Why not tonight tho? I'm going a bit crazy here.

I just need a bit of time. Will you be okay? Can someone stay with you?

I'll survive.

Survival. Is that where we are? A few short months ago I sat at this desk and read an email from Karma and Michelle and thought that it was the answer to my problems. If I could laugh, I would. But I can't. I need to figure out what the hell is happening, and for that I need backup. Someone who isn't tied up in this in the way I and the rest of the members of the Pride are.

I need Dan.

CHAPTER 29

Exile

Now—October

I leave the office early and wait anxiously for Dan to get to the apartment. I didn't tell him I'd be here early; I just packed up my things for the weekend and came home.

Home. Ha. This isn't home. It's a showroom. The concrete walls echo with my impatient footsteps. I always feel cold here, no matter how high I turn the heat.

Was I seduced to move into this place? It's hard to find another explanation. Because the apartment is beautiful, yes. But not something I'd normally have been attracted to.

I open my computer and go to the security page app for the building. I can watch the lobby and hallway feeds, a feature I've never checked out before, but it'll give me some warning for when Dan arrives. Why do I need a warning, though? Dan's not the enemy. I'm the one who brought danger into the house. And yet I feel a simmering anger at him. Part of what made us vulnerable was his family. If Penny had left the instructions she'd said she was going to, we wouldn't be in this mess. Or if Katherine hadn't been such a grasping bitch. Either one, and the dominoes would still be standing.

I know these thoughts are unfair even as they bloom in my mind, but I can't help them.

But that isn't true, my questioning brain shoots back. They have other ways to trap me—the file, the compromising photos with Mark, things I probably don't even know about yet. What part of my life don't they have control over? This apartment is the cherry on the sundae.

But it must have a purpose. Why do they want us here? What's the point?

To contain, to control. To watch.

Feeling sick, I click through the security footage menus, looking for an archive. It's there. Months' worth of video coverage of the front door and the lobby. I'm surprised they keep this much footage, but that's a choice I don't have time to investigate.

I start with the oldest entries and work through them methodically. I get to the day Dan and I visited with the real estate agent. I study our faces on the surprisingly clear images. I seem happy, Dan looks wary. I should've noticed, but I didn't. I'm a terrible wife. Selfish and self-absorbed. I have a million apologies to make to him, and I don't know where to start.

I move to the next day and then the next. I find it on the third. Gary coming into the lobby. His face is shrouded but I recognize his posture. He's less circumspect when he gets to my front door. He enters without any hesitation. Did he have the key? Of course. Connie gave it to him.

What did you do in my apartment, Gary?

I think back to the instructions I received from Karma the other night. All those precise commands. The cameras that must be in Athena's apartment. Athena's, which also belongs to Connie.

I don't know how to identify hidden cameras, so I google it. What shapes to look for, the usual places to hide them. Armed with some knowledge, I'm about to start searching when I stop. Cameras mean someone could be watching. Is that happening right now? Does Panthera have enough manpower to watch every member?

Or do they keep their resources for people they're worried about, like me?

I can't take the risk. I have to assume Karma is watching me. I didn't send her the draft affidavit today when she asked, telling her that it wasn't complete yet and that I was worried about sending it electronically, given the bombshells it contained. I assured her that Athena was cooperating, that I'd file a motion to introduce the evidence shortly. She'd seemed mollified, but who knew?

How can I tell, though, if I can't find the cameras?

Maybe there's a simpler way to determine how closely they're monitoring me.

I grab my purse and go into my bedroom. I root around for the Panthera pin I'd stashed there this morning and take it out. It looks innocent, but how can it be? I try to imagine where a camera might be in this room. Surely there isn't one in the closet? I take the pin inside it, cupped in my hand, and think about how it had pricked me that night in July. My blood was wiped away on a cloth. Was that on purpose, too? Had they kept it to have my DNA? How paranoid do I need to be?

I examine the pin. Based on my research, it isn't large enough to house a camera, but a microphone? A tracker? I don't know enough, and the only way I can find out—smashing it open—will reveal what I'm up to. The pin isn't going to help me figure out what I need to know, so I find a shoe box and place it inside. If I'm asked about it, I'll say I lost it somewhere, and how can they prove otherwise without letting me know that they know where it is?

My watch buzzes with a Panthera message. Shit. Maybe there *are* cameras in the closet?

I try to quell my breathing and pick up my phone.

It's Karma. **Why did you leave the office early?**

How do you know that?

I called your office. Answer the question.

I'm tired. I need a break. It's been . . . a lot.

You can have a break after the trial.

What if I can't make it till then?

There's a pause from Karma, and then a series of photos pop into the thread. Me in the lobby of Athena's building. Me entering her apartment. Me standing over Jack's body. Me in the basement fishing the gun out of the dumpster, only it looks like I might be putting it there.

My mind leaps forward, a moment of insight.

Karma and Michelle had a deliberate plan when they put Jack in Athena's path. They were behind the attack. Maybe they didn't intend for Jack to die, but they clearly meant to compromise Athena. *This is the Test*, she'd said. But what's being tested? Her loyalty, mine? How far we'd go to protect ourselves?

How far we'd go to protect them?

That has to be it. That's what Karma meant, though I haven't fully gotten it until now. Back at the pin ceremony, she'd said that there was a way through the Test if we acted together and didn't question why it was happening. Blind obedience is what she wanted, and that's what they wanted to test. What they could get us to do if we simply said yes, no matter the consequences.

What do I do? Just submit?

No. It's gone too far for that. I've compromised too much of myself already. I need to find a way out of this. I need time. Time to formulate a plan without my every move being watched.

You don't need to threaten me, I write. **I'm doing what you want.**

It does not feel that way. Regardless, this is your last warning. Do you understand?

Yes.

Athena will be testifying. See to it that it is done.

Yes.

There is only one way out of this, Karma writes. **Follow our instructions.**

I understand, I write, keeping my face as still as I can, knowing for certain that they're watching me. I check the time. It's coming up on five. Dan will be leaving work soon. I need to head him off, meet him somewhere else. I need to get in touch with him in a way that isn't being monitored. I have to assume that everything I own—my phone, my computer, all of it—is compromised. And while apps like Signal are supposed to be secure, I have no assurance that Connie hasn't found a way to penetrate that system.

I will myself to think while I do something innocuous and get a Diet Coke from the fridge. How can I reach out to Dan without them knowing? There must be a way—

Oh. The burner phone Dan got me when I went to the retreat. It's still in my suitcase.

I take a drink of my Coke, walk calmly to the hall closet, and go right into it, closing the door behind me. I don't turn on the light. Instead, I feel around in the dark until I find the phone in my suitcase. When I turn it on, it still has a charge, enough juice to send Dan a text.

Meet me at our old place.

Why? And why are you texting me from this phone?

I can't explain now. Just do it, okay? And maybe leave your phone at the office.

What?

I'll explain everything when I see you, I promise.

Dan doesn't write back immediately. I can imagine him sitting at his desk, wondering if his wife has gone mad. And she has, she has, and she needs his help.

Please, I write.

Okay, I'll be there in an hour. Are you okay?

No, but we will be.

I turn off the phone and push it deep into my pocket. I grab a coat and leave the closet, looking puzzled, then examine the door and the handle to give the impression that it closed behind me without me wanting it to. I shake my head, then shrug and walk away.

Will whoever's watching buy this act? I'll find out soon enough.

*   *   *

I pack a backpack as surreptitiously as I can, then send a dummy text to Dan saying we should stay in a hotel for the weekend to spend some quality time together. Then I go online and book a room at the Benjamin.

I try to think about all the things you're supposed to do to stay off the grid. I have a couple of hundred dollars in cash, which I'd taken out to pay the cleaner. My phone and laptop are out, but I have an old laptop that I haven't used in years which is in my bedroom closet. I put that in the backpack along with a change of clothes. In the bathroom, I write down the numbers for the people I need in a small notebook, praying that they didn't put cameras in there too, then put my phone down on the counter in the kitchen. Will they believe I've forgotten it? Does it matter if they can't find me?

Or maybe there's another way.

I pick up the phone and text Karma.

I'm going to book into a hotel for a few days.

Why?

I need a quiet place to work so I can get this trial ready. Somewhere I can totally immerse myself and get some rest. It's too hard for me to do that here.

I forward her my booking at the Benjamin, hoping it's enough to convince her.

You're strong, Nicole.

Thank you.

We wouldn't have picked you if you were not up to the task. Trust us.

Good lord. Is Karma so deluded that she thinks I could ever do that again?

I do.

You may go. I expect Athena's proposed testimony to be filed on Monday.

It will be.

I put down the phone and breathe a sigh of relief. I pull out a suitcase and pack, hoping no one notices that I'm putting things for

Dan in as well. I wheel the bag out of our room with my backpack on my shoulder. I leave my phone in the kitchen; the burner phone is in my pocket.

Outside, in the cold blustery day, I feel free for the first time in weeks.

It's a fleeting sensation, but it's something to build on.

I never should've given my freedom away.

CHAPTER 30

The Old Apartment

Now—October

"**W**hat the hell is going on?" Dan asks as he barrels into Penny's apartment. I arrived twenty minutes ago, almost begging Katherine to let me up. She was her usual frosty self at first, but when she saw the state I was in—sweatpants, an old sweater of Dan's, skin pale from stress and lack of sleep—she let me in and poured me a large glass of wine.

"Can you get him something to drink, Katherine?"

"Sure," she says, and goes into the kitchen. We're in the dining room, which is not so different than how it was when we lived here. I wonder what happened to all her grand plans to redecorate.

Dan sits across from me at the dining room table. He looks washed-out and tired. He's still in his suit from work, though he's taken off his tie and opened the top button on his dress shirt.

I reach across the table to hold his hand.

He takes it, squeezing it tight. "Why the weird texts? Why are you using the burner phone? Why are we here?"

I try to smile in a reassuring way. "All excellent questions."

"Does this have something to do with where you were last night?"

"Yes."

Dan casts his eyes down. "Not work."

"No."

"Was it that guy? Mark?"

I squeeze his hand harder. "No." I take a ragged breath. "Wait, did someone say something to you?"

Katherine comes back with a bottle of red wine and three glasses. "Should I leave you two alone?"

Dan nods, but I interject.

"No, Katherine, I think this involves you too."

"It does?" Dan says.

"Why don't you sit," I say to Katherine. She's wearing a pair of leggings and a lightweight sweater, and her hair is up in a ballet bun. Without makeup and the WASPy clothes she wears when she's with her mother, she looks much more human.

Katherine takes a seat at the table and pours out the wine. Dan gives me a look. I know what it means—*What's gotten into you?* He doesn't know the quarter of it.

"I wanted to ask you, Katherine, why you decided to move to New York."

"I told you—I got a job offer from Linnaeus."

Linnaeus. Linnaeus. Something about that name is niggling at me. "What do they do?"

"Part of their business is mass production of generic drugs, like the family company, only on a much larger scale. But they're also doing some very interesting research on a new protein that's made by immune cells. If the research pans out, it could be a game changer for allergy sufferers and the immunocompromised."

"Do you know who owns them?"

"It's owned by a holding company."

"Give me a second." I leave briefly to grab my backpack and take out the old laptop stashed inside. I plug it in and boot it up, and when I'm connected to the internet, I do a quick search on Linnaeus. Carl Linnaeus was one of the first scientists to describe lions in a scientific way in 1758. Linnaeus is owned by a numbered company, that's owned by another company, that's owned by Felidae.

Connie's company.

"Why does it matter?" Dan asks.

"Connie Chu owns that company."

"Oh shit."

"Who's Connie Chu?" Katherine says, her eyes darting back and forth between us.

"I'll explain in a minute. Did you apply for this job?"

"No. I was recruited."

"Why did you take it? I thought you were happy in Cincinnati."

"I've been running our company profitably for five years, but the bank doesn't want to scale up or step back. And no one takes me seriously there. Because my name's on the building, they assume I didn't deserve the job. But I have an MBA from Wharton. I'm good at what I do. I've been looking for something else for a while, and when this came along, it seemed like the perfect fit. But what's this all about? What does Connie have to do with it?"

"In June, I got approached to join a women's organization. It was billed as a networking opportunity, and they asked me at the right time. I'd received some bad news at work, and I needed a boost. So, I went to their retreat in Colorado in July. And that's where I met Connie Chu."

"That's odd."

"Not odd," I say, "deliberate. They recruited me because they wanted me to be their lawyer in a piece of litigation that's very important to them."

"SulliVent?" Dan says.

"That's right."

"But why?" Dan asks. "I mean, that guy is a creep, but why's it so important to them?"

"Sullivan tried to take over Good Karma five years ago."

"Good Karma," Katherine says. "The wellness company?"

"It's much more than that. They have their hand in a lot of pies, the health and beauty products being the most public. Karma Rosen is one of the founders of the group."

"What is this group?" Katherine says. "It sounds like something I should join."

"That's what I thought. But I was wrong."

"I'm confused. What's going on, exactly?"

"You're not the only one," Dan says.

I take a deep drink of wine, but it's not helping. "I don't even know where to start. But I need your help. Both of you. I'm in trouble."

It sounds so melodramatic saying this in the safety of Penny's apartment. In an odd way, I feel more at peace than I have in months in these familiar surroundings. Then I flash back to the events in Athena's apartment, the dead body on the floor, the things I did at Karma's command, and I know I have to come clean to Dan, and to Katherine, too. That what I just said is more than a fact—it's a plea.

"Will you help me?"

Katherine and Dan exchange a look, an image of complicity that I've seen in family photographs but never in person.

"We will," Dan says. "But first we need to know everything."

• • •

Many hours later, Dan and I climb into the guest bed. This is the room that smells the most like when Penny lived here—the lavender she used to keep it fresh has seeped into the wood, the floors, the air. It used to bother me, but tonight, I'm happy for the familiar embrace.

"In the morning," Dan says, "we go to the police."

I've told them everything. All the things that happened at the retreat. What's taken place since I got back. The warning signs I ignored. The slow march to the other night.

Dan and Katherine listened and asked questions, and Dan eventually started taking notes on a legal pad. For a part of the evening, it felt like old times, or that one old time when our firms were co-defendants on a case, and we got to work together. Dan is smart and good at this, as good as me, and smarter probably because he's found a way to be happy with less success. Somehow, along the way, I forgot about that, that a lot of his initial appeal was his intelligence.

But this, I can't agree with this.

"We can't do that."

"We can't cover up a murder."

I shiver under the covers. "It wasn't murder."

"She shot him."

"Yes, but, if it happened, it was self-defense."

"If?"

"I know it sounds crazy, but . . ."

"What?"

I prop myself up on a pillow. "Something has been haunting me since that night. How she seemed so sure that this was a test. *The Test*, she said. If that's true, then it was a circumstance that was created by PL to see how we'd handle it. So if it's manufactured, is that what really happened? If even Athena and Jack's meeting was arranged by them—and it had to be, given that he isn't who he said he was, and oh . . ." I flash back to the scene in Athena's bedroom. Jack on his back, his arms splayed out. The small hole in his chest. "There wasn't enough blood."

"What?"

"When we turned him over to roll him into the tarp. If he was shot through the chest, there would've been buckets of it. And Gary didn't do anything to clean up in there. If he was really dead, if they were trying to cover it up, then there would've had to have been a whole cleaning crew to get his DNA out of there."

"What are you saying? That they staged a fake death? All because of a court case?"

"That can't be the only reason. There must be something else. But yes, I think Jack is alive."

"How do we prove that?"

"I'm not sure." But something else is bugging me. Something I saw today when I was researching Jack. "Can I have your iPad? I want to check something."

"You're not making any sense."

"I know. It will in a second, I think."

He hands me his iPad, and I navigate to Instagram and look up Jack's page again. It's full of his daily posts. Workouts, food, random street views.

Dan watches what I'm doing over my shoulder. "Is that the guy? Jack?"

"Do you recognize him?"

"No, but hold on a sec." He taps on Jack's most recent photo, one of him at a gym. "That's the Flex Gym near my old office."

"Are you sure?"

"I recognize that setup—I used it for years. And the poster on the wall behind him."

I study the photo, searching for clues, trying to figure out what it was that drew me back to this page. Something I saw and ignored, or something I missed? He'd written *Fit life* and the hashtags #workout #fit #daily. The post had six likes. And . . .

"OMG. Look at this . . ." I point to the bottom of the post. "He posted this today."

"Wait, what?"

I tap the screen where it says the photograph was posted ten hours ago. I hadn't noticed it this morning; the time tag is so small it must've only registered in my subconscious. "He's alive."

"Come on. Maybe he scheduled the post before he died? Can you do that on Instagram? Or it's a glitch?"

"I don't think you can schedule posts on Instagram without using some kind of third-party app, which I guess is possible, but why would he do that? And his posting today fits with the facts. The Test. The fact that Gary barely cleaned up the apartment. All he did was get Jack out of there. It wasn't enough, not if a real crime had occurred."

"Okay, say it's true. Why would Jack go along with it? Who'd let themselves be caught up in that?"

"He's an actor, isn't he? I guess he was paid."

"You'd have to pay me a lot of money to do something like that."

"Yes, but they have a lot of money."

Dan runs his hands through his hair. "If you're right, then it hasn't really worked, has it? Not if it's so easy to establish that he's alive. I mean, why let him post today? Doesn't that undo everything they did?"

"I bet they didn't expect anyone to go looking. The point of the Test is to put you in a situation where they control your behavior, to see if you'll do what they want. They wanted to show Athena that they could control every aspect of her life, so she'd do what they needed her to do. Once they'd flexed that muscle, Athena wasn't going to go looking into whether he was truly dead. They didn't think I would either."

"They took a big risk."

"Did they, though? They've been two steps ahead of me this whole time. More. Everything that's happened to me since the management committee reduced my points has been manipulated by them. Hell, they're probably even behind that, too."

"How?"

"A lot of research and planning and a lot of money. But you see that we can't go to the police, right? Not until we know more."

"But how are we going to do anything about this?"

"I'm not sure. But I think I know where to start." I tap the iPad. "The gym. Let's go there tomorrow and see what we can find out."

Dan frowns. "We're not TV detectives. These people are dangerous."

"Then we'll have to be very, very careful."

CHAPTER 31

Teamwork

Now—October

In the morning, we decide that it makes more sense for Dan to go to the gym alone. If someone is watching, then they'll be expecting me, not Dan. He dresses in sweats and an old ball cap and leaves me with Katherine in the kitchen. I fill her in on the fact that we think that Jack is alive, and the concern that's creasing her face relaxes, then re-forms.

"This all sounds nuts."

I wrap my hands around my coffee mug. "I know. I feel like I'm going crazy."

"Are you?"

"I've thought of that. But no, I don't think so." Katherine finishes the omelet she's making and puts it on a plate for me. "Thank you."

"No problem. I like cooking."

"How's the job going?"

Katherine gives me a wry look. "You mean the one I only got as a way to fuck with you?"

"You're angry."

"No, I just . . ." Katherine sits down at the table, cradling her own mug. "I thought I'd gotten that on my own. That I earned it."

"I'm sorry."

"Are you?"

"I didn't want any of this to happen."

"You're always so hostile, though. To me, my mom."

"No, I . . ." I stop myself from saying that they were always so hostile to me, ever since Dan introduced me to them six months after we started dating.

Katherine picks up her fork. "You think we were the unfriendly ones."

"Weren't you?"

"I'm not saying my family is all warm and fuzzy. Dan is the nicest of all of us. But it was like you were expecting us to hate you. You had this armor up. And at the same time, you kind of looked down on us."

I want to fight her on that one, but maybe she's right. We could both be in the wrong. It takes two to fight. "I'm sorry I made you feel that way."

"It's okay."

"Not really. And I am truly sorry that you're caught up in this mess. I appreciate you taking us in. It means a lot."

"You're family."

My throat tightens. This is the nicest thing she's ever said to me, but I've never said anything nice to her, either. This conversation is like a mirror being held up to reflect my worst qualities. "Thank you."

"Everything okay with you and Dan?"

"How would you react if your spouse did what I did?"

"Hard to know when I don't have a spouse."

I watch Katherine while she slowly eats her eggs. She seems matter-of-fact about this, not hurt or upset. And good for her. Too many of us get our worth from our relationship status.

"Well, I've learned one thing about dating," I say.

"What's that?"

"Stay off the internet."

Katherine starts to laugh, and I join her. It has a hysterical tinge to it, but it's one of those laughs that grabs you by the belly and doesn't let go. Soon tears are running down my face and hers too.

I clench my stomach, getting control of myself. "We shouldn't be laughing."

"No."

"Someone might be dead."

She wipes the tears from her cheeks. "But probably not, right? You said."

"Probably not. But the rest of it is almost as bad."

"But you're trying to fix it. That's what you do."

"I do?"

"I don't know you that well, but yeah, that's always been my impression. You see a problem and try to solve it. I admire that about you."

"Thank you."

"So what's the fix here?"

I lift my shoulders. "I don't know. I'm more in the mode of trying to fully figure out what's going on first. I don't have the full picture."

"What's the next step, then?"

"Let's see what Dan comes back with."

"Can I help?"

"It's nice of you to offer, but I think it's better if you stay out of it for now. You don't want to be taken down with me if it doesn't work."

"You know, they have this saying at Linnaeus. It was repeated a million times in our new-hire training: *You can only fix what you know is a problem.*"

I pick up my fork and dig into the omelet. "Oh, I know I have a problem."

"Well, yeah, but it feels like you're just reacting, not trying to get ahead of it."

"You're right, I have been doing that. It's hard to get ahead of something when I don't even know how big it is."

"When do you think they started planning this?"

"It must go back a while. When did Linnaeus first approach you?"

"March or April. They wanted to get me here in New York, right? So you'd have to move out of the apartment?"

"Yes, but that raises so many questions." I raise my fingers to count them off. "How did they know that would happen? How did they even know there was an apartment to fight over? How did they know about Penny's will?"

Katherine nods. "How did they know Penny was sick at all?"

"Penny was diagnosed as terminal in March. That's when she told us she spoke to her lawyer to make sure everything was in order. That's why we assumed that there were instructions to sell us the apartment when Ms. Coates told us about the will." I sit back in my chair. "Ms. Coates. Her lawyer. She must be in Panthera."

"You think she changed the will?"

"She wouldn't have needed to do that, but . . . she could've just ignored Penny's instructions about the apartment if they weren't in the will."

"Why do that?"

"To make me vulnerable. The place we're living in is owned by Connie. I'm pretty sure it's bugged."

Katherine shudders. "That's creepy."

"Which is why we're staying here. Thank you for that." I sit back in my chair. "Getting us out of Penny's was a two-step process, though. Who recruited you?"

"The executive VP of Linnaeus. A woman named Kerry Miller."

I pull the computer toward me and google her. She's in her mid-forties and has an impressive résumé. On instinct, I check the images tab. I flip through a couple of photos until I find it. I click on the image and increase its size.

Kerry's wearing a PL pin.

"Was it your idea to take over the apartment when you moved here?" I ask.

"I . . ."

"It's okay. I know you resented us being in here. But what made you ask to take it over?"

She thinks about it. "Kerry might have suggested it."

"And that didn't raise a red flag?"

"It happened organically. She came to Cincinnati for the final interview, and we spent the day together. I showed her around the factory, and then we went out to dinner. She was engaging and nice and easy to talk to."

"And there was wine?"

"So much wine. I don't normally drink in work situations, but she told me I already had the job. She made it into a celebration."

"I get it."

"At some point we were discussing where I'd live in New York, what neighborhoods to consider, and I told her about Penny's apartment. How I'd always wanted to live there, but that my brother did instead, and Penny had always favored him." She casts her eyes down.

"Penny did favor Dan," I say lightly. "She admitted it to me. That must've been hard."

"Except it's Dan. I'd favor him, too." She twists her mouth. "Anyway, I told her Penny was dying and that maybe you guys were going to buy the apartment. I don't even remember everything I said, but the next morning when I woke up, I thought, why can't *I* have the apartment? So I asked Mom about the will. You know the rest."

— Penny's diagnosis.
— The job offer to Katherine.
— The drunken thought planted to take the apartment for herself.

It has all worked out exactly the way they wanted. You almost have to admire the precision of it.

"It's scary to think about," Katherine says. "How easily I fell for it."

"I did too."

"They took some risks, though. They couldn't know when Penny was going to die, or that I'd take the apartment."

"I'm sure they had a backup plan."

"All this for a lawsuit?"

"For revenge, I think. Karma wants to punish Sullivan."

"Even if you win the lawsuit, though, that's only money. He might be out at SulliVent, but he still has Nexia, right? What are they accomplishing?"

"You're right." I stare at my plate. The eggs have gone cold and are unappealing. And then I have one of those moments, like looking at a meaningless pattern of dots, and an image emerges.

The connections all make sense to me now. I know why I was brought into this, who I am on the chessboard and the others too.

Karma doesn't just want to expose Sullivan; she wants to take something from him just like he'd tried to take something from her. She doesn't just want him out at SulliVent.

She wants Nexia.

* * *

Later, I'm at my office putting together the material I'll need for the meeting I've arranged with Athena and Samantha. I took a risk, coming to the office, but it's a graveyard on Saturdays, and so far, I haven't seen a soul.

As I'm downloading files onto the laptop, Dan calls.

"You were right." He sounds excited and out of breath.

My heart accelerates. I knew it, but to hear it confirmed still takes me by surprise. "Jack was there?"

"Yesterday, and again this morning. The desk clerk confirmed he checked in using his membership."

"How did you get that information?"

Dan chuckles. "You think I'm not charming enough to get someone to give up their secrets?"

"No, I know you are. I'm touched that you're using that charm for me."

"You're welcome."

"Did you get the evidence that he was there?"

"I got a screenshot of the login and she even gave me a clip of camera footage from the part of the gym where he works out."

"Wow, you're more persuasive than I imagined."

"I think he's been rude to her in the past, so she was more than happy to help me when I told her he'd been harassing my wife."

"Revenge. It's our theme."

"Pretty much."

I sit on the edge of my desk. "I figured some stuff out this morning. I've arranged an off-site meeting later today to try to put all of this together. I'll text you the address. If you still want to help."

"Stop asking that, okay? You're my wife. We're in this together."

"Thank you for not saying it."

"What?"

"'I told you so.'"

He chuckles. "It's fine."

"You were thinking it, though."

"I'll see you later."

I end the call, then straighten up and check my reflection in my screen. There I am, same as ever. I don't know what I expected to see, but it's reassuring in a way. I can still get back to the person I was before all of this started, if I play my cards right.

"I wrote the memo," Julia says behind me.

I wheel around. "Oh, great. Can you email it to me?"

She nods but doesn't say anything. She's wearing yoga pants and a loose sweatshirt and looks about twenty years old. Vulnerable.

"What is it, Julia?"

"You're in that group, right? My mom's group?"

I don't see any point in denying it. "Yes, why?"

"Panthera isn't good. It does bad things."

"Such as?"

She meets my eyes quickly then looks away. "My mother, Karma—they're not nice people."

"In what way?" I asked carefully.

"No one ever believes me when I tell them that. But you know how my mother left her career behind and went to Africa? How she had this great spiritual awakening? Well, that was me she was leaving behind too. I was ten."

"I'm sorry. That's terrible."

"It was terrible. That's what I'm trying to tell you. That's who you're involved with. Someone who'd leave her daughter behind and ask you to be happy for her because it's what she needed to do for *her*. It didn't matter what happened to *me*. And Karma, she encouraged all of it."

I don't have any trouble believing that about Karma, but Michelle seems softer, less threatening. Then again, I wasn't abandoned by her, and she's in this with Karma, however soft she may appear.

"Why are you telling me this?"

"Because I can tell you're in trouble. Everyone around them is always in trouble."

"I'm okay."

"You're not. People lie to me like I can't tell. But I can. I always could."

I wonder if it's true. It could be useful to have her around for the next few days. But do I risk it? How can I trust someone who was planted on my team to spy on me?

"Have you been telling your mom or Karma what you've been working on here?"

"No. I told you."

"Can I trust you?"

"You're asking me?"

"I am, Julia. I am asking you. Because you're right—your mother and Karma are up to no good, and I could use your help. But I need to know if I can rely on you. I need you to be on my side, not theirs."

"I can do that," she says. "But what about you?"

"What about me?"

"You're in Panthera, not me."

"I was only trying to get a leg up in my career. I didn't know . . . I thought the group was about helping each other."

She juts out her chin. "People should get things because they deserve it. Not because of some secret organization."

"I get it, but one thing your mother and Karma have brought into focus is that a lot of people have a leg up in this world. If you use connections to get ahead, then you're just doing what everyone is doing. And maybe that seems cynical, but I do still believe in the ostensible purpose of their organization."

"Which is?"

"To be like men in the world. Not to question how or why we get things, because they never do."

"We should be better than them, not adopt their methods."

I shake my head. "So you'll be resigning from your position? Give back your Harvard degree? Only take what you have one hundred percent earned for yourself? How would you even measure that?"

"I don't know. But—"

"But what?" Julia clamps her jaw shut, and I instantly regret my tone. "I'm sorry, Julia. I didn't mean to snap at you. I'm under a lot of stress."

"Okay."

"I want things to be fair too. I do. But it might not look like the kind of justice you learned about in law school. Is that okay with you?"

"Will people get hurt?"

"They might. Only bad people hopefully, but I can't guarantee that."

"I understand."

"So do you want to help? It's entirely your decision."

"Is my mother going to be hurt?"

"If this works, yes; she might."

She considers it, but only for a moment. "I'm in."

CHAPTER 32

I Love It When a Plan
Comes Together

Now—October

Later that afternoon, Dan, Athena, Samantha, Julia, and I are holed up in Athena's district office. The room we're sitting in is charmless and windowless. It's their secure room and is swept regularly for listening devices, Athena tells me. There's a wall of whiteboards streaked with old strategic plans and the stench of stale food clings to the air. We've ordered in sandwiches and soft drinks and now we're ready to get down to business.

I haven't logged on to the Wi-Fi. Our operating principle is that everything we use is bugged or otherwise tracked, but Athena has an air-gapped laptop that her head of voting outreach uses to protect their mailing lists. It's not connected to the internet, and it's supposedly impenetrable. Julia's working with it.

"Athena," I say. "Please tell us from the beginning what happened that night."

Athena nods in a determined way. "We went to dinner like we have plenty of times before, but he was acting different."

"Different how?"

"On our other dates he'd been a bit standoffish. Fun, flirty, but it felt like he was going through the motions."

"Why did you go on more than one date with him then?" Samantha asks. She came directly from a barre class, and she looks like a dancer, her hair in a tight bun, her arms sinewy and strong.

"It's hard for me to meet nice men. He felt harmless. And it was good to have someone to have dinner with once in a while."

"What was different that night?" I ask.

"He was much more aggressive. Not overtly at first, but he had a different feel to him. It's hard to explain, but I thought it meant that he wanted to have sex."

"Which you hadn't before?"

"No. But I wanted to." She smiled shyly. "That had been a while too."

"It's okay, Athena. Go on."

"We had dinner and he suggested going back to my place and I said yes. We came upstairs and I poured us some wine. That's when things went sideways."

"How so?"

"I think he put something in my drink. I felt woozy, but I'd only had one glass of wine at dinner, so that's the only thing that makes sense."

I kick myself. What happened to those glasses of wine on the counter at Athena's the other night? I'm drawing a blank. "Did you keep the glasses?"

"No, I only realized the next morning when I was washing them out after you'd left. It was too late to keep a sample, but I'm sure. It's the only thing that explains, well, everything that happened after."

It makes sense to me too. She *had* seemed drugged that night. I'd attributed it to the shock, but drugs fit her behavior better. "What did happen?"

"I told him I wasn't feeling well, and when I stood, I was dizzy, so he said he'd help me upstairs. He'd backed off as soon as we got to my apartment, so I let him." She stares straight ahead. "When we got to the bedroom, he grabbed me and tried to kiss me. I pushed him away. He grabbed me again. I told him to go. He said he would after he finished. I got myself away from him and to the nightstand where my gun was. I took it out. I told him to leave, to stay away from me. But he kept coming and coming. He wouldn't listen. I pulled the trigger and he dropped to the floor. There was blood. You saw. I was sure he was dead."

Dan coughs at the other end of the table. "Did Karma or Michelle know you had a gun?"

"They knew I'd learned to shoot because of the threats that I get."

"The ones you get?" he asks. "Or the ones you were getting? Had you been getting more threats in the last six months?"

"There was a series of particularly awful ones last fall. That's why I got my license in the first place. Why I learned to shoot and moved into that apartment. This guy was sort of stalking me, and he broke into my old place."

"Did Karma suggest that you get a gun?" I say. "That you get trained to use it?"

"She did."

"God," Dan says. "How long have they been planning this?"

"A long time, I'll bet. You had a file on me when we met, right, Athena? On the plane?"

Athena looks guilty. "How did you know?"

"It was too much of a coincidence that you were seated next to me and you knew things about me, like my name when I hadn't told you what it was. And when we were on that hike together, you said something about the points committee, even though I hadn't told you about that. Did you have a file on each of us? Me, Samantha, and Heather?"

"Yes. They gave them to me and Connie."

"Did they tell you what they were putting the Pride together for?"

"Only that they were reshuffling things. Expanding and including new members."

"Clearly a lie," Dan says. "Samantha and Athena were included because they were Sullivan's victims, Heather because of the take-over, and Nicole for the trial."

"Where is Heather?" Samantha asks.

"I haven't looped her in yet," I say.

"Why not?"

"I wanted to keep the circle as small as possible for now. If they're monitoring us, I can justify this group because we're prep-ping for trial. But if I bring Heather in, they'll know we're up to something."

"Why do you think they picked you?" Julia asks.

"I'm sure they had their eye on a couple of possibilities. They needed someone that they could put in a vulnerable position. My points were cut right before they approached me to join. I'm not sure how they manipulated that, but . . ." I trail off as another piece of the puzzle falls into place.

"What?" Dan asks.

"Radius."

"What's that?"

"It's the dating site where Athena met Jack. But remember that first night we looked together, Athena? Thomas was on there."

"Thomas was on a dating site?" Dan says. "Isn't he married?"

"He is. And he's the head of the points committee. If he didn't de-fend me in the meeting, it could explain why my points were lowered so much. And he's the one who made me feel so bad about myself right before I got the invitation to join the group."

"They must be blackmailing him," Dan says. "But how would they know he was on Radius?"

"Sandy must've told them." I turn to Athena and Samantha. "His wife. She's a lawyer too."

"Sandy Philips?" Athena asks.

"Yes."

"She was in my first Pride in Panthera."

I sink in my seat. "Jesus."

We sit in silence for a minute, absorbing this new information.

"What happened next?" Julia says eventually. "That night, Athena, with Jack?"

Athena rubs her hands up and down her arms. "I felt so sick and out of it. I sat there in disbelief for a few minutes. And then I called Karma and asked for help."

"Why?"

"She's always saying to me in our check-ins that I should rely on her for whatever I need. Her suggestion stuck."

"You told her what happened?"

"Yes. She said she'd take care of it. To go downstairs and leave the front door unlocked." Athena places her hands flat on the table.

"And then to text me?"

"She said to text you and ask for help."

"And the gun, did she tell you to put it down the garbage chute?"

"I did that on my own. After I opened the door, I realized it was in my hand, so I put it down there. And then I went to take a shower because I felt dirty."

Dan rattles his legal pad. "So, to summarize, Karma and Michelle arranged for you to meet Jack—I assume Connie helped them with the tech side of things, getting you and him to match on Radius."

Athena expels a deep breath. "Connie's the one who told me about Radius."

I turn to Julia. "Find out who owns Radius."

"Good idea," she says, and makes a note.

"Okay," I say. "You meet Jack, you go on dates, they make sure that you have a gun in your home, and when the timing is right, they get you to pull the trigger."

"But what about the blood? The shot? How is he alive?" Dan asks.

"He's an actor. I assume the blood was fake. Maybe he even took something to slow his heart rate down, to put him in a deep sleep so it would seem like he was dead. And the shot must've been a blank. At some point, they sent someone into your apartment to change out the bullets. Connie has a key. They probably used Gary to do it. Karma called him in like she did Wednesday night."

Athena shudders. "That guy gives me the creeps."

"Me too. I wonder what his role is? Why would he help Karma and Michelle like this?"

"I know," Julia says. "I know why he would help them."

"Why?"

"Gary is married to Karma."

CHAPTER 33

One Man, One Vote

Now—October

"**G**ary's Karma's husband?" I say. "Are you sure?"

"Completely," Julia says.

Flashcards of my interactions with Gary flick through my mind.

- —His silence in the van as he drove us from the airport to the ranch.
- —The way he took our phones from us at dinner.
- —His cold manner in Athena's apartment the other night.
- —How certain he'd seemed that Jack was dead.

Jack wasn't the only actor involved in this plot.

"Why do they hide it?" I ask.

"Karma likes to project an Amazonian persona," Julia says. "That she's solely in charge and doesn't need men. But she and Gary started Good Karma together. I guess they decided then that they'd keep him a secret. It made for better marketing."

"Did you know this, Athena?"

"I'm as shocked as you are."

God, what else don't I know? How am I going to find out everything I need to in time?

"What about Connie?" I ask. "What's her role in all of this?"

"I've only met her a few times," Julia says. "But she's been in the group since the beginning, I think. When my mom came back from Tanzania and she started working with Karma, that's when I met Connie."

"Is she in on the plan with Michelle and Karma?"

Athena bites her lip. "She must be. The apartments. Radius. She's on the board of SulliVent. She has to know some of what's going on."

"More than some of it, I think," Dan says. "They couldn't do it without her."

"You're right."

"Why are you helping us, Julia?" Dan asks. "Going against your own family?"

"What they're doing is wrong. Manipulating the court system. Manipulating people."

"You included?"

Julia's cheeks are tinged with pink. "Yes, obviously."

"They underestimated you."

"People always do."

"Their mistake." Dan holds up the legal yellow pad he's been scratching at. "So we know what Samantha and Athena and Gary and Nicole are doing in this little play. This part of the plan was the backup in case you didn't want to go along, Athena, right? You told them you didn't want to testify when they first asked you to?"

"That's right."

"Why did they need to go this far? Why didn't you just agree to do what they wanted?"

Athena places her hands in her lap. "Because that would destroy everything I thought we were working for together."

"How did they know about you and Sullivan?"

"The same way they found Samantha. They combed through personnel records searching for abrupt departures. Sullivan had a type and a pattern. When Karma first brought it up, it was like she already knew exactly what had happened."

"Me too," Samantha says. "When Connie approached me, she already knew also. Or it seemed like she did. She'd researched me, knew I'd gone to therapy, that the person I'd posted about in relation to #MeToo was him."

"She presented a guess as fact," I say. "It's a courtroom tactic. If you state something you believe firmly enough, you can often get a witness to accept it, because they're convinced you know the truth even if you don't."

"That makes sense," Athena says.

"When did you first tell them that you wouldn't testify?"

"Last fall."

"What about you, Samantha?" Dans asks. "When were you approached?"

"January."

"And you agreed to testify?"

"I did. My role on *District Attorney* was finishing and Connie got me in to audition for *Law & Order*. Connie also made sure that the production company knew I was going to testify. They promised it wouldn't be an issue for them. They wanted an opportunity to stand behind a woman who was speaking out, and I was it."

"So it was easy for you to say yes."

"It was."

"And if you hadn't? Do you think they had something in store for you?"

"I'm sure some doors would've been shut. Nothing I'd ever be able to prove. You can never tell why you get a part and why you don't; it's maddening."

"When did the lawsuit start?" Dan asks.

I know the file by heart. "Jennifer Naughton came forward three years ago, which prompted an internal investigation. She filed her lawsuit shortly after SulliVent's internal investigation concluded and Sullivan was ousted from the company."

"And Connie would've known that because she's on the board," Dan states.

"Yes, I'm sure she did."

"And the board made the decision to fire him."

"Absolutely. Firing the CEO is a board-level decision. Sullivan doesn't have a majority stake in the company, so he couldn't fend it off."

"Do we know when Connie joined SulliVent's board?"

"Can't check that in here," I say, "but I bet it's four years ago."

"You think Connie got on that board on purpose, and she and Karma and Michelle got Naughton to come forward to give them an opportunity to get him fired?"

"I do."

"Karma asked me to join Panthera four years ago," Athena says. "Before the complaint about Sullivan."

"But that's not when she brought up Sullivan?"

"No, that was more recent, but she must've known. That's why I was recruited."

"Clearly. So Sullivan pisses off Karma five years ago. She starts to plot her revenge. She's heard that he might have a problem with women. It was 2017—the height of #MeToo. She searches out victims with Connie's help, gathers you close, and they prompt the first complaint. He gets dismissed with Connie likely pushing for that at the board level."

"But the evidence isn't that strong. So he sues over it."

"Pretty predictable for a guy like Sullivan."

"Okay, so then he sues. But why does Karma care about the outcome of the lawsuit?"

"Karma hates Sullivan," Julia says. "He tried to take her company away from her."

"She wants to make sure he isn't reinstated?" Dan asks. "Is he even asking for that?"

"No," I say. "Regardless of the outcome of the lawsuit, he's out at SulliVent. But he's still at Nexia."

"Nexia?" Samantha says, her voice quavering slightly. Nexia is where she was assaulted.

"What's Nexia?" Dan asks.

"His nanotech company. They're trying to revolutionize drug delivery systems. If it works, it's a game changer."

"Why would they want that company?"

"There must be synergies with Good Karma, but mostly, I think they want to destroy him."

"But what's the lawsuit have to do with taking over Nexia?" Athena asks.

"It's where Heather comes in."

. . .

We have a short debate about whether Heather can be trusted. Connie is out of the question, but Heather doesn't seem like the sort who'd be easily cowed by Panthera.

That's the wrong way to look at it, though. We all have vulnerabilities. Just because I don't know what Heather's is doesn't mean she doesn't have one. But I'm a litigator, and Heather is the expert in takeovers, and I need her to find a way to do what I want. We have to take a risk.

So after some back and forth, Athena calls Heather and tells her that she needs her help ASAP to work on a "mailing to constituents"— the same cover story that she and Samantha are using to be in the office in case anyone is paying attention.

I feel nervous, but I tell myself Panthera isn't big enough to be watching us twenty-four seven. It's not the Soviet Union, one minder for each person. Besides, they think they're about to get what they want. Their guard should be down. Even if it isn't, I'm not sure they can stop us now.

I meet Heather at the entrance, waiting inside the door. Some of the leaves are starting to fall from the trees, and they're tossing in the wind. Heather arrives wrapped in a blanket shawl, her cheeks rosy, curiosity in her face. I raise a finger to my lips and whisper, "Where's your pin?"

"Oh, that old thing? I never remember to wear it. Michelle's always scolding me."

I smile and hold out a box where I indicate she should put her cell phone. She raises her eyebrows and I mouth that I'll explain in a minute. She puts her phone in with a shrug, and I turn it off, then leave the box in Athena's office. Heather follows me into the conference room and stops short in the doorway, taking in the participants.

"What's going on here?"

"You know my husband, Dan, and this is Julia. She works at my firm and is Michelle's daughter."

Heather laughs. "That's why you looked familiar."

"No one thinks we look alike. I look like my dad."

"I meant I think I saw your picture in her office once."

Julia doesn't say anything, and I take my seat at the table. "I'll explain everything in a moment, but if you don't mind, can I ask you some questions first?" I indicate an empty seat, and she sits and unwinds her shawl. I offer her some sandwiches, which she declines, but she takes a Diet Coke, clicking open the can with a sharp fizz.

"All right, go ahead."

"What was the first Panthera event that you attended?"

"July of last year. They have one every July, I think, right, Athena?"

"That's right."

"And you were recruited by Connie?"

"Yes." Heather takes a sip of her Diet Coke. "We started talking at a cocktail party, one of those mixer things, and then we had lunch. Soon afterwards, the invitation from Michelle and Karma arrived in my email. I ignored it for a couple of weeks, but then Connie contacted me and convinced me to join."

"What happened at that first retreat? Why did you really leave?"

"Like I told you, I had to leave for a work thing."

"When did you leave?"

Heather sits back in her seat. "The second day. So I went through the opening gathering or whatever and a few activities and then the call came, and I left."

"And you left to work on a deal?"

"Yes."

"A takeover attempt," I guess.

"Yes."

I leave her answer there for a moment. "Who was there with you?"

"Connie, and three other women I've never seen again because I didn't join their Pride. Karma, Michelle, and Gary."

"And then you got invited again?"

"Yeah, in the spring. What's all this about?"

"The takeover."

"What takeover?"

"Of Nexia."

Athena stirs in her seat, then reaches for a can of Coke, nearly knocking it over.

Heather sits upright. "How do you know about that?"

"It's the only thing that makes sense."

"Makes sense of what?"

I let out a sigh. I'm so tired. I don't have the energy to explain it all again to Heather.

"Can we trust you?" I ask.

"Trust me to do what?"

"Not to tell Michelle, Karma, and Connie."

"Why would I tell them anything?"

I stand and grab a Coke out of the mini fridge in the corner and take a long sip, hoping the caffeine and sugar will give me the energy I need.

"This is all a plot," I say. "A long con. PL. Our involvement in it." I sit back down and explain to her as succinctly as I can what's been going on.

—Sullivan's original attempt to take over Good Karma.
—How Karma and Michelle decided to get revenge.
—Their search for leverage over him, which led them to Athena.
—Putting Connie in place on the SulliVent board, waiting for Sullivan to screw up.
—How they got him fired from SulliVent.
—How, when he sued, they decided to take it up a notch.
—The way they recruited Heather, me, and Samantha and put us together with Athena and Connie.
—The leverage they built over me and Athena.
—That terrible night with Jack.

"So that's the plan. And the final step is Nexia. They need to make sure that Sullivan loses his lawsuit, and not just loses, but loses badly enough that it will affect both his standing with the board and Nexia's stock price."

"How do they do that?" Heather asks.

"By getting more witnesses to testify against him. One woman was enough to get him removed from SulliVent, but not to take him down. But when you add Samantha and Athena into the mix, women who are powerful and known, then it starts a wave."

"His own personal #MeToo."

"Yes."

"And that brings us to me," Heather says.

"They needed someone who could spearhead the takeover once the stock price plunges after their testimony comes out at trial. You've been buying Nexia stock, right?"

"Yes."

"Have you been shorting it? So you can get it cheaply when bad news hits?"

"That's part of the takeover strategy," Heather says slowly.

"Is that public information?"

Heather glances at Athena, then away. "The aggregate short position is easy to look up. That's why you need to do something like that over time, so it doesn't set off any alarm bells. Takeovers are delicate. You don't want to raise any suspicions until you're ready."

"Remind me how many shares you need to own to do a takeover," I say. "I slept through corporate law."

"You can bid without owning a single share, but then the other shareholders can turn it down. If you have a large block of shares—or a large block of shares that you know will vote with you—then you're in the best position to take over the company."

"So you can just buy up a company's shares and then take it over?" Samantha asks.

"It's not that simple. There are lots of rules, but to simplify, you can buy up to five percent of a company anonymously. Then you have to disclose."

"What about using proxies?" I ask. "If this plan has been in the works for a long time, then there'd be enough time to get allies to buy shares or get a seat on the board like Connie did with SulliVent."

"Good point," Heather says. "That could work."

"Is that what your client is doing?"

"Some of it, yes."

"Who is your client?"

"You know I can't tell you that. I've already told you too much."

"It must be Karma and Michelle." I put up a hand. "Don't worry, you don't have to confirm it. Even if you're not dealing with them directly, they're involved. And Connie. It's the only thing that makes sense."

"I agree," Dan says. "And we should stop it."

"Stop what?" Athena says.

"The takeover."

"Why?" Samantha says. "Who cares what happens to Sullivan or his companies?"

"Karma does," I say. "And if we're going to get her and Michelle out of our lives, if we're going to be free of them, we need to stop their plan. You want that, right?" I look at Athena, then Samantha, then Heather. Each of them is troubled, scared. It's how I feel too, but I can't spend the rest of my life like this. I don't believe Karma. She's not going to let me go when this is over. There will always be something else I have to do for them, some new demand.

"What are you suggesting?" Athena asks.

"If you don't testify," I say, "then the plan can't work. The existing evidence alone is not enough to bring down Sullivan."

"But then they'll release all the stuff they have on us," Athena says. "We have to testify."

"No, I don't think so. I think there's a way that we can get out of this, maybe even turn the tables on Karma and Michelle."

Samantha draws in a deep breath. "Do you think that's wise?"

"It has to be better than letting them slowly take over every aspect of our lives. We're all their prisoners. Somehow, we've ended up in . . ." I make eye contact with Dan. "We've ended up in the corporate equivalent of a cult, and they're not going to let us leave quietly. Even if we go along with their plan and it works, it won't be the end. So that gives us two options. We stay or we blow it up. And I don't want to stay."

"Explosions can be messy," Dan says gently.

"That's why we have to be out of the way when it goes off."

CHAPTER 34

Coming Home to Roost

Now—October

Monday afternoon and I feel ready.

We spent the rest of the weekend working out the details, the role each of us is to play, coming up with a plan to stop Karma and Michelle and maybe turn the tables on them. We went over it and over it, questioning, testing, until it was as airtight as it could be.

Sunday night, Julia and I worked in the office, putting together the binder of evidence we'd need to execute phase one. Then I emailed Karma and told her that Athena's evidence would be filed shortly, and I expected a hearing at the end of the week to admit it. She responded immediately, pleased, and asked for an in-person meeting with her and Michelle on Tuesday. I agreed.

Then I called Mark Fiori and told him I thought there might be an opportunity to settle with Sullivan. He expressed disbelief but said I should go ahead. I asked him not to brief the board until we'd reached a deal. I was worried that Sullivan might get wind of it, I told him, because he still had allies in the company. Mark said he'd wait for my call and that I had the authority I needed.

Then I called John Taylor, Sullivan's counsel, a guy who I knew from previous files always worked on Sundays.

—I told him to bring Sullivan in for a settlement meeting.

—That he'd regret it if he didn't.

—That I was about to file explosive new evidence.

He agreed to get Sullivan there.

So here I am, walking into a conference room, trying to muster the self-confidence to pull this off. Julia follows me in. The binders she prepared are on the conference table in front of Sullivan, who's arrogant and well-pressed in a five-thousand-dollar suit.

He's an attractive man in his mid-fifties, full of the assurance that comes from having made it a long time ago. A billionaire, an inventor, a man with ten million Twitter followers. He's never married, tends to date models and singers on their way up. He started his first company at twenty-three and has a flair for marketing. With a different set of choices, he might've been a politician. Instead, he chose to worship at the altar of money. Would he have become quite so corrupt without it? Did the money feed the rot, or was it always there, a malignant growth ready to spring into action when opportunity arose?

"Good morning, gentlemen. This is Julia Sanders, the associate working with me on the file."

I shake John Taylor's hand. He's a mostly decent guy in his early forties who's never mistaken me for my assistant or made an off-color joke in my presence. My record against him is 3–2.

I move on to Sullivan. A head of thick dark hair shot with gray. Light-blue eyes. The tan of the rich who don't have to suffer weather. His hand is cold, but not clammy. A firm shake, eye contact, then a dismissal. He's here but he's not happy about it.

I take a seat and Julia sits next to me. I open my binder. "Mr. Sullivan, thank you for agreeing to come to this settlement discussion."

"From what I understand, you didn't give my attorney much choice."

"Well, thank you just the same."

Sullivan examines his manicure. "Where's your client?"

"I have the authority I need. And I'm sure you'll appreciate fewer people knowing the details."

Sullivan raises an eyebrow. "And what details are those?"

"If you open the binder in front of you, you'll find our motion to present additional evidence of prior bad acts and our motion for a sealing order. Behind that you'll find an affidavit from Athena Williams, whom I believe you're acquainted with?"

Sullivan doesn't say anything, just narrows his eyes as if he is trying to think of a way to escape. But he can't invent something to get away from what he did. Or from me.

"I'll take that as a yes."

"Just get on with it," John says.

"All right. Athena alleges that you sexually assaulted her in a work setting."

"I deny it."

"I'm sure you do. But it's starting to be a pattern now, isn't it? Three women? And once someone like Athena Williams comes forward . . . well, the wheels are going to start to fall off your denial train."

"We'll see."

"No, I don't think we will."

"How's that?"

"You're going to settle this case."

"Why would I do that?"

He's a cool customer, I have to give him that.

"Because you haven't thought this through. This testimony is going to come out, whether or not the judge grants my motion to admit it. Once I file the motion, the affidavit will be in the public domain. You're going to lose more than your court case."

"Idle threats."

"No. There's a plan to take away your company."

Sullivan's mask falls. His eyes turn flinty. "What?"

"Consider it. When these allegations get out, the first thing that's going to happen is that Nexia is going to call a board meeting to discuss your future at the company."

"How do you know that?"

"It stands to reason. But also, at least one member of your board has been waiting for this."

"Who?"

"Does it matter? Trust me, a member of your board will insist on a meeting and will call for your resignation when these allegations come out."

"They won't have the votes."

"Won't they? You've been through this before, and this isn't ten years ago, or even five. Multiple accusations of sexual assault? That's not just boys being boys. And I checked. Nexia's board is fifty percent women. Very progressive of you. But it's going to be your downfall."

"That's ridiculous. The company is mine."

I flip to another page in the binder. "Well, that's not quite true, is it? Since Nexia went public, you own a plurality of the shares, but not an outright majority."

"So?"

"Have you not noticed the increase in the stock's short position? The increased trading volume over the last year? Someone is poised for a hostile takeover. They're waiting for you to be vulnerable."

He goes perfectly still, taking in what I'm saying. For all his terrible flaws, he's a brilliant man. He processes data rapidly and sees connections. "Who is it?"

"You should be able to work that one out yourself."

His eyes narrow and release. "Karma Rosen?"

"That's right. Good Karma is going to buy you out."

"It won't happen."

"She has the resources. I've included the public records in the binder in front of you—she owns almost five percent of your company. When your stock price goes down after the allegations become public, she's going to scoop up another significant amount of stock at a bargain. She most certainly has proxies in a similar position.

There's someone friendly to her on the board. And think of the optics. Bad man removed and replaced by do-good woman with feel-good products."

"I'll fight it."

"You'll lose."

Sullivan thinks again about what I am saying, playing it out like a chess match in his mind. Seeing twenty moves ahead, forty. He's been checked and the checkmate is inevitable.

Or maybe not quite.

"She wants our tech?"

"I'm sure she does. But mostly, she doesn't appreciate what you did to her. Trying to take her company."

"That was business."

"And so is this."

"It feels bigger than that."

"Karma thinks big."

He closes the binder. "How do you know so much?"

"That's a long story."

"You're in on it with her."

I don't say anything. I let silence tell the lie I won't say out loud.

Sullivan nods. "So if I settle the case, I get to keep my company?"

"No."

He leans back in his chair. "No deal, then."

"I don't think you're quite getting it. If you want to do something else with your life, you'll make this deal. Remember that the assaults are still within the statute of limitations for criminal prosecution."

"This is blackmail."

"Is it? I'm not asking for anything for myself."

"But you are asking for something."

"Naturally." I glance at the list I have in front of me, though I have it memorized. "You're going to step down and appoint a successor."

Sullivan's voice is tight. "That's ridiculous. Everyone will know something is wrong if I do that."

"Not if you say that you're dealing with a health issue."

"I'm perfectly fine."

"No one will know that, though. Pick something, a minor cancer, for instance, and say you need to step back for six months. Then, when you return healthy and glowing, you can talk about your shifting priorities and start something new. You can sell it. It's what you do."

He plays with the binder's cover, flipping it open, then closed, while he considers what I'm saying.

"Who is supposed to replace me?"

"Her name is Katherine Rawleigh."

"Who is she?"

"She's a VP of a large pharmaceutical company."

"I mean, who is she to you?"

"Why does it matter? You're going to resign later today and advise the board to immediately appoint her as your successor. You'll use your influence to convince them she's the right woman for the job."

"How do I know she's qualified?"

"Please. She can't be worse than you."

He shakes his head. "Is that all?"

"One last thing. You're going to give me the proxy for the stock you own in Good Karma." Sullivan had purchased 5 percent of Good Karma as part of his own takeover attempt, and he'd held on to the stock all these years.

"You personally?"

"That's right."

"I could just drop the case and walk away and not do any of this."

I smile. "You're right. But the information will come out anyway. You'll still lose your company. This is happening regardless of the lawsuit."

"This is bullshit."

My anger is bubbling beneath the surface, but I do my best to control it. "No, it's retribution. Stop sexually assaulting women."

"I never—"

"Spare me."

He narrows his eyes. I can feel his malevolence like a force, but

I'm not going to bend. He's spent too much time scaring women, and I'm not going to be one of them.

"You're taking everything I have."

"I'm keeping you out of jail. And you can go on your merry way with your reputation sort of intact, and your freedom and your money. You have a chance to start over with the billions of dollars you still have. Do something good in the world."

"Is that what you're doing?"

"This isn't about me."

He laughs bitterly. "No? Sure, right. You say so."

"I'm not here to argue with you. Do we have a deal or not?"

He looks at John, who's been impassive this whole time, reading the affidavit and other material in the binder. I've been in his position, unable to cover over that sick feeling every lawyer gets when presented with proof of their client's lying. I could feel sympathy for him, and I do, but in this exact moment, what I need is for him to back me up.

"We could fight it," John says. "Report her to the bar, hold a press conference, try to get out in front of it."

"But the women could still come forward."

"We can't stop them from speaking out if they want to. I did warn you about that when you took this case . . ."

Sullivan takes a long moment to consider it. "All right, then, but I need assurances too."

"Such as?"

"That the women will sign a nondisclosure and an agreement not to prosecute."

"Of course."

He shakes his head and I think he's going to bolt. But he has no real options. Whatever the pain of this, I'm still his best option. "We have a deal."

I put out my hand. As he reaches across the table to shake it, I try not to think about this deal with the devil I'm making and why. I try to take a Karma attitude about it all—if it doesn't bother the man in the equation, then why is it bothering me?

CHAPTER 35

The Calm Before the Storm

Now—October

I come home exhausted. Master Machiavellian plotter is not my métier, and the energy required to think of each step—see three, six, ten moves ahead—is significant.

It's cold out, getting dark earlier and earlier. Winter will be here before we know it. But what will my life look like in a new season? Where will we even be living?

Dan and I have returned to our apartment, mindful of the potential for microphones and cameras. I'm waiting in a mental crouch for the shit to hit the fan. For Karma and Michelle to find out that I've thwarted their plan for the lawsuit, even though I asked Mark to hold off telling the board until noon tomorrow.

I have a meeting tomorrow morning with Karma and Michelle, and I'm hoping for the element of surprise to make it go smoothly. But the papers are signed and witnessed, including Sullivan's withdrawal of the lawsuit, which will be filed in the morning. There's nothing Karma and Michelle can do now to stop it.

As to the rest? Only tomorrow will tell.

So Dan and I chat about benign things over takeout and have

another conversation with our eyes. Then we crawl into bed and hide under the covers, staring at each other in the hazy darkness.

"What are we going to do after this?" I say in the lowest whisper I can manage.

"What do you want to do?" Dan whispers back. His features are unreadable in this light, but his arms are holding me close.

"Remember during the lockdown, how bored we were?"

"I do remember. It seems so long ago now."

"Remember how we said when we could we were going to go places and do things?"

"We did, didn't we?"

"We did. But then we didn't do that."

"We took that one trip to Maine."

I smile, remembering. It was a sun-kissed week in a beach house. We started drinking at noon and laid out on a float. We went paddle boarding and got food at the local farmer's market. I also did three hours of work every morning.

"Weren't we going to go to Europe? And Australia? Weren't we going to go somewhere where we couldn't be reached?"

Dan rubs his nose against mine. "You said those things, yes."

"And?"

"You didn't mean them, did you?"

"Why would you think that?"

"Experience." He pulls me closer. "Come on, Nic. You like to work. That's when you're happiest. When you have a purpose. You get restless on vacation. And it's okay—I get it. I always knew that about you."

"And it's one of my endearing qualities?"

"Well . . ."

"We should do that. We should go somewhere no one can find us." I snuggle closer to him. "I'm scared," I say so softly I'm not sure he can hear me.

"I know; me too," he says into my ear.

"What are we doing?"

"I thought you had a plan?"

"I do, it's just . . . I forgot to ask: Did you find Jack?"

"Yeah."

"You talked to him?"

"I did," he says, and his words are a caress. It must be the relief of knowing that we were right, that Jack is not dead and that I didn't help paper over a murder.

"What did he say?"

"Well, he took a bit of convincing, since he's been paid rather well to shut up, but in the end, I persuaded him that he wanted to do the right thing. He signed an affidavit explaining everything."

"You didn't get in a fight, did you?"

His hand rubs my back. "No, no, don't worry. I used a page from your playbook and told him I'd go to the police."

"Why did he do it?"

"He was told it was all a training exercise for Athena. Like an advanced personal safety scenario."

"He bought that?" I ask.

"He's an out-of-work actor and they threw a lot of money at him. He made it make the sense he needed it to, to carry it out."

"Did he drug her?"

Dan nods against my forehead. "He put a sedative in her drink."

"And provoked her?"

"Yes. All the ways she described. He took something too, so that after the gun went off, he'd appear dead. And he had a rig that actors use on set to make it look like he'd been shot. It was some kind of animal blood."

I shivered. "He didn't think that was crazy?"

"He did, but they paid him a hundred grand."

"Jesus."

Dan slipped his hand under my T-shirt, touching the soft skin at the base of my spine. "He was supposed to go out of town for several months, but he decided not to."

"Why?"

"He got an audition."

"Oh my God." I laugh quietly. "Actors. Who hired him?"

"Gary, by the sounds of it."

"What a crazy risk they took."

"Was it, though?" Dan kisses me, leaving his lips against mine. "It's what you said. They knew Athena wasn't going to go searching for answers. It probably didn't even matter if she believed it or not, in the end. They'd have all the leverage they needed over her either way."

I kiss him back, scooting closer so our bodies are in full contact. "I guess you're right."

"They just didn't count on you."

"Ha. No."

"That was their mistake."

I rest my head against his. "Karma and Michelle are going to try to ruin us when I tell them what's happened."

Dan starts to make slow circles on my skin. "That's why you have the Good Karma proxy, isn't it? And all the other evidence you've gathered of their plan. They'll fall in line like Sullivan did."

"I hope so. Are you mad about Mark?"

Dan pulls back. "You said nothing happened."

"Nothing did."

"So no, I'm not mad."

I squeeze him tightly. "And what about kids? You still want that?"

"I was never sure I did. I only wanted to have a conversation."

"Okay."

"But maybe not now, right?" His lips touch mine again as his fingers press more insistently.

"Not right now."

We make love as quietly as we can, and afterwards, we curl up together and he falls easily to sleep. My rest is not so quick in coming, as I go over the details again and again.

Have I seen the board clearly enough, or is there some other plan afoot that I've missed?

. . .

I decided to host the showdown with Karma and Michelle at my office. So once again, I'm walking into our main boardroom with the amazing view and the wall of glass, thinking one thing's going to happen and getting another.

And once again it all starts with Thomas.

"What's this I hear that you're thinking of leaving the firm?" he asks before I've even taken a seat. Michelle and Karma are almost unrecognizable, sitting at the other end of the table in business suits, their hair professionally done, makeup on. I've seen Karma like this before, but seeing Michelle out of her Mother Earth attire is a first.

My heart starts to thud. I've missed something. Something crucial. "What?"

"We apprised Thomas that you were going to be leaving the profession," Karma says, her voice even, almost flat.

"Well, you're mistaken. I'm not going anywhere." I sit down and place the binder I'm holding on the table. "Why would I?"

Thomas smiles. "That's what I wanted to know. After all I, I mean, we . . ."

"Have done for me?"

"Yes."

"Precisely." I look past Thomas to Michelle. I wonder for the first time how much she knows. None of the threats have come from her. It's always been Karma that's been the hammer.

"Well, that is good news indeed," Thomas says, making no move to leave.

"Why are you here, Thomas?"

"I thought I'd come and say hello when I heard who was coming in."

I keep my face as neutral as possible. "You know each other?"

"I've known Karma for a long time. She and my wife are good friends." And there it is, the confirmation I didn't need that Thomas was involved. When I'd mentioned Panthera and Karma in our conversation about my expense reports, he'd feigned ignorance. I'm almost impressed by his ability to lie.

"I had the impression you didn't know who she was when I first mentioned Panthera to you," I say.

"Did you?" Thomas says, his face innocent.

"My mistake." I could drop the word "Radius" into this conversation like a bomb, but I need to save my ammunition for later. "Now, if you don't mind, I have some things to discuss with Karma and Michelle."

"Oh yes." He stands and smooths his tie. "Carry on." He walks to the door and stops. "Ladies."

When he's gone, I turn back to Karma and Michelle. Michelle seems nervous, but Karma is calm, her hands folded on the table in front of her.

"What was that all about with Thomas?" I ask. "Why did you tell him I'm leaving the firm?"

Karma raises her left shoulder. "You said you wanted out. I assumed that meant the law too."

Unbelievable. "That's not your decision to make or announce."

"As you say. Now, we'd like a full update on the Sullivan file."

I pause, savoring the moment. "The case is settled."

Karma's composure slips. "What? How did that happen?"

I let her stew while I observe Michelle. Her cheeks are flushed, but her expression is innocent. I swivel back to Karma. "Because I know what you're trying to do, and I'm not going to be involved in it."

"Involved in what? Defeating an evil man?"

"Is that what you've been doing?"

"Of course," Michelle says softly. "Mr. Sullivan is a terrible person. When I think about what he did to that girl, to Samantha and Athena . . ." She looks genuinely upset, and perhaps she is. It doesn't matter.

"This isn't about what happened at SulliVent or even what happened to his victims. It's about Nexia."

Karma pales under her makeup. Michelle looks confused. "What's Nexia?"

"Sullivan's other company. Right, Karma?"

She stays quiet.

"You didn't know, Michelle? What this is all about?"

"What are you talking about?" She twists in her chair. "Karma?"

Is this a performance? She's capable of giving one, but maybe she's being genuine. It doesn't matter. "This whole case is part of a scheme to get Nexia from Sullivan."

"What?"

"Karma wants the company. For revenge, for profit, for both. So, she's been manipulating me. Manipulating all of us to do what she wants to weaken Sullivan so she can take over Nexia. But the plan isn't going to work. Sullivan's withdrawn his case. The documents are being filed as we speak."

Karma's jaw is tight. "You're letting him go?"

"He's stepping down from the company."

"That's not enough. Not for what he's done."

"He needs justice," Michelle says. "He's hurt so many women."

"That was never going to happen. Civil trials are about money, not justice."

"That's cynical," Karma says.

"More cynical than dragging three women over the coals in court, their lives picked over like the trash just so you can win a court case? Would you want that for your daughter?" I look at Michelle when I say this. Can I penetrate the fog that she lives in? Or am I the one in the fog?

"They were willing to stand up," Michelle says.

"They were threatened and trapped."

"What?"

I close my eyes for a second. "Do you want to tell her, Karma, or should I?"

Karma's eyes narrow. "You're making a mistake."

"You made the mistake when you decided that you could manipulate me like you were manipulating the others, and that I'd just go along with it."

"You don't know what you're talking about."

"No, well, let me lay it out for you. Are you listening, Michelle? Five years ago, Sullivan tried to take over Good Karma. He failed, and Karma was so angry she decided to retaliate. You knew, Karma, somehow, that he abused women—maybe you made an educated guess because it was the height of #MeToo. Maybe you heard a rumor. Regardless, you were right. So you used your network of women to help you. You got Connie installed on the SulliVent board. You worked with her to find victims. Once you did, Connie encouraged Jennifer Naughton to bring her complaint and got Sullivan fired. When he sued, you upped the ante and decided to take Nexia away from him. Perhaps that was the plan all along. You recruited Heather, bought up Nexia's stock, and applied pressure to get Samantha and Athena to testify. Then you brought me on to manage the whole thing."

Karma is perfectly still. Michelle looks like she might pass out.

"But you miscalculated. You went too far. When Athena resisted, you put a darker plan in motion, arranging for her to meet a man that you'd planted, and eventually manufacturing a confrontation that would leave him dead and allow you to blackmail Athena and me."

"Dead?" Michelle bleats. "Someone's dead?"

"No," I say. "He's not. We were only meant to think he was."

Karma clenches her jaw, but she doesn't speak.

"It was all part of the plan. Just like getting my sister-in-law to come to New York to oust Dan and me from our apartment. Working with Thomas to put me in a vulnerable position with the points committee. All of it so Sullivan would lose his lawsuit and Good Karma could take over his company when the bad press led to his inevitable removal." I lean forward. "What does Nexia have that you want so badly? Or is it only revenge? The power of it all?"

"I don't have to answer your questions."

"You're right; you don't. But it also doesn't matter. Because you're going to let all of us—all of this—go."

"What?"

"You're going to release us. Tell Thomas to stop his campaign against me in the partnership and stop blackmailing him for cheating on his wife. Turn over all the information you have on Samantha and Athena and Heather. Dismantle Panthera and go back to your life before any of this happened. And if you don't, then I'll do to you what you tried to do to Sullivan. I'll take your company from you."

Karma brought her chin up. "And how will you do that?"

"Just like you were going to do to Sullivan."

"You don't have the shares or the votes."

"I do."

Michelle put her hand on Karma's arm. "Is all of this true? Is what Nicole's saying right?"

"No."

"No?" I say. "What part, Karma? What did I miss?"

She meets my gaze. "Why don't you bring your friends in here and I'll tell you. They're here, aren't they?"

"Who?"

"Athena, Samantha, Heather."

I don't bother asking how she knows this. But they're waiting in my office. I was going to call them in once I had her agreement.

"Yes." I pick up my phone and text my assistant. I tell her to bring Julia, too. Then I sit back and watch the two women who've put me in this situation. Michelle seems dazed, almost disconnected from reality. Karma's harder to figure out. Is she plotting her next move or simply trying to absorb that she's lost? Either way I feel nervous, the worry that I missed something ringing in my mind like a bell.

We don't speak until Samantha, Heather, Athena, and Julia enter. Michelle seems stunned to see Julia, but a surprise for me comes with them: Connie. Seeing her increases my nerves and seems to reassure Karma. But our plan is solid. The lawsuit is over. All that's left to haggle over are the consequences.

Everyone takes their seat, all eyes on me.

"So they're here," I say to Karma. "Now what?"

Karma looks at Heather. "Are you going to tell her, or should I?"

I turn to ice. Oh shit. Oh no. I've read this whole board wrong.

Heather's face hardens. "You can go ahead."

Karma's lip curls in pleasure. "It's interesting, isn't it, how one person can get so much right and yet miss one key fact that changes everything?"

She lets her words lie there as I look around the room at Athena, Connie, Samantha, and Heather, and now I know. Karma doesn't need to tell me.

I am not one of many pieces being moved around the board by a single player.

I'm the target. The weak prey stalked by the pride.

And now they're moving in for the kill.

CHAPTER 36

Check

Now—October

I try to remain calm.

"Heather?" I say, my voice wavering. "You're in on this with them?"

Heather smiles with pleasure. "You thought Karma and Michelle could pull all this off on their own?"

"Why?"

"You wouldn't understand."

"Heather," Athena warns. "She deserves an explanation."

"What's to explain?" Heather says. "We came up with a plan and we're executing it."

I swivel toward Athena. "You too?" I confirm. She nods sadly. "Jack, the plan, all of it?" She nods again.

Samantha won't make eye contact, and Connie seems to be gloating. Even Julia's features are different, more knowing, less innocent.

It's all of them. They are all in on this but me.

— Jennifer Naughton, Sullivan's ouster, the plot to take over Nexia.
— Putting together the Pride, the lawsuit strategy, recruiting me.
— Taking over my life, hiring Jack, faking his death.

None of it was a surprise to any of them. It was only a surprise to me.

"When did you start planning this?"

Heather lays her hands flat on the boardroom table. I think back to the lunches we had, the pitter-patter of idle conversation when Heather dropped her sarcastic exterior and seemed to open up. But this Heather, this is a person I've never seen before. Cold, calculating, angry.

"It started when I worked on the SulliVent deal when he was trying to acquire Good Karma five years ago."

A lightbulb goes off. "Are you the reason it didn't happen?"

"That's right."

"How did you do it?"

"I went to Karma. I told her what was coming in time for her to marshal her defenses and stave him off."

"You put your job in jeopardy?"

"Well, he put my life in jeopardy, so . . ."

"Oh." So that's it. One of the things I've never been able to figure out. How did Karma and Michelle know Sullivan was a serial sexual abuser? What made them go looking in the first place? "What happened?"

Heather's chin is quivering. "Same as everyone. I was working with him on the deal. We were at the office late one night, and he offered me a lift home. You've heard what happens next."

"Did you go to the police?"

"Please! Only two percent of rapes actually end up with a conviction. It's basically legal to sexually assault people in this country. I wasn't going to be a statistic."

"So you decided to kill his deal? Wasn't that risky?"

"He'd already done the worst he could to me. I had nothing to lose." She's pale, and I almost feel sorry for her. No, I do feel sorry for her, but I'm also angry. Angry and disappointed in myself that I didn't see this coming and that I don't know how to stop it.

"Karma brought you in at that point?" I say to Connie. "You had the resources to help her."

"That's right," Connie says. In contrast to Heather, she is calm and sure of herself. "I worked with Karma and Heather to stop the takeover."

My brain is trying to catch up. I thought I knew Connie, Heather, and Athena. I thought I knew what we were doing. But I'd overlooked one of the fundamental lessons I learned years ago in court. If you don't have external proof, then you never know when someone's lying. Human lie detectors don't exist. We are easily taken advantage of.

"And once you pulled that off, you decided to go further. You used Panthera to create a trap for Sullivan."

"We'd only been tapping into part of its potential," Karma says with a measure of pride. "It was time to move it to the next level."

"It was supposed to be about women's empowerment," Michelle says, her voice trembling. "Not revenge."

"You can't separate the two, Michelle. You know that."

Michelle's hands are shaking, and she balls them into fists. "But this? Everything that Nicole has been saying? I never would have agreed to this."

"Which is why we left you out of it, dear."

I catch movement from Julia out of the side of my vision. When I turn toward her, her face is filled with contempt.

"I never asked for that." Michelle slumps down in her seat. "I only wanted to make things better."

"And we have," Karma says. "Don't you see?"

"I don't see," I say.

"Come on, Nic," Samantha says. "Sullivan is a terrible person. Think about how many women we're going to save from the same fate if he's stripped of his power."

"Which you could've done by going to the police or making your stories public. Taking Nexia from him doesn't accomplish that. He's free to sin again."

"But he knows we're on to him. The power we have. If we'd gone to the police, we would've been public too. You don't understand. This didn't happen to you."

"But now it is, right? You're involving me in it."

Samantha smiles sadly. "We needed one more. One more to finish the plan."

I turn back to Heather. "So you went to Karma, and she staved off the merger and then what? You decided that wasn't enough?"

"That's right," Heather says. "He had to lose all the things he cared about."

"That's when you joined Panthera. Not this summer with me. Not last year."

"Yes."

"You too, Samantha?"

"That's right." Samantha nods. "I've been in it for years."

"Why the cover story? Why deceive me about that?"

"We thought it would be easier to fold you in if you didn't think you were the only new person in the group."

"In our experience, it's harder to coalesce a Pride if someone feels like an outsider," Karma says.

It's all been lies. Everything. Everyone.

"What about you, Julia? How did you get involved in this?"

"I've known Karma for years. And Connie too. Connie helped me get into Harvard. She's helped me in a lot of ways."

I breathe out slowly. How could I have missed this? How could I be so blind?

"So you decided to get revenge and you went looking for other victims?" I say to Karma.

Karma tilts her head to the side. "Once Heather told me what happened, I knew there had to be others. His whole routine was too pat. It couldn't have been the first time he'd done it."

"You found Athena like you said before? Looking at personnel records?"

"Yes," Athena says. "Not everything we told you was a lie."

"Only the important parts."

Of everyone, I'm the most shocked about her. I thought we were friends. But I have no friends in this room.

"The whole thing with Jack. His death staged. That wasn't the Test for you, was it? It was the Test for me."

"You were bucking," Athena says. "We needed to keep you in line."

"And what about Jennifer Naughton? Did anything actually happen to her?"

"We didn't have to make anything up where that was concerned."

"Is she in Panthera?"

"No. Like we told you, she wasn't at the level we recruit from. It wasn't necessary to bring her into the Pride, or the wider plan. She thinks Connie found her by investigating for the board. And Connie helped her find a new job at an ally's company. She doesn't know anything more than that."

"Why me, then? You already had a lawyer. Why did you need to involve me?"

Connie raises a shoulder. "We made a mistake initially, using someone outside of Panthera."

I thought about their original lawyer. The man who'd written a cover-your-ass memo advising them to settle. "He was someone you didn't have leverage on, you mean?"

"As you say."

"He wouldn't bring Samantha's evidence?" I guess. "Or Athena's?"

"That's right," Connie says. "He didn't think the court would admit it. And he found it suspicious that we'd found two additional witnesses when the outside investigators SulliVent had hired after Naughton came forward found none."

"Why didn't they find Samantha and Athena?"

"That investigation was out of my hands," Connie said. "And confined to SulliVent only."

"But Samantha's and Athena's stories are real?" I ask.

"Nic, come on," Athena says. "We wouldn't make something like that up."

"Wouldn't you?"

Athena won't look me in the eye, but Samantha is steady. "It happened to both of us, just like we told you. We just needed you to believe us. That other lawyer didn't. He was an asshole."

"So you fed the witnesses to me one by one. You made Athena reluctant to testify so I'd buy it when she finally caved. That's what Jack was for too, yes? All part of the theater to make me swallow the coincidences."

No one says anything, and I'm not even sure I'm talking to them anymore. I sift through what I've learned, trying to make it add up. But something isn't sitting right: Karma was shocked when I told her about the settlement with Sullivan, that her plan wasn't working, that her own company was in jeopardy again. I was in the dark, but she might be too.

I'm only halfway through untangling this.

"Was the settlement part of the plan all along?" I ask Athena.

"No, that's *not* what we wanted," Karma says. "This must be—"

I raise my hand to stop her. "Athena?"

She stares back at me. "What do you think?"

I turn to Julia. "You gave me the idea to try to keep the testimony confidential. And then to use that as leverage to get him to settle."

"I did," Julia responds calmly.

"Athena, Samantha—you wanted to use your testimony to get him to give up Nexia voluntarily. You didn't want to have to go through the trial."

"That's right."

"Or risk the merger going wrong."

Heather nods. "Mergers are unpredictable. Sullivan might've fended it off. It was better to get the settlement and convince him to go voluntarily. As an added bonus, Samantha and Athena wouldn't have to testify."

That tracks. During our strategy sessions over the weekend, Heather had been the one to suggest using the threat of the takeover to get Sullivan to capitulate.

"So what now?" I say, the energy draining out of me. "Am I free to go?"

"We were hoping you'd join us," Athena says.

"Join you?"

"When we take over Good Karma," Samantha adds. "We'd like you to be general counsel."

"Excuse me?" Karma raps the table. "What is going on? I demand answers."

"It's quite simple," Connie says to Karma in a calm voice. "We own or control thirty percent of Good Karma. You only own twenty-five percent. We'll be replacing the board and then you as the CEO."

"What? How?"

"I've been buying up stock for years. So have Samantha, Athena, and Heather. We each have five percent as of this morning."

"That's only twenty percent."

"They have my five percent too," Julia says. "Mom gave it to me when I turned twenty-one."

Michelle's face falls. "That was for your future."

Julia's features go flat. "You never cared about my future. You gave me those shares out of guilt. You abandoned me. You left me with Dad and his drugs and the girls that changed every week, when you went away. You hid me from the world. You missed ten years of my life."

Michelle reaches out to her across the table. "I explained that. I needed to work on myself to be a good mother to you."

"Please. That's not how it works. You aren't a mother if you aren't there for your children. You can't walk away from your responsibilities and expect no consequences."

"Is that why you're doing this?" I ask Julia. "To get revenge on your mom?"

Julia's eyes slide in my direction. "Bad people need to be punished, I told you."

"So this is justice?"

"You told me there wasn't any such thing. That justice doesn't happen."

"That's not what I meant."

"It's true, isn't it?"

A counterargument starts to form in my mind, but then I dismiss it. "This isn't justice. It's revenge."

"What's the difference?"

I turn away. There's no point in arguing with her. "Why are you turning on Karma after working with her for so long?" I ask Connie.

"My question exactly," Karma says, her anger raw but her power already diminished.

Connie makes a dismissive gesture. "We don't need her anymore."

"That can't be it."

This must be about Good Karma. What does Good Karma have that Connie might want?

"This is about Linnaeus, isn't it? That protein Linnaeus is working on. The one that can boost immune systems?"

"Did Katherine tell you about that?" Connie says.

"She did. And with Good Karma, you'd have a built-in distribution network to manufacture and sell it."

"If we sell it as an herbal remedy, we don't have to go through the tedious regulatory process with the FDA."

"And Nexia. Their nanotech—that's a part of this too?"

"It's an effective delivery device."

"Which you could sell to the government?"

"I didn't want to do that," Karma says, realization hitting her. "When Connie said it was something we could do with Nexia once we took it over, I told her I didn't trust the government. They'll find a way to weaponize it, like they always do. They won't help people."

"And you're helping people with your bath bombs and natural remedies?" Connie says scornfully. "Please."

"Can you use the compound to manipulate the immune system, destroy it?" I ask. "Turn it into a biological weapon that's delivered by Nexia's nanotech?"

"Like most things, the compound can be used in many ways and for many purposes, depending on what you want to accomplish."

"And by selling it to the government, you'll make a killing on it both ways: in the wellness market and as a potential weapon."

Women Killing It. Way too accurate.

"We all will," Heather says. "Once we control Good Karma *and* Nexia, the sky's the limit."

"But you've come up short," Karma says, regaining a bit of confidence. "You only control twenty-five percent of Good Karma. I'll marshal the board and we'll defeat this evil attempt to get me out. It didn't work last time and it won't work this time."

"No," Connie says. "We have thirty. And once we control the board, your twenty-five percent won't be relevant."

"Who has the final five?"

"I do," I say. "I have Sullivan's proxy for his five percent of the company." I turn to Heather. "That's why you wanted me to get that. Not to negotiate our freedom."

Heather smiles and it's scary. "Think of it, Nicole. All the anxiety, the striving, the worry, the work . . . It can all be resolved now. You can be general counsel for Good Karma. Connie's apartment will be signed over to you. You'll be set for life."

I stare at her. At all of them. "But I don't want that."

"I don't think you have much choice, Nicole," Athena says gently.

"Why are you going along with this, Athena? What do you get out of it?"

"I'm taking my power back. You think I want to stay allied to someone like Karma? Someone who'd be willing to set me up, blackmail me for the rest of my life to get what she wants?"

"But you were in on it."

"It's who she is, though. She did it to you too, remember?"

I switch to Samantha. "And you, Samantha?"

Her face is impassioned. "I tried being altruistic for years. I volunteered at women's shelters and donated money, and nothing changes. #MeToo didn't take out all the bad men; it only skimmed a few off the top. So fuck it. Fuck them. It's time to do something different and see if that works."

"By getting rich?"

"By controlling things. If we're not in charge, then this will keep happening to us over and over."

"Well said, Samantha," Athena says. "Are you with us, Nicole?"

My mind is racing. There has to be a way out of this. Something they've forgotten or haven't thought of.

And then I realize what it is. The way out.

"No, I'm not."

"You don't have much choice," Julia points out.

"You're wrong. You've made a mistake, all of you."

"Which is?" Heather asks, sounding not worried at all.

"You're not going to get Nexia. And you're not going to get me to join you."

CHAPTER 37

Mate

Now—October

I'm met with a table full of incredulous faces, but I'm determined.

"If you don't want to join us, fine," Heather says dismissively. "But we're going to need your proxy for those shares."

She's hit on it. The leverage I have. The leverage I was using to get myself out of the trap I thought I was in can get me out of the trap I *am* in. And a fact they don't know about. Something I'd improvised during my meeting with Sullivan.

"No, Sullivan gave that to me. I can't sign it over to you."

They look to Julia for confirmation.

"She's right," Julia says. "Proxies are not transferable."

"That was a mistake," Connie says. "Why didn't you tell us that?"

Julia crosses her arms. "She was on our side. You said she was going to be on our side."

Athena speaks gently. "It's fine, Julia. We miscalculated; that's not on you."

"So get Sullivan to give it to one of us, then," Heather says to me.

"The deal is set. Sullivan is not going to agree to change any of it. And I'm not going to ask."

"And I'm not going to take this lying down," Karma says, standing up. "Come on, Michelle. Let's go."

Michelle looks up at her. I watch twenty years of belief cross her face. Twenty years of trust that's been eroded.

Michelle rises slowly, her face trained on Julia. "I'm sorry, Julia. I love you."

Julia scoffs. "You love yourself. That's what this whole thing has always been about."

Michelle smiles at her sadly but follows Karma out, the door to the conference room clanging shut with a bang.

"We're going to need to contain them," Athena says to Connie. "There are still things they can do to stave us off."

Connie raises her phone to her ear. "I'll take care of it." She stands and leaves, already speaking to whoever her fixer is, I assume.

"Now," Athena says, addressing me. "We need to find a way to get Sullivan to change the proxy."

"He'll never agree. All the paperwork is already done. You signed your NDA and so did Samantha. The court paperwork has been filed. The case is settled. I don't have any leverage anymore."

"I could come out with my story," Heather says. "That's leverage."

"The day after a court case settled? You'd have no credibility. You'd look like you were trying to jump on the bandwagon and get money."

"Some people would believe me."

"Not enough to get Sullivan to act the way you want him to. Besides, if the story is public, he has no incentive to do anything you want him to."

"There has to be a way," Heather says, more to herself than to me.

"I'm not going to help you. And neither is Nexia."

"What does that mean?"

"Nexia knows it's a target for a takeover."

"How?"

"I told Sullivan in the negotiations."

Athena waves her hand dismissively. "That doesn't matter. He's out. They won't have had time to do anything."

"Right," I say. "But the new president also knows. She was installed yesterday and immediately advised the board of Good Karma's plan."

"She?" Athena asks as Connie comes back into the room.

"Katherine Rawleigh."

"Your sister-in-law?" Connie says. "What's she got to do with this?"

"You got her a job at Linnaeus, remember? You sent your executive VP in to woo her and bring her to New York. You even planted the idea for her to take Penny's apartment when she died."

"What's she got to do with any of this?" Heather asks.

"When Sullivan stepped down, someone had to replace him as president. I suggested Katherine."

"Suggested?"

"Insisted. I thought it would help to have a friend inside Nexia in case Karma tried to go ahead with the takeover anyway. Katherine's already started working to stop it."

"We didn't tell you to do that," Heather says through gritted teeth.

"Someone had to take over. I thought we were trying to prevent Good Karma from getting Nexia. I put measures in place to help achieve that."

Connie appraises me for a second. "We'll get you disbarred."

"For what?"

"You blackmailed Sullivan into settling his case."

"He'll never file a complaint. That would expose him. And I'm the one who's been blackmailed and manipulated. By you."

"You don't have any proof of that. It would be your word against ours."

"I do. I have Jack."

This lands like the grenade I was hoping for. I'd kept this detail to myself, too. Only Dan and Katherine know that we found him and have his affidavit. I wasn't sure why I kept it from them, other than my litigator's instinct never to reveal all my cards at once.

"What do you mean?" Athena asks, her voice shaking.

"You left a loose end. He was supposed to leave town, only he didn't. We have an affidavit from him that sets out the whole plan."

"He never spoke to any of us," Heather says. "Only to Gary."

"Yes, but with all the evidence I have—the texts in the Panthera thread, my testimony and Katherine's—I could easily go to the police or the press."

"We're going to go to jail?" Samantha says, her lip quivering.

"Hush, Samantha. No one's going to jail. Right, Nicole?"

Connie and I share a long stare. "Not if you do what I want."

"So it's your turn to blackmail now?"

"If that's what you want to call it."

"What do you want?"

"Undo what you did to my life, put me back where I belong. Where I was before all of this. Let me go and walk away from Nexia and you can go free. All of you."

"What about Good Karma?" Heather asks.

"I don't care what you do with it. Take it over, bankrupt them, whatever you want. But Panthera . . . Karma and Michelle still control it." I lean back in my chair. Do I care if Panthera continues? Probably not the best idea to have a secretive organization out there that wants revenge on me. "You weren't going to leave it with them, were you?"

"No," Connie says.

"How were you going to take it over?"

"I have the list. I set up the security infrastructure they use to monitor everyone."

"The pins," I say. "The Panthera pins. That's how you do it, right?"

"They are a tracker and a microphone, yes."

"You and Samantha weren't wearing yours the day you came to my office the first time. I wondered about that. You didn't want Karma listening in?"

"That's right."

There are too many things I'd overlooked with these women. I'm going to spend years unpacking why that was.

"And what about Michelle?" I say. "Is she as innocent as she pretends to be?"

"She goes along with whatever Karma wants. Karma doesn't fill her in on the more sordid details."

"They shouldn't be left in control of the organization, but you shouldn't have it either."

"What are you saying?" Athena says.

"Give me the list."

"No," Connie says.

"Turn it over to me or I'll go to the police. And just in case, I'm going to leave a copy of the evidence I have with a neutral party with instructions to release it if anything happens to me, or Dan or Katherine or Jack. You do what I say, and I'll let you be."

"How dramatic," Athena says.

"Really, Athena?"

She puts her hands up. "Fine, fine." She looks at Connie, then Samantha, then Heather. One by one they nod in agreement. "You have our word."

Is that enough? Their "word" is useless. But I have my evidence. Releasing it might destroy me, but it will certainly destroy them. Mutually assured destruction. The basis of more than one détente. "And you have mine."

Athena stands and walks toward me. I rise to meet her. She's holding out her hand. I take it. "You were a worthy opponent."

Another beat of disappointment. This has been a game to her. To them. Is it over, or are they still playing and I've missed some move? Is this what defeat or victory looks like?

Too early to say.

"As fate would have it?" I respond.

"As fate would have it," they echo.

• • •

When the day is over, I walk home, my coat tucked tight against my body. It's dark, and the air is cold and swirling. Cars honk and yellow taxis flash by, their meters reflecting off the glass buildings. I'm exhausted, but as I put distance between myself and the office, between myself and *them*, I start to feel lighter. Like when I took my pack off after that day of hiking at the ranch, I am light on my toes, almost floating along these streets, the sounds of the city the music that guides me.

I don't know what happens next. Will I be able to go back to my life without any consequences? That's unlikely, and I'm not even sure it's what I want. I had what I thought I wanted before any of this happened, what I'd worked for, but I wasn't happy. I don't know if I can go back to the whims of the points committee and the constant stress of having to do more, more, more.

At least now I have choices.

—Dan is waiting for me at Penny's.
—Katherine will find her own space, and we'll have the apartment we love so much and our memories of Penny.
—Katherine is a friend now, and maybe together we can change things.

We prevailed. Come what may, Dan and I are strong enough to weather this life.

I did something good today. Something to build on.

Something to hold close, like this coat.

This was the Test. My test.

Hopefully I passed with flying colors.

Dear _____,

Have you ever wondered why your career hasn't progressed
as far as it should?

Why others have continued to climb the corporate ladder
while you've been stuck in place?

We've been there.

Despite years of hard work and all the talent in the world,
our careers were stalled too.

Why?

Because the boys' club still exists. No one wants to talk
about it, but it's true.

Something had to be done about it, and that's how
Panthera Leo was born. Women helping women succeed the
way men have for centuries. Now we're a network of CEOs,
managing partners, executives, and money managers—every
successful woman you know is probably one of us.

And that's why we're writing to you. You've been
recommended to us, and we'd be delighted if you'd
become a member. All it takes is a few minutes of your
time to complete our application, which can be found at
www.pantheraleo.com.

A few minutes, and everything you always wanted could
be yours.

Our next experience is happening soon. Please join us.

Best,
Nicole & Katherine

Acknowledgments

I hope you enjoyed Book 13! A common author trait—we tend to think of our books in terms of the number of them. Bizarre, right?

Anyhoo! I did it! I wrote another book! And you read it! Thank you. It's still hard to believe that things I write go out into the world and get read by anyone.

I'd also like to thank my editors, Kaitlin Olson and Laurie Grassi—your comments and suggestions helped make this novel so much better. Ditto for the production team, copy editors, and proofreaders—you find all my mistakes and make my words look pretty.

The marketing, publicity, and sales teams at Atria and Simon & Schuster Canada—for getting my books out there in the world.

My writing buddies—Elyssa Friedland, Carol Mason, Rachel Stuhler, Liz Fenton, and Shawn Klomparens. You help me survive this crazy business.

My agent, Abigail Koons—this is our eleventh book together (at least?)! An amazing milestone.

My family—for reading, encouragement, and attending too many Zooms.

David—after twenty-seven years together, we made it through fifteen months of quarantine. That's something!

And speaking of quarantine, I wrote this during it. I can't end this without thanking the women who kept me sane through it: Tasha, Sara, Christie, Candice, Janet, Ilana, Rhonda, and Tanya. Thanks to Zooms, runs, walks, tennis, wine, and laughs, we made it. Love you forever.

About the Author

CATHERINE McKENZIE was born and raised in Montreal, Canada. A graduate of McGill University in history and law, Catherine practiced law for twenty years before leaving to write full time. An avid runner, skier, and tennis player, she is the author of numerous bestsellers, including *I'll Never Tell* and *The Good Liar*. Her works have been translated into multiple languages and *I'll Never Tell*, *You Can't Catch Me*, and *Please Join Us* have all been optioned for development into television series. Visit her at **www.catherinemckenzie.com** or follow her on Twitter **@CEMcKenzie1** or Instagram **@catherinemckenzieauthor**.

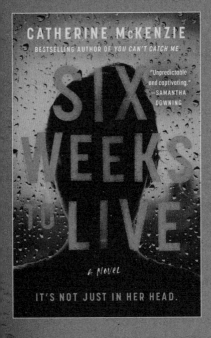